Agnes Mary Frances Robinson

The Life of Ernest Renan

Agnes Mary Frances Robinson

The Life of Ernest Renan

ISBN/EAN: 9783337333522

Printed in Europe, USA, Canada, Australia, Japan

Cover: Foto ©Raphael Reischuk / pixelio.de

More available books at **www.hansebooks.com**

THE LIFE OF
ERNEST RENAN

BY

MADAME JAMES DARMESTETER
(A. Mary F. Robinson)

METHUEN & CO.
36 ESSEX STREET W.C.
LONDON
1898

To

MADAME JEAN PSICHARI
(NOÉMI RENAN)

I DEDICATE THIS PORTRAIT

OF HER FATHER,

WHICH OWES TO HER DEVOTED HAND

ITS MOST LIFE-LIKE

TOUCHES

CONTENTS

PART I

PART IV

PART 1

CHAPTER I

TRÉGUIER

E RNEST RENAN was born at Tréguier, in the Côtes du Nord, on the 28th of February 1823. For the third time in sixty years Brittany gave birth to a man-child who should transform and renew the religious temper of his times.

Chateaubriand and Lamennais were scarcely past their prime when the young Renan first went to school in Tréguier. In him, as in them, the racial strain is strong. Under the exuberance of Chateaubriand, the revolt of Lamennais, the sentiment and irony of Renan, we meet the same irregular genius, mobile and sensitive beyond the like of woman, yet, in the last resort, stubborn as Breton granite under its careless grace of flowers.

All these were great writers, but in their style, as in their intellectual quality, they have small share in that Latin order which is the birthright of a Bossuet, a Racine, or even a Voltaire. Their genius is a sort of hippogriff, as Renan used to say of himself, belonging to no known

3

race of mortal herds. Their style is a midsummer medley saved from incongruity by an
infallible grace. Romance and Antiquity meet
there, and the old world and the ultra-modern
—the harp of Tristan and the echo of Paris.
Celtic magicians, they see the world through
a haze of their own, at once dim and dazzling,
full of uncertain glimpses and brilliant mists,
like the variable weather of their moors.

There are men of genius whose birthplace is
of no moment. Who remembers that Shelley
was born in Sussex? But Renan is as Breton as
Merlin himself. Those who know nothing of Celtic
places must find it hard to understand him. When
I write: "Renan was born at Tréguier," I would
desire that my readers should call up, not necessarily Tréguier, but the grey steepness of any large
hill-town in Brittany, Scotland, Northumberland,
Wales, Ireland, or Cornwall. Let them remember
not only the gaunt and solitary aspect of the
place, but the kind of persons who dwell in these
small grey cities, at once so damp and so scantily
foliaged, under the incessant droppings of the
uncertain heaven. There is a great indifference
to worldly things. And the dreamer—we may
count him as ten per cent. of the population—be

he poet, saint, beggar, or merely drunkard—is capable of a pure detachment from material interests which no Buddhist sage could surpass. There is a vibrating " other worldliness " in the air ; the gift of prayer is constant ; religious eloquence the brightest privilege, and religious fervour a commonplace. Yet, all round, in the high places and the country holy-wells, Mab and Merlin, the fairies and the witches, keep their devotees. And over all the grey, veiled, melancholy distinction, which first strikes us as the note of such a place, there is the special poetic, Celtic quality, the almost immaterial beauty which has so lingering a charm. Many landscapes surely are lovelier than these weatherbeaten moors of wet heath and harsh gorse, of wild broom and juniper. Look at them, overhung by the wreathing hill-mists, traversed and seamed across by the deep-sunken river valleys which hide such unsuspected wealth of hanging woods. There is scarce a tree on the upper level—a stunted pine, perhaps here and there, or half-a-dozen lady-birches, mixed with thorn, clustered round some *menhir* by the yellow upland tarn. The keen sea wind has torn and twisted the scanty trees and blown their branches all one way. The purple heather barely hides the rock which pierces the sterile soil, as a bony arm frays a worn-out garment. The ocean, the melancholy ocean of a Celtic shore, bounds the horizon with its illimitable grey. The Breton coast near Tréguier is the softest, the prettiest, of these typical Celtic landscapes. But even there the country wears a barren grace. Yet what Norman pasture or Burgundy vineyard can boast the strong attraction of the moors?

The same quality — neither rich nor sound but infinitely sweet—clings about the people. The men in the fields gaze at you with stern dark faces in an almost animal placidity. In Renan's youth, they were still almost as wild as their country, strange rude men, with flowing hair, wrapped up in goatskins in wintertime. The girls are charming—it is difficult to say why— their slender and yet rough-hewn figures have no more grace of curve than a thirteenth century church saint in her niche. Their pale faces, with down-dropped lids and delicate pointed chins, have very little bloom. In their black dresses and white coifs they have the austere distinction, the demure reserve, of very young novices who renounce they know not what.

This Breton race, apparently so severe, is one of the most pleasure-loving, and one of the most garrulous in France: a very storehouse of myth and legend, of song and story, of jest and gibe.

These melancholy men and maids, visible emblems
of renunciation, are capable of mirth and wit and
passion. Fond of the glass, quick to repartee,
they glory in the gift of the gab, but only when
the door is shut on strangers. The extraordinary strength of idealism, the infinite delicacy of
sentiment, which form the inmost quintessence of
the Celt, impose on him an image of seemliness,
a pure decorum, to which he incessantly con-
forms the old Adam rebellious in his heart.
Reserve and passion, prudence and poetry, are
equally inherent in him. The very sinner who
trangressed most flagrantly at last week's wake
or "Pardon," will show to-day in every act and
every word a serene tranquillity, a justness of
thought and phrase which is no more hypocritical
than was the passionate fantasy of his falling-
away.

Tréguier is an ancient cathedral city set high
upon a hill at the confluence of two lovely rivers.
A solitary place whose quiet streets are bordered
with blank convent walls over which the garden
tree-tops wave at intervals. The steep and silent
city is crowned by a Gothic cathedral, an admirable structure whose simple lines soar upwards
from a broad and massive base, ever slenderer,
ever narrowing, till they terminate in a spire of
extraordinary delicacy and loftiness, a land-mark

for many miles around. Beautiful cloisters, as old as the church itself, surround the grassy churchyard. But the glory of the cathedral is the large tomb of St Ives which it contains. The patron saint of Brittany, who is at once the patron of Truth and the patron of Rhetoric, is buried there.

Such is Tréguier on the hill. Two steep streets connect this "haunt of ancient peace" with the seaport of Tréguier, a busy place, yet opening quietly, not on the full sport and hurry of the ocean, but on a land-locked estuary folded between tranquil promontories wooded to the water's edge. Tréguier port traffics in fish and grain, and the trading population centres round the quay. But this stir of life is hushed as we mount the hill. Only a few retired sea-captains, a sprinkling of the local gentry, and the numerous clergy, find on that peaceful summit an undisturbed asylum.

In the first quarter of the present century, a certain Renan, of the fisher-clan of the Renans of Goelo, having made some money by his fishing-smack, bought and inhabited a pleasant house on the hill, near the cathedral and the desecrated Episcopal Palace. The house we speak of is a tall, narrow, irregular building, no two windows of a line, whose gable-casements command a pleasant view of hills and woods seen across an abrupt hill-side flight of steep-pitched roofs.

"Captain" Renan (*i.e.*, captain of his fishing-smack) was a feckless, musing man, an obstinate dreamer, convinced of his gift for practical affairs. Yet a man of character, of a silent tenderness of sentiment, with a strain of melancholy even in his happiest affections. The name he bore was well known in Tréguier, for his father was one of the most ardent among the Republicans of the place. In those days, when Charles X. was on the throne, Republican opinions were out of fashion ; but Charles X. had no less devoted subject than the elder Renan. He too was a sailor : it is the Bretons who chiefly man the navy of France. On the very morrow of the Coronation this obstinate old skipper walked down Tréguier High Street adorned by an immense tricoloured cockade.

"I should like to know who will snatch these colours from me ! " cried he.

"No one, Skipper ! No one ! " answered the townsfolk of Tréguier, and taking him by the elbow, they led him home. For though party passion ran high in Tréguier—aye, even scaffold-high !—a general neighbourliness tempered preju-dice ; and men who had threatened each other's heads a short while back, showed a willingness to render each other any kindly service, while fully aware that on the morrow the old political quarrel might break out afresh.

In one of these hours of truce, the son of this staunch old sailor, Captain Renan — a good Republican himself—had married the daughter of a respectable Lannion trader. She had been reared in the religion of the altar and the throne. Her mother's house had been, throughout the Terror, the devoted hiding-place of non-juring priests. But the brilliance and the success of post-revolutionary adventure had left Captain Renan's bride of a more modern way of thinking. She was a Philippist—an Orleanist, as we should say to-day :—a little lively gipsy of a woman, black as a prune from Agen, and with Gascon blood in her. She had ever a witty answer ready, and knew how to defend her opinions and bring the laugh on her side. Her sharp brilliance formed the strongest possible contrast to the dreamy melancholy of her gentle husband.

The Celt is not only religious and political, he is also innately superstitious. There were wonder-working saints and fairies, and wise-women in plenty, on all the moors round Tréguier. When Ernest Renan was born,—a seven months' child, —his anxious mother feared he could not live. Old Gude, the witch, took the babe's little shirt and dipped it in a country holy-well. She came back radiant: "He will live after all!" she cried, "the two little arms stretched out, and you should have seen the whole garment swell and float: he means to live!" The fairies loved the child, declared old Gude, and had touched him with their wand before his birth.

Wise old dame, she saw from the first the strength and the charm of Ernest Renan; a sort of natural magic, a sort of immaterial grace. There was the fairies' kiss! Renan almost certainly exaggerated his debt to a Celtic ancestry. But this much at least he owed them: this, and that obstinate sweetness, that rare fidelity of his, which contrasted so strangely with the liveliest impressionability of the nerves. And some whilom bard, most surely, bequeathed him the peculiar music of his style, clear as the bell about the neck of Tristan's hound, which rang so sweet that whoso heard it forgot forthwith his cares and all his sorrow.

Seven hundred years ago the Celtic poets invented a new way of loving. They discovered a sentiment more vague, more tender, than any the Latins or the Germans knew, penetrating to the very source of tears, and at once an infinite aspiration, a mystery, an enigma, a caress. They discovered "l'amour courtois." Yesterday their descendant, Ernest Renan, would fain have invented a new way of believing. . . . The "amour fine" of Launcelot has passed from our books into our hearts; we feel with a finer shade to-day because those Celtic harpers lived and sang. I dare not say that Renan has done as much for Faith—that he has transported it far from the perishable world of creeds and dogmas into the undying domain of a pure feeling. But, at least, the attempt was worthy of a Celt and an idealist.

CHAPTER II

HENRIETTE

W E have spoken of fairies. The true fairy—
the guardian angel, rather—of Ernest
Renan's youth was his only sister, Henriette.
Henriette had already one brother, Alain, an
excellent lad of fourteen, sober, just, and silent.
She was twelve years old when Ernest was born,
a little woman already, troubled about many
things, dimly aware of the struggle for life and
able to understand her mother's tears, as she
watched her rock the baby on her knees, weeping
passionately over this second son, so long desired,
and now born, as it seemed, into a world of sordid
misfortune. Already the head of the family, in his
dreamy but obstinate unworldliness, had half ruined
the little household. Henriette, who inherited
her father's silent and tenacious character, bore
him a child's absolute devotion. She adored him
and understood his moody reserve, as ruin
gathered closer. She loved the vivacious mother
whom she so little resembled, and who showed

the plain child but scanty tenderness.   Above all, she hugged to her inmost heart this new-born brother, as though she felt that for him, through him, and in him, she should attain to a completer existence than any she had dreamed of heretofore.

Henriette was neither quick nor brilliant.   She was not at all pretty, in the usual sense of fresh country prettiness.   We might say of her, as it was said of the Maid of Siena, "*speciositas naturaliter in ea non inerat excessive.*"   Her delicate features were marred by a birthmark. But she had eyes of the sweetest, long, white beautiful hands, and even in childhood a bearing of modest distinction.   A sort of innocent dignity was hers—a dove-like dignity made of mildness and quiet and reserve.   Nothing of the poetic charm of her birth-place was lost upon the pensive child.   The shadow of the convent walls, the stillness, broken at intervals by the clash of church bells, the distant moan of the sea, the half-understood Latin sentences which the good Sisters taught her in the psalter, all were things to be pondered in her heart,—subtle influences to mould her tender nature.   Her education, if limited, was exquisite.   As she grew out of childhood, the noble families of Tréguier, banished by the Revolution, crept back, one by one, fatigued and penniless, to wither in their ruined homesteads. Many single ladies of the most authentic nobility, were glad to earn their bread by giving lessons—a praiseworthy habit they had contracted during the Emigration. One of these impoverished damsels completed the training of Henriette Renan, and added to her natural sweetness that touch of good breeding which enhances every grace. Henriette, sensitive to every refinement, quickly caught the trick of unspoken and apparently deferent authority. While she was still a mere child, she was in great request as a tamer of wild spirits, and the young madcaps of the place yielded to her tranquil charm. She was born to guide, to soothe, and to educate. And when she was twelve years old she began the education of Ernest Renan.

"She attached herself to me with the whole strength of her tender and timid heart, athirst for love. I still remember my baby tyrannies ; she never chafed at them. Dressed to go out to some girlish party, she would come to kiss me good-bye, and I would cling to her frock, beseech her to turn back, not to leave me ! And she would turn round, take off her best gown and sit at home with me. One day, half in fun, half as a penalty for some childish offence, she threatened to die if I would not be good, and thereupon she leaned back in her arm-chair, closed her eyes and made believe to be dead. I have never felt anything so vivid as the pang of terror with which I saw my dear one, immovable, absent—for our destiny did not permit that I should watch her last moments. Wild with grief I sprang at her and bit my teeth in her arm. I can still hear her scream ! But I could only say, in answer to all reproaches ; ' Why did you die ? Oh, will you ever die again ? ' " [1]

When Ernest Renan was five years old and his sister just turned seventeen, their father's ship came into Tréguier port without a skipper. None has solved the mystery of the end of Captain Renan. Did the sea wash him overboard ? Did he seek in suicide the bitter remedy for his troubles ? His body was washed ashore off the sandy coast of Erqui. He died in debt. Not mere anxiety, but real poverty, was henceforth the portion of his little household.

Everyone at Tréguier knew and respected the Renans. The widow was left undisturbed in her little home ; her creditors were confident she would pay off, little by little, her heavy inheritance. But it is difficult for an inexperienced woman to earn, for the mother of three children

[1] " Ma Sœur Henriette," p. 13.

to save. I suppose they had some thoughts of letting the little Tréguier home, for after the unhappy skipper's death, when Alain left to make his way in Paris, Madame Renan, Henriette, and Ernest removed to Lannion, where the widow had the support and comfort of her own family, respectable and well-to-do people of the trading class. Neither Henriette nor Ernest liked the change.

.√ The country between the sea and Lannion is the very cradle of romance. On the sandy shore near Plestin, King Arthur fought the dragon ; at Kerdluel he held his court. Scarce a gun-shot from the coast there gleams the isle of Avalon. But in the most romantic neighbourhood, the life of a country town is essentially commonplace. The uncles and aunts of the little Renans had not much in common with Launcelot or Enid.

These small shop-keepers, in their trivial and difficult prosperity, these worthy Marthas troubled about many things, had little in common, either, with our two immature idealists. Henriette especially felt the transplantation. Her delicate and tender spirit seemed to soar ever upward, like the distant spire of Tréguier, further, further, from this too solid earth. Home-sick for Tréguier and heart-sick for her dead father, Henriette Renan

B

saw nothing in this world to tempt her from her wish to enter a convent. Ernest was the confidant of her vocation, and their happiest moments were these winter evenings when they would slip away to church together, the tall sister walking briskly with little Ernest completely hidden under the ample folds of her Breton cloak. Which was the happier then? She, God in her heart, the child she loved at her knees? Or the little lad himself, delighted to move in this warm loving darkness, clinging to his sister's skirts, crunching under his feet the fresh, firm snow? Long afterwards, this would still be their relation, on the one side a tender guidance, on the other a confident and happy clinging; and, as long as she lived, the cloak of Henriette Renan comforted her brother in this frosty world.

It was Ernest, after all, who proved the chief obstacle to Henriette's vocation: Ernest's future and her father's memory. The poor child, with her delicate sense of honour, could not rest happy till those debts were paid. How was her mother to pay them? Or Alain, in his 'prentice years? It was all very well for the creditors to be patient: until the last sou was paid her father's name was that of a bankrupt. And then, Ernest!

One day Henriette noticed a certain careful awkwardness in the gait of her little brother, always a slow and heavy child. Her attention discovered his timid endeavour to hide an unseemly rent in his baby garments. Poor child! Such a humble little effort to be decent in tatters, was too much for Henriette's vocation. From that moment the convent was done with. She burst into tears and vowed to devote herself henceforth to the welfare of this patient brother, who, with delicate instincts, seemed destined to cope unaided with the sordid struggle for existence.

From that moment, Henriette Renan was the head of the household. Young as she was, a mere girl, inexperienced, she resolved to get the better of ill-fortune. The resolve of a Breton is a very dogged thing. Like that stone which a Yorkshireman keeps seven years in his pocket before he turns it, and then seven years more before he flings it, the resolve of a Breton is a thing which can bide its time. None of the British Celts possess that union of a tenacious obstinacy with a very sweet and tranquil temper which is the strength of the Breton. To go on willing the same thing for years, quietly, without making yourself or other people unnecessarily miserable about it, is, it must be owned, a great secret. And if the Breton neither drank nor dreamed—if the Breton cared in the least for success—there would be no pulling against him in the race. Henriette's early efforts were all unavailing. First she attempted the thing which lay to her hand: she went back to Tréguier with her mother and Ernest and tried to set up a school in their old home. Then in 1835, she started for Paris, as governess in an establishment for young ladies. Before leaving her dear Tréguier on this desolate adventure, she received an unexpectedly brilliant offer of marriage from a man, much her elder, who felt the charm and rare devotedness of this fragile creature. But a hint that he did not mean to espouse her relations alarmed the high-strung Henriette and sent her off at a tangent on her career of self-sacrifice. She felt, it seems, some inclination for the kind and wealthy neighbour who shared her tastes and who offered her a Breton home. But, her father's debts—but, Ernest's future! How could she forsake the two most helpless things in the world, the dead, and a child? She thought of them. As for the happiness of Mademoiselle Renan and her establishment in life, these were very secondary considerations. It was unfortunate, doubtless, that she was so morbidly timid, so afraid of strangers, so easily home-sick. She must try to overcome these failings. So she packed her trunk, pinned on her old green shawl, kissed a long good-bye to all she loved on earth, and, with a last cruel wrench as she crossed the threshold, she took her place in the Paris coach and watched the spire of Tréguier till it faded to a smoke-line in the distance.

CHAPTER III

THE SEMINARY

MADAME RENAN was no less religious than her children. But she wore her religion with a difference. A bourgeoise of Lannion, with a quarter-strain of Gascon in her, she was less dreamy than the family she had married into: these Renans, obstinate, ruminating men—skippers like her husband and her father-in-law, or bards and vagabonds like Pierre, her brother-in-law. Madame Renan's faith was, naturally enough, a little different from her daughter's; less a perpetual elevation of the soul by thought and prayer than a convenient guide to life and death, cheerful on the whole, abundantly illustrated with all the most agreeable legends. She was an excellent churchwoman. She had brought up her eldest son to trade, but the dear desire of her heart was that her Benjamin—her last born gifted darling—should become a priest.

Ernest was not six years old when first his mother placed him under the protection of the saints. When the child's father had been brought

home and buried, she took the little lad by the
hand and led him outside the town to the shrine
of St Ives. St Ives is the greatest saint in
Brittany—the advocate of all good Bretons in the
heavenly courts. Madame Renan confided her
fatherless son to the guardianship of the immortal
lawyer. With what feelings since then, we may
wonder, has St Ives surveyed the career of his
ward and fellow-townsman? The point is nice ;
for St Ives, let us remember, is the patron saint
of truth. *Saint Yves de la Vérité* may pardon
some heretical shortcomings to one who chose for
his epitaph *Veritatem dilexi.*

In 1829 Ernest Renan was six years old. The
child must be taught to read and write, and must
learn his prayers in Latin. Who so fit as the
priests of the seminary to educate the ward and
pupil of St Ives? When, shortly after 1830,
the Renans returned from Lannion to Tréguier,
in order for Henriette to prosecute her scheme of
school keeping, Ernest was placed under the care
of the priests. There is an excellent seminary at
Tréguier : Renan never ceased to commend the
virtue, the simplicity, the kindness, the intellectual
integrity of his earliest pastors and masters. These
ecclesiastics taught him mathematics and Latin ;
they taught him little else. The notes of the
teachers of Ernest Renan are still in the posses-

sion of his family. They are excellent notes;
docile, patient, diligent, thorough, are adjectives
which recur. We read, however, that "Ernest
Renan is sometimes inattentive during service in
church."

Renan never ceased to extol the education
given him by the priests. "They taught me the
love of truth, the respect for reason, the earnestness of life. And these are the one thing in
which I have never varied. I left their hands
with a soul so tried and fashioned by them that
the light arts of Paris could only gild the jewel :
they could not change it. I believe no longer
that the Christian dogma is the supernatural
epitome of the sum of human knowledge : but I
do believe, I do still believe, that our existence
is the most frivolous of things, unless we conceive
it as a grand and perpetual duty. Old and dear
masters, nearly all of you dead to-day, whose
image often visits my dreams—not as a reproach,
but as a mild and charming memory, I have not
been as unfaithful to you as you think ! At heart
I am still your disciple."

Twice a day, regular as clockwork, Ernest
Renan might have been seen walking slowly
up the steep High Street to the college. The
years went by, the child of eight or nine became
a lad of fourteen, but the mien never altered, nor

the slow, sober gait, already a little rheumatic, nor the amiable unremarking gaze lost in some pleasant dream. Be sure that he took never a glance nor a step more than was needful ; for this child, so curious in all matters moral or intellectual, was the least observant of mortals. Renan was a gifted rather than a clever lad, more meditative than brilliant, honest and profound rather than quick or versatile. His lighter gifts and graces came to him when youth was over. A certain heaviness and slowness, always characteristic of his appearance, appeared as yet to cling round his intrinsic genius, like the protecting envelope about the unripe burgeon. Laborious, conscientious, eager to please, he was not only the gifted but the good boy of the college.

No child was more studious, more docile, more easily contented. When the day's task was done, no game, no long walk, no birds-nesting or black-berrying excursion tempted this odd schoolboy, always difficult to stir and averse to movement. He would take his book and sit in the inglenook on winter afternoons, or in the summer he would saunter round the cloister and watch the one old cow tethered amid the thick grass of the tombs. Life was full of interesting things. His mother's narrow house contained treasures of amusement. The child knew how to make a great deal of happiness out of little things. He had brought back from Lannion wonderful archives of old bills found in his grandmother's garret : the quaint Gothic letterings of the headings filled his baby-soul already with the true historian's feeling for the Past. "There has been a deal of love spent on these," he used to say. Then there were long political discussions with Marie-Jeanne, the little maid-of-all-work ; interminable musings over an odd volume of the " Cantiques de Marseille"; best of all there were the vast histories, the complicated and intricate Breton souvenirs and legends which would fall, hour after hour, from the lips of " Maman " as she sat busy with her sewing or her knitting. Belovéd " Maman," gayest and happiest of women, from whom the child inherited his temper of serene contentment, I think she taught him more, with her fund of myths and legends, than the good fathers up at the college, with all their Latin ! For here, in the peaceful house - place, the future historian of religions learned, as unconsciously as a child learns his mother's tongue, how the unknown becomes the supernatural in a rustic imagination, and how, in another wise, a fact becomes a faith.

He learned other lessons which were to shape his life no less. Every influence taught him the duty of honour, the value of disinterestedness.

These qualities were not merely elemental virtues, but the privilege of a superior intelligence. All the boys at Tréguier College who showed an unusual aptitude were destined to the priesthood, unless they happened to be nobles, born thereby to certain other superior duties of their own, based on the same foundation of honourable disinterestedness. Commerce, money-getting, un-inherited wealth, were the pursuits and the compensations of men who had failed in their studies. Had they been quicker at their Latin grammar, they would certainly have chosen to be priests. For the self-made man was an inferior creature, half-educated, fond of gain, fond of his own opinion, harsh to the defenceless, pushing, and frequently discourteous; doubtless useful enough in his proper sphere, infinitely below that of the priest or the noble. The man who seriously respects himself must give his best labours to an ideal cause, far removed from his own desires and necessities, wholly unconnected with his personal profit. No other life can be beneficent or noble. . . . Such was the conviction formed in child-hood which was to guide Ernest Renan throughout his life. But in childhood he translated this idea into the limited vocabulary of his age. He looked round him: the most disinterested, virtuous and studious persons of his acquaintance were the priests at the Tréguier Seminary.

His mother was enchanted, the good priests smiled acquiescence, when this unpractical, delicate, sedentary lad, who was always first in the class-room and last in the play-ground, said, " I mean to be a priest ! " Of course Ernest Renan meant to be a priest : and, later on, Professor at Tréguier, and, later still, perhaps, Canon of St Brieux. He would become the worthy emulator of his teachers ; and, since he loved books, —who knows ?—he might compile or edit some history in the style of Rollin. " Maman " would live with him always, and keep his house, and mend his cassock while she told him stories.

Man proposes. . . . In the summer of 1838 Ernest Renan carried off all the prizes at Tréguier College. We can imagine the joy of Henriette, withering and paling up in Paris from sheer hard work and home-sickness. All her heart was in her dear child. The news of his triumph flushed her and expanded her, and renewed her youth. The silent and reserved young governess could not keep *this* wonderful piece of news to herself. Her prophetic heart foretold great things for Ernest ! The doctor of the school where she taught was among the confidants of her discreet and tender enthusiasm, and

the good man, touched by the unwonted fire of
this quiet creature, interested also in her Breton
Phœnix, spoke to some of his friends about the
marvellous boy of Trèguier.

Among others he spoke to Monsieur Dupanloup, an elegant and brilliant—nay, the most
elegant and the most brilliant — Parisian ecclesiastic. At that moment Monsieur Dupanloup
was superior of a Parisian seminary which he had
founded in order to give educational advantages,
of an altogether exceptional kind, to young nobles
and theological students. St Nicholas du Chardonnet was meant to be a hot-bed of Catholic fervour
and Catholic genius. Success, brilliance, talent,
were among the evangelical virtues specially culti-
vated there. In the eyes of Monsieur Dupanloup
the glory of God, the mysterious Shechina, was
a very visible and glittering light of a somewhat
superficial radiance. This Parisian recruiter of
Catholic genius was quite aware that good things
might come out of Brittany. . . . Chateaubriand
. . . Lamennais . . . When he heard of the Phœnix
of Tréguier, " Send him to me at once ! " he
decreed.

Renan was fifteen and a half.

" I was spending the holidays wtth a friend
near Tréguier. On the afternoon of the 4th of

September a messenger came to fetch me in great haste. I remember it all as if it were yesterday! We had a walk of about five miles through the country fields, then, as we came in sight of Tréguier, the pious cadence of the Angelus, pealing in response from parish tower to parish tower, fell through the evening air with an inexpressible calm and melancholy. It was an image of the life I was about to quit for ever.

"On the morrow I left for Paris. All that I saw there was as strange to me as I had been suddenly projected into the wilds of Tahiti or Timbuctoo." [1]

In Paris, at the seminary of St Nicholas du Chardonnet, the Phœnix of Tréguier appeared but an awkward youth. Pale, sickly, ungainly, his stooping shoulders crowned by a head disproportionately large, the unprepossessing lad was as dull in manner as plain of face. He went musing all alone, brooding ever in a solitary reverie, his fine eyes seldom lifted from the ground, his subtle, humorous, delicate smile extinguished in utter homesickness.

Every now and then Henriette, in her old green shawl that spoke of Tréguier, would call to see him in the parlour. And the rest of the time the unhappy boy struggled and stifled in the Slough

---

[1] "Souvenirs d'enfance et de Jeunesse," p. 171.

of Despond, where the foot sinks hourly deeper, whence the soul, past hope, desires no escape. The professors at the seminary must have been sorely disappointed in their Breton prodigy. But, one morning, the priest committed to read the letters written by the pupils to their parents, was struck by the profound, the yearning tenderness and heartbreak of Ernest Renan's outpouring to his mother. He set the letter apart and showed it, in some surprise, to the director, Monsieur Dupanloup. That evening contained the weekly hour appointed to read out, in presence of Monsieur, the list of the places taken by the boys in their different forms. Renan was fifth or sixth in composition.

"Ah!" cried the director, "had the theme been the subject of a letter I read this morning, Ernest Renan would have been first!"

From that hour he followed the lad in his studies, guided, supported, bewildered, enchanted him, and made the new interest of his life. Ernest Renan was not to die of nostalgia, after all. But something died in him all the same. "The Breton died in me!" he used to say. The transition had been too brusque for his honest heart, for his solid and logical mind. What was there in common between the archaic faith of the Tréguier priests and this brilliant, decorative, literary and quasi-scientific Catholicism of Paris? Nothing which seemed important in the eyes of Monsieur Dupanloup appeared supremely needful to those Breton saints. How could the same august and sacred name shelter two incompatible spirits? If the one were true, the other must be false. If the one were false, the other might be false. If both were true, then Truth was no longer a thing one, simple and sole, but complex, infinite, susceptible of variation. These were the thoughts which darkened the mind of the young seminarist. He repulsed them as temptations, and redoubled his religious practices.

" He was," writes the Abbé Cognat, " one of the most devout of us in his pious reserve : chorister, writer of hymns, dignitary of the Brotherhood of Mary. Nor was he without a touch of superstition in his piety : never, for instance, did he forget to introduce a cross in the flourish which terminated his signature." [1]

If the Breton died at St Nicholas du Chardonnet —and I, for one, stoutly deny that he died—" the Gascon in me," wrote M. Renan much later, " saw abundant reasons to live."

The atmosphere of St Nicholas was no longer the still and humid air of Tréguier cloister. The breath of the boulevards penetrated through

---

[1] Abbé Cognat : M. Renan. Hier et Aujourdhui.

a thousand fissures into the closed circle of the seminary. Rollin was no longer the ideal man of letters, for the students discussed with passion Michelet, Lamartine, Victor Hugo, those rising glories of the hour.

"I discovered that there was a contemporary literature. I learned with stupor that knowledge was not a privilege of the Church. My masters at Tréguier had been far more advanced in Latin and mathematics than my new professors. But they dwelt sealed in a catacomb underground. Here, in Paris, the air of the outer world circulated freely. New ideas dawned upon me. I awoke to the meaning of the words, talent, fame, celebrity. A new ideal swam into my ken. This, perhaps, was what I had longed for so vainly, so vaguely, in the dim cathedral aisles of Tréguier!"[1]

[1] "Souvenirs," p. 185.

CHAPTER IV

A DOUBTFUL VOCATION

LIFE, which already had set a dozen fatal questions to germinate in Ernest Renan's mind, had shaken the very foundations of the faith -of Henriette. Already at Lannion, on the very morrow of her vocation resisted, she had begun to doubt of the truth of Christianity—a strange thing when one thinks of the girl's age and her environment. Unhappy as a governess, she no longer desired to be a nun. The Paradise of her old dreams appeared to her as a poor piece of man's work, a projection of the human fancy; and the adorable Mary, the hierarchies of saints, nay even the Good Shepherd, in whom she had believed, seemed so many sacred and pitiful ghosts. But out of the ashes of this old faith, reverently lifted on to the high places of the soul, there leapt a brighter flame, a new religion, imprecise, without text or dogma, and almost wholly moral: a belief in the vast order of the universe, speeding through cycles of time towards some Divine intent, and furthered in its grand and gracious plan by every private act of mercy or renouncement, by all the tendency of effort which makes for righteousness.

Thus believing, however reverent towards the faith which had nurtured and prepared her soul, Henriette beheld with much misgiving her brother's progress towards the altar. How should a boy of fifteen appreciate the sacrifice demanded of him? The lips said: *abrenuntio!* but the child knew not what he renounced. Most sisters would have thought, first of all, that he cut himself. off from love, but I believe Henriette's instinctive thought was that he cut himself off from liberty: that the child bound the man to think as the child,—that the child bound the man to obey as the child, and bound him into an intricate and inextricable fabric from which there could be no subsequent deliverance save at such a cost of good name, public respect, and ancient friendship as made her pale to think of. But Henriette was aware that the only fruitful change in spiritual matters, is that which begins within. Her meddling could do no good, only harm. The child might take his vows and keep them all his life long in perfect inner liberty, his heart remaining in accordance with his rule. She said nothing, therefore, only in silence vowed him her devoted sympathy if this should *not* be the case.

Half hoping, half fearing, lest he should outgrow the vocation so placidly accepted, she went week after week to see him in the parlour of St Nicholas, and let no word pass her lips that might hasten the issue.

But there came an end to these visits. Henriette found the struggle for life hard in Paris. Few were the savings she could send to Tréguier. When Count and Countess Andrew Zamoyski offered her a brilliant situation, amply paid, she accepted. She went out into exile in Poland, trebly far way in those days of post-chaise and travelling-coach—into a climate peculiarly unsuited to her fragile constitution—into a foreign country which, among its population, contained not one friendly face. Poor timid soul, the ten years of her engagement, the last ten years of her youth thus offered up in filial sacrifice, must have appeared in the prospect longer than all her past. Yet she set out, in 1840. Doubtless, when she bid good-bye to the dear young brother whom at their next meeting she should find a man, she did not dream that, from the vantage point of distance, she should become more familiarly his confidant, far more intimately his guide and true Egeria, than in the happiest days of their companionship. All that Jacqueline Pascal was to the great tormented soul of her

brother, Henriette was gradually to grow to
Ernest Renan.

Some short while after Henriette's departure,
Ernest Renan was promoted from the seminary
of St Nicholas to the more advanced college of
Issy, in the suburbs of Paris. There is no class
of philosophy at St Nicholas. In the French
University our fifth form corresponds to the
class of rhetoric, our sixth or highest form
to the class of philosophy, which is the direct
portal to the Sorbonne, the Ecole Normale, or
one of the various special schools of law, medi-
cine, engineering, and the art of war. Something
of this order is maintained in the seminaries.
After the class of rhetoric, St Nicholas sends
such of its pupils as are destined for Holy Orders
to study philosophy in the great diocesan seminary
of St Sulpice, which reserves for their accommoda-
tion its country house at Issy. Two years later,
the seminarists are received into the vast
establishment of the square St Sulpice at Paris,
where they are initiated into the mysteries of
theology.

Issy is an old French country house — a
small suburban palace which belonged from 1606
to 1615 to Queen Margot of gallant memory.
The worthy fathers have since added a few
wings, a few aureoles, a blue mantle or so, to the

mythological personages on the walls, and nothing
else has been altered in the pavilion of the Queen.
The long, low house looks on to a park planted
in the usual French fashion with clipped alleys
of lime and hornbeam enclosing wide irregular
lawns where the flowers spring and the hay grows
and ripens as nature wills. Not only in hay-
time, but right through the autumn and on sunny
winter days, Ernest Renan might have been found,
spending his hours of recreation on a stone bench
under the leafless limes, wrapt in a great *houppe-
lande* or French Inverness-cloak. There, imper-
vious to cold and damp, he read his book, without
a glance, without a word, for aught around him.
Every now and then M. Pinault, the reverend
professor of mathematics, would stop to gibe at
him :

"O, the dear little treasure! Look at him,
don't disturb him. Now, pray, don't disturb
him. See how completely he has rolled himself
in his form! *Mon Dieu!* he will always be like
that! He will study!—study!—study! Poor
sinful souls will appeal to him for help. He will
go on studying. He will murmur: Leave me!
Leave me! I am just at such an interesting
point!"

Ernest Renan would look up at his tormentors,
a little troubled by the acuteness of the shaft,

would heave a sigh, and would, in fact, go on studying.

Renan had entered Issy with a passion for Catholic scholasticism. The seriousness of his intelligence was satisfied by the vast and solid fabric of Catholic theology. Here was a subject more to his mind than Monsieur Dupanloup's course of rhetoric; more to his mind even than those first fevered readings of modern romantic literature, though these had left an ineffaceable impression on his talent. But now he had come to the heart of things. "I had left words for facts. I was about to examine the foundations, to analyse in all its details, this Christian religion which appeared to me the centre of all truth."

And hand in hand with the Catholic "philosophy of Lyons," Renan studied the Scotch metaphysicians. For some months Reid remained his ideal :—" My dream was the peaceable life of a laborious ecclesiastic—Reid or Malebranche—attached to his duties, relieved from his parish work on account of the value of his researches. Not until later did I perceive—with that degree of certainty which soon was to leave my mind no room for choice—the essential contradiction between these metaphysical studies and the Christian Religion."[1]

[1] "Souvenirs," p. 217.

After Reid came Malebranche, then Hegel, Kant, and Herder. From the first page, these more audacious and more universal thinkers exercised on Renan's mind an irresistible attraction. " I studied the Germans," he has written more than once, " and I thought I entered a Temple ! " A temple, indeed, vaster than any church. . . . At the two remotest poles of human thought there are situate two opposite conceptions of the universe. Orthodox and traditional transcendentalism shows us a definite act of creation, a living God, a Providence which guides the world, and the infinite army of the immortal souls of men. At the furthest extremity of metaphysical science exists the mystical doctrine of immanence, which, in place of a definite creation, explains the universe by the gradual evolution of a germ. All Being is Becoming : an eternal process, an infinite continuance, over which an unconscious deity broods in the abyss. The universe is animated by one single Soul, in whom all living beings share, but of which, so to speak, they only enjoy the usufruct, since they fade and vanish like sparks that fly upwards, while It remains eternal. Of these two creeds, Renan was bound in honour to believe the first. Little by little, he inclined towards the second.

The retentive and tenacious mind of Renan

let nothing slip of these early readings.   All his
philosophy is there in germ.   The mystical
pantheism of Herder, the Hegelian idea of
development, supplied him with the theory of
evolution—of a world perpetually in travail of
a superior transformation.   Kant renewed for
him the impelling principle of Duty.   And
Renan's theology is contained in a phrase of
Malebranche's—*Dieu n'agit pas par des volontés
particulières:* God does not act by special pro-
vidences.

"I greatly like your German thinkers (he
wrote to his sister in September 1842), though
they be somewhat pantheist and sceptic. . . .
One's first impression of philosophy is that it tends
towards a universal scepticism.   One is struck
by the uncertainty of human knowledge, the
slight foundation for all opinions save those based
on reason.   What we had always taken for
Truth appears mere prejudice and error. . . .
Philosophy excites, and only half satisfies the
appetite for Truth.   I am eager for mathematics!"[1]

Nothing could be more characteristic of Renan's
peculiar intellectual constitution than the manner
in which this very appetite for proof served to re-
strain his scepticism.   He appears to have decided,

[1] Ernest et Henriette Renan : "Lettres intimes," pp. 88, 96, 97.

almost immediately, that the pure toil of the
human intellect in the void could produce no
solution of the eternal problem.   He demanded,
not a system, but a proof; and while continuing
to read Kant and Herder, and especially Malebranche, he devoted no less a part of his time and
strength to the pursuit of mathematics and natural
science. " Who shall criticise the Eternal without
knowledge ? " he cried with Job. . . . By a sort of
instinct which had not yet found its right outlet,
Ernest Renan sought in exact science an answer
to the terrible problems which philosophy had set
him, and which the approximative or historical
sciences were at length to resolve.

In this state of suspense, voluntarily imposed,
there were moments when Renan relinquished
all his doubts with the great cry of Faust:
Gefühl ist alles! His heart had never wavered
an instant in its absolute attachment to the
Catholic Church. If faith be a sentiment, if we
know God only by the heart, then Renan was
a Christian. No life to him appeared so beautiful,
so desirable, so true to the highest ideal, as the
life of a priest. " Even if Christianity be only a
dream," he writes to his sister in September 1842,
" Even if Christianity be only a dream, the
priesthood remains a divine type." Your true
vocation is revealed by a certain inaptitude for

any other career. Renan, with his passionate love of study, his taste for seclusion, his complete incapacity for practical affairs,—Renan, with his vague and lofty aspirations towards the infinite, seemed born to be a priest. From Issy, in 1843, he wrote to Henriette :—" In fact I am only fit for *one* sort of life—a life of study and reflection, retired and tranquil. All the ordinary occupations of mankind appear insipid to me ; their duties taste flat against my palate and their pleasures are a weariness. The motives that guide them are odious to me. It is clear that I am not born for a life of action.

" A private life would be my happiness. But that a man should live merely to himself taints his retirement with egoism. Even if it were possible that I should live so, and not be a burden on those I love ! The priestly life offers all I desire without any compensating disadvantage. The priest lives for his fellows : he is their repositary of wisdom and good counsel. He is a man of study and much meditation, and, at the same time, a brother unto his brethren. And this is in my eyes the ideal life.

" I am deep in philosophy and physics—deep in Malebranche, the finest dreamer, the most implacable logician who ever existed. Yet he was a priest. More than that ; he was a monk.

And he lived unmolested in an age when Rome
was jealous of her powers. See how man, by the
mere impetus of his own weight, is constantly
carried up the steeps of Hope!"[1]

But for Henriette, vehement and tender, he
would, no doubt, have given way. She, with her
piercing insight, her wide prescient outlook, her
innate incapacity for compromise in a case of
conscience, was for ever exhorting him, enjoining,
remonstrating. More than once his heart fails:
"Ah, Henriette, I am weak!" She will have
no mercy! She sees, she feels, all that is fatally
ignoble, hypocritical, and arid in the life, and at last,
in the mind even, of the unbelieving priest. That
vocation which Ernest beheld on its ideal side
only, she saw in all the formidable consequences
of its limitless subordination. Can an ecclesiastic
dispose of his own soul? Is he not subject, even
in spiritual things, to the direction of his superiors?
Should he see the better part, is he always free to
chose it? Is he not bound to follow in a track
made to suit the common herd? Must not the
tyranny of custom and number drag down to the
level of the majority the rare devotees of an ideal
duty? Anxiously, eagerly, she entreats her
brother to assume no bond too soon, to wait until
he be of man's estate before he take upon himself

[1] "Lettres intimes," p. 118.

the vows and service of a man. "Above all, do
not think of us—of our family well-being! There
is no true claim there. I can suffice!" She proposes to him other prospects. As a professor or
as a public schoolmaster he might live the life of
study he desires, and be useful to his fellows—
and yet be free! She promises to find some
sure solution—not, no doubt, the ideal of his
dream. "But that ideal does not exist, I fear,
upon our work-a-day earth. Life is a struggle.
Life is hard and painful. Yet, let us not lose
courage. If the road be steep we have within us
a great strength; we shall surmount our stum-
bling-blocks! It is enough if we possess our
conscience in rectitude, if our aim be noble, our
will firm and constant. Let happen what may,
on that foundation we can build up our lives."

Meanwhile, at Issy, other influences, no less
determined, no less sincere, were concentrated
upon the unstable soul of Renan. In June
1843, Renan, towards the end of his course at
Issy, was informed that he was among the chosen
few admitted to the tonsure. The young man
implored a delay, immediately granted: "But
keep this affair," said his director, "separate from
the question of your vocation. They are distinct,
and you know my opinion as to the second."

"And would you believe," writes Renan in-

genuously to his sister, "that I too am now much
more assured of my vocation. All my directors
are convinced of it. . . . As for the question
of intellectual liberty, I have answered myself :
there are two sorts of independence ; the one
presumptuous and bold, railing at all that is
respectable, — this is indeed denied me by
priestly duty : but in any case, my conscience
and my desire for truth would forbid me such
audacities ; of this sort of independence, there
can, therefore, be no question. There is, however,
an independence of another fashion, wise, sage,
respecting what is worthy of respect, despising
neither beliefs nor persons, examining all things
calmly, in good faith, using reason as a divine
gift, and neither accepting nor rejecting any
conclusion on the mere sanction of a human
authority. Such independence is open to all
men, and why not to a priest? It is true that
in the case of a priest this liberty is subject to
a certain restriction from which other men are
free. The priest must know when to be silent!
He must place a guard upon his lips. He must
not scandalize the weaker brethren ; for their
name is legion who take umbrage at that which
they can not comprehend. But, after all, is it so
hard to keep one's mind to oneself in solitude?
It is often a secret movement of vanity which

leads us to communicate our opinions. The law of silence ought, perchance, to be the chosen portion of the lover of peace. 'We must have a silent opinion at the back of our mind,' said Pascal, 'which is our secret standard in all things, while we speak the language understanded of the people.' "

CHAPTER V

A GREAT RESOLUTION

IN this frame of mind Renan left the seminary at Issy, and proceeded in due form to the great College of St Sulpice, in order to take his degree in theology prior to entering the Church. Here he began to study Hebrew. From the first he displayed a singular gift for semitic philology. And this appeared to simplify his career. It seemed so obvious that Renan was destined to be professor of Oriental languages in a Catholic seminary. But in reality, every month of study led him further and further from the Church. Here, in these questions of date, in this patient study of those inflections which serve to prove a date,—here was that certainty, that proof positive, for which he had so vainly craved in the throes of his doubts. Renan, by natural gift, was not a pure thinker, but a historian. The proofs of history were, in his eyes, the only authentic proofs. And these were all against the Church. No impartial philologist can maintain that the second part of Isaiah is due to the same hand as the first. The Book

of Daniel is clearly apocryphal. Who can suppose that the grammar or the history of the
Pentateuch date from the period of Moses?
Admit one error in a Revealed Text and you
incriminate the whole. In another order of facts
it is clear that many a dogma of the Church
reposes on the erroneous translations of the
Vulgate. The Church, like the Scriptures, was
therefore fallible !

Meanwhile, St Sulpice laid the accent on
philology, insisted on Renan's peculiar gift,
and gave him every possible advantage. A
special permission allowed him to follow M.
Quatremère's course of Hebrew and Syro-Chaldaic
tongues at the College of France. In 1844 he
was intrusted with a preparatory class of Hebrew
grammar at St Sulpice. At twenty-two years of
age the young professor applied to the Semitic
languages the system which Bopp had recently
deduced from the comparison of the different
Indo-European tongues. Renan's *General History
of Semitic Languages* was to spring from this class
at St Sulpice.

The young scholar tried to stifle his doubts, to
apply himself relentlessly to exact studies, to pay the
least possible attention to his religious convictions.
A professor in a seminary would not need the living
faith of the simple parish priest. Alas, his exact and

D

patient mind assimilated all the knowledge afforded
him by the College of France, and by his masters
at St Sulpice, and found therein new material
for disbelief.   But while his reason disengaged
itself day by day from the authority of the
Church, his heart found every day some new
reason to be grateful.   Rome has never disregarded the talents of her servitors.   In our
time she is especially tender to such of them
as show a superior capacity for science : since
at that outpost she is most frequently attacked.
The directors of St Sulpice were not at all inclined to under-rate their pupil, they were ready
to make almost any sacrifice in order to keep
him where his talents were so greatly needed.
They hoped also, doubtless, that science would
prove a derivative, a happy counter-irritant, likely
to allay the excess of German metaphysics—and
this shows their sincerity : they could not suppose
the truth upon the other side !   Who can blame
their zeal ?   They were not only wise and prudent,
according to their generation ; they were charitable
with an eternal charity.   Their work of faith and
rescue was, to them, none the less a work of faith
and rescue, because it was accomplished with
an ulterior aim and an extraordinary diplomacy.

It was of no avail.   Renan was honest, and at
the other end of Europe there was Henriette

ceaselessly exhorting him to honesty. In his experience, science had confirmed the doubts aroused by speculation. He knew what was the essential minimum of Catholic belief: and he knew that he did not possess it. In this mood he returned to Tréguier in 1845, to spend the summer vacation with his mother.

"Ah, dear Henriette, the future fills me with fear. I, so weak, so inexperienced, so lonely, so unsupported,—with only you, five hundred leagues away, to help me—how am I to shatter bonds so mighty, and to wrench myself from a path whither a superior power has led me! I tremble when I think of it; but I shall not fail. And then—do you think I tear my faith out of my heart without a pang? Do you think I quit, without reluctance, these projects which for so many years have made up my life and my happiness? And all this world of mine, in which I was so at home, will cast me out for a renegade? And that other world—will it accept me? The first loved me, and made much of me : what does it not promise even to-day? Henriette, my good Henriette, keep me in heart! Oh, how sad and barren life appears to me in these moments! . . . Oh, my God, into what a snare hast Thou led my feet. I can only free myself by piercing my mother's heart. Oh, mother! Mother! I do

all I can to paint the future, to cheer her as best
I may, to soothe her fears. . . . How often have
I resolved to cast my doubts and scruples to the
winds and go straight ahead! She is there, two
paces away! God knows if I love and revere
her : it is but a torture the more.[1]

    .   .   .   .   .   .

"Her endearments break my heart ; her day
dreams—which she is for ever repeating, and
which I never find the cruel courage to gainsay—
are a continual grief. Ah, if she only understood!
I would sacrifice everything to make her happy—
everything except my conscience and my duty.
Ah, why was I not born a Protestant in Germany!
Herder was a bishop, and he was barely a
Christian. But in the Catholic Church there is
no room for heresy.

    .   .   .   .   .   .

"My German philosophers are my resource.
There I behold the continuation of Jesus Christ!
What sweetness and what strength! Christ
will come from the North at His Second Advent. . . .

"I still believe. I pray. I repeat the *Pater*
with rapture. I love to be in church. Pure,
simple, artless religion touches me profoundly
in my lucid moments : then I feel the perfume of

[1] " Lettres intimes."

God. Yes, I am pious, fervidly pious, sometimes, in spite of all my doubts. I think I shall always remain pious in any case. Piety has surely a value of its own—be it merely subjective.

" Here they take me for a good little seminarist, very religious, very gentle. God forgive me, it is not my fault! How could I make them understand! I could never put so much German into the heads of my honest Bretons.

" There are moments when I think I will amputate my reason, and live only for the mystic life. Except my judgment, except the faculty which weighs and criticises, the Catholic Church responds to every function of my soul. I must therefore sacrifice either the Church or my judgment . . . a difficult and cruel operation, but God knows I would perform it if I could think it His will. Ah! how I dread the end of the vacation! When it comes to practice, what shall I decide? "[1]

This young Hamlet of the Inner Life was none the less a Breton, with a spring of resolve in him on which he did not count enough. More than once in his career the man who—in the phrase of Montaigne—was among all others " undulating and diverse," was to exhibit this same admirable obstinacy for conscience' sake. He left Tréguier

[1] Letters to the Abbé Cognat : " Souvenirs," p. 382 *et seq.*

on the 9th of October 1845, and returned to
St Sulpice prepared to temporize and dally, far
from certain of his future choice. A sort of
innocent duplicity made the constraint of pious
practices not entirely odious to him ; a certain
artless macchiavellism, which he never lost, made
the difficult and mortal game he played rather
interesting, than merely cruel, or repugnant.
Moreover, the beauty of Catholicism satisfied
his artistic instincts, his tender sensibility. And
his education had fostered in him his natural
optimism, so that he still sometimes envisaged, as
quite practicable, heaven knows what chimaeric
fusion between an inward sincerity and an outward observance of the Noble Lie. But his religious
education had also fostered in him an extraordinary strength of conscience—backed at the last
extremity, as we have said, by the Breton's
doggedness.

It was evening when Renan arrived in the
square of St Sulpice. A surprise awaited him.
The directors, who had dallied and gone saunter-
ing long enough, thought the moment had come
for a brusque tightening of the rein, for a flying
leap over the hedge. Renan found himself no
longer a pupil of the seminary. During his
absence he had been appointed professor in the
Archbishop of Paris's new Carmelite College.

To accept was to give a pledge of good faith to the Church. To refuse so honourable a position was inexplicable. Renan sought his superiors, explained his whole position, his doubts, his scruples, which, instead of diminishing, increased with every month. Once at bay he stood firm, refused to temporize, and showed the obstinate grit in him. The Fathers immediately gave way; their bonds apparently fell from him. The same evening, without any sort of scene or storm, desperately alone, but not outcast, the young seminarist crossed the threshold of the seminary, traversed the square, and entered a small semi-clerical hotel at the north-western corner of it.

"A man of much talent said once of M. Renan :—

"'Renan thinks like a man, feels like a woman, and acts like a child.'"

"Did he act like a child, the poor young Breton who fled from St Sulpice aghast because he no longer thought the lessons of his masters all quite true? It was, perhaps, a piece of childish folly to renounce the splendid future which awaited him in his chosen path, to affront extreme poverty, without resources, without prospects, sustained by the sole impossibility of living for aught else than a conviction. Those who think that the hall-mark of a man is his sincerity in regard to the world and his own soul, will grant that on that occasion the child showed himself twice a man." [1]

[1] James Darmesteter : Ernest Renan. " Critique et Politique," p. 63.

CHAPTER VI

DOMINUS PARS

· PARIS, RUE DU POT-DE-FER
October 13*th*, 1845.

" $\mathbf{A}$ T last, my Henriette, my dearest friend, I
can pour out all my heart, I can tell you
all the trouble which corrodes my soul! The
last few days count in the record of my life ;
perhaps they are the most decisive, certainly the
most painful I have experienced. So many
events have crossed each other in this narrow
space that the mere recital of them will imply all
my feelings. And it will console me to tell you
everything, for here, now, my isolation is terrible,
and my lonely, tired heart finds an infinite sweetness in resting upon yours.

" Only one word first, dear, of this last vacation ;
a sweet and cruel time for me. My position was
of the strangest. To enjoy the companionship of
my kind mother, to wait on her, caress her, cheer
her by my day dreams, is so delightful a pastime to
me that I believe there is no trouble, no anxiety,

that I could not forget in her society. And then, a peculiar indefinable sense of well-being hangs about my native place. All my childhood, so simple, so pure, so heedless, survives in its atmosphere, and this revival of my past charms me almost to tears. The life of that country is but a common, vulgar life, I know. But there is a repose about it, a quiet well-being, in which thought and feeling, when not prisoned in the narrow circle of our daily round, are able to exercise their sweet gift of healing. Ah, how I feel to the core that vanished sweetness! I am weak, my dear Henriette. I sometimes think I could be quite happy in a simple, common life which I should ennoble from within. Then I think of you and I look higher.

"Yet in this mild and calm atmosphere of Tréguier, you can easily see how difficult was my position with regard to mamma. She had but the faintest suspicion of my state of mind, and she tried to trace my secret thought under the least of my words and actions. And I was afraid to let her see the truth and yet I felt I ought not to conceal it. Think how I suffered! The *necessity* of telling her all, the fear of her cruel disappointment, led me, hour by hour, into almost contradictory courses. And our good mother, with a disastrous cleverness, interpreted them all accord-

ing to the desire of her heart. She would take
no hint, no mere suggestion. At last one day—
one hour—which I shall never forget, I was
forced to be more explicit. I said clearly that
my vocation was *doubtful* . . . that I must exact
a *delay*. Well, from that hour she had been more
calm. She is less afraid when I speak of studying in the Paris University, when I speak of a
possible journey to Germany. I knew how to
turn all these projects in harmony with her dearest
scheme—our meeting, the progress of my studies,
&c. Do not mention to her that I am at an inn!
Ah, dear mother, how dear she is to me—my
greatest happiness but also my greatest trouble.
I should hate to be vulgar in any part or parcel
of my inner nature ; but I am sure that I am not,
in my love for her!

"I arrived in Paris on the 9th of October, in
the evening. That same night I slept at the hotel.
The next days I passed with all due gravity and
decorum in terminating my connection with St
Sulpice. I was charmed by the esteem and the
affection which the fathers showed me. My
Hebrew professor has promised to recommend
me very warmly to M. Quatremère: he holds to
me as to his favourite pupil. I could not have
imagined so much broadness of view in the
strictest orthodoxy. They are persuaded that I

shall return to St Sulpice, and,—would you believe
it, dear Henriette ?—I like to think so myself,
and was enchanted to hear them say so.   Accuse
me of weakness if you like.   I am not of those
who take a side, and never lose hold, whatever
they may think, whatever Science prove.   And
Christianity is so large a thing, a man may well
hold more than one opinion concerning it, according to the different degrees of his instruction.
Still, at this moment, I do not see how I can in
conscience become a Catholic priest.

" I have seen Monsieur Dupanloup: he was
delightful !   He granted me an interview of an
hour and a half—a thing he never does.   How
well he understood me at once !   He did me so
much good !   He replaced me in my lost high
sphere, whence these practical preoccupations
had caused me to fall in some degree.   I
was quite frank and explicit with him, and he
was very pleased with me.   I recognised the
superior mind in his advice, so clear and to
the point.   He promised to do *his utmost* for
me. . . .

" You must let me assure you, dearest, that, say
what you will, I cannot spend all this year at
your expense.   I have quite decided to accept
some post which will not encroach too much upon
my time and may even be useful to me. . . .

" I have been to see the directors of Stanislas
College. I had the best of references. Some of
my old comrades are there and had spoken of me.
I allow that I should like, best of all, to enter as
a teacher at Stanislas. There, my dear, I should
be treated honourably and morally. Perhaps you
do not like the prospect, as the college is directed
by ecclesiastics ; but it is formed exactly on the
model of the University. And I have been most
frank. I have explained to the provisor the
reason of my leaving St Sulpice. And think
what an admirable transition ! No one would be
astonished to see me pass from St Sulpice to
Stanislas, and no one would be astonished to see
me move on from Stanislas to another college
of the university ! And mamma would be delighted : it was one of her ideas."

Stanislas is in fact a Jesuit college participating
in the examinations and other advantages of the
lay public schools of Paris. In the touching and
honourable engagement which the venerable Order
of St Sulpice was fighting with an inexperienced
governess in Poland for the soul of Ernest Renan,
the last rally had not yet been sounded. The
Church did not by any means despair of her
acolyte. And he, perhaps, had never felt more
drawn towards the House of God.

" I spend my evenings in the church of St

Sulpice," he wrote to his friend, the Abbé Cognat. [1]
. . . There is no more happiness for me on earth.
. . . I remember my mother, my little room, my
books, my dreams, my quiet walks at my mother's
side. . . . All the colour seems to have faded
out of life."

It is probable that the Fathers counted on this
reaction and were well aware that the towers of
St Sulpice never look more noble than from the
other side of the square—from the windows, say,
of Mademoiselle Céleste's stuffy but respectable
small clerical hotel.   Nor can we wonder at their
error. They knew their pupil in his sweet
humour and his docility, in his attachment to
themselves and to the Church : they knew him
as an imaginative, serene, and hopeful child; they
did not recognise as yet that granite resistance
which underlay this graciousness of disposition,
and which it was impossible to undermine. Un-
impassioned, sincere, curious above all things of
the truth, Ernest Renan was not to be led in
any path but that he saw before him. Even
while the reverend ecclesiastics of Stanislas and
St Sulpice were putting their heads together in
a charitable purpose of friendly circumvention,
Renan was writing to his sister concerning "the

---

[1] Renan's letters to the Abbé Cognat, during the years 1845-6,
are reprinted in the Appendix to his "Souvenirs de Jeunesse."

singularity of his relations with them, which
afforded him the opportunity of making the most
valuable psychological observations." He was
interested, and touched, and sceptical, and heart-
broken, with equal sincerity. The fathers,
strangely enough, knew little of his religious
scruples: Monsieur Dupanloup alone asserted that
they amounted to a total loss of faith. Prompted
by a reserve which made him dread to exhibit in
public his inmost wound,—and, perhaps, inspired
by that morbid horror of the commonplace which
haunted Renan throughout his youth,—he kept to
himself the moral and philosophical origin of his
doubts, and put forward only his scientific scruples.
He was acutely conscious (the theme recurs again
and again in his letters), that the recalcitrant
seminarist is rarely a heroic personage. If he
had to doubt, at least he meant to doubt with
distinction and originality.

So he spoke to the astonished Fathers of the
inexact philology of the Vulgate, or the erroneous
date assigned by the Church to the Book of
Daniel. St Sulpice knew how to deal with the
mere sensuous backslider; it knew how to deplore,
to deprecate, and if need be to imprecate, the
torments of revolt, the passionate despair, of a
Lamennais. It could not take these niceties of
scholarship so seriously — a mitigated contact

with reality would soon, it opined, bring the fancies of a dreamer within bounds.

And doubtless St Sulpice counted also on the contrast between the warm kindness of the Church and the shrewdness of the world, ever suspicious of the unfrocked clerical. Monsieur Dupanloup offered his purse to Renan. He can not have been quite pleased to hear that, out of her savings, Mademoiselle Renan had already sent her brother a sum of eight and forty pounds. Moreover, by some prodigy of feminine ingenuity, the little governess at Zamocz had obtained for her brother letters of introduction to the most eminent scholars of the day. She had thus made Renan in some measure independent of the Church.

The worst of his trial was now, in truth, over for Renan. His great act of resolution had, as it were, cleared the air. There was no more compromising. Like many naturally undecided persons, Renan pursued tenaciously a course of conduct once adopted, knowing in what an eddy of ceaseless irresolution he would be flung by another change of front. Those who met him at the moment of his secession from St Sulpice observed in him none of the poignant anxiety of the Christian who feels his faith slip from him. He had the look of a young philosopher, calm, resolute, smiling, who sees new immense horizons open before him. For the moment he was pre-occupied by his practical affairs which he took seriously, although not tragically.

It is characteristic of Renan's complex, curious and quiet-tempered nature that his change of opinion provoked in him no aversion towards his lost ideal. He did not desire to burn what he had once adored. He went on adoring with a difference. He maintained his fealty to M. Le Hir as a spiritual superior and chose him for his confessor—for this strange apostate continued to confess himself and to receive absolution. " It does me good, and is a great consolation. I will confess myself to you when you are in orders," he writes to his friend. He was on terms of intimacy—almost of unction—with the Abbé Gratry, the Superior of Stanislas. For Renan entered Stanislas, as St Sulpice intended him to do, much to the distrust and discomfort of Henriette. The young usher, at six-and-twenty pounds a year, admitted to terms of such flattering familiarity with his directors, saw Stanislas at first through rose-coloured spectacles. . . . Henriette's fears are a mythical survival, interesting to the scientific observer.

" Because it is a College of Jes— . . . Oh, my dear Henriette, is it possible that a clever woman in the nineteenth century can amuse herself with

E

such nursery tales? In truth, I myself am no partisan of the Society : in all the force of the term, I do not *love* it. But from the bottom of my heart I laugh at the fantastic imagination which sees in it a sort of ogre-scarecrow to frighten babes with. It is a really remarkable item of psychology, a product of the faculty which gave us Bluebeard and other tales of wonder. 'Tis the love of mystery, the human need of the fantastic which has produced the legend of the Society of Jesus." All the same, a few days later our young psychologist left Stanislas, as he had left St Sulpice. He had been very happy with the Jesuits. But his lucidity saw through their judicious wiles. " 'Tis a duty to go. I have made a great sacrifice : it would be absurd to hesitate before a small one."

When, therefore, Renan was required to wear a cassock and conform, merely in outward things of course, to his ecclesiastical environment, he sighed—but went away. "They were very nearly taking me again in their net," he wrote to Henriette. But he left them, shut upon him with a pang of regret the door of the House of the Lord, and sought that world of laymen which appeared to him so sordid, almost immoral, and unfriendly. " For I need an atmosphere of moral feeling," he remarked to his sister. What he needed still more was an atmosphere of independence, in which to work out his own salvation. That at least he found in the school for young gentlemen where he was admitted as parlour-boarder—or rather as a sort of pupil-teacher, since he received his board in return for the lessons he gave.

The house was in a steep street of the Montagne Sainte Geneviève, known to-day as the Rue de l'Abbé de l'Epée. In those days it was called the Rue des deux Eglises. Renan must often have smiled as he read the name. For God had led him indeed into the Street of Two Churches, nor was the second, in his eyes, less holy than the first.

"Long ago," he writes to the Abbé Cognat, "already when I went up to the altar to receive the tonsure, I was tormented by terrible doubts. But my superior urged me on, and I had always heard that it was my duty to obey. So I went up, but God is my witness that in the intention of my heart, I took for my portion that Truth which is the hidden God! I dedicated myself to her quest, for her sake I renounced all profane motives and ambitions—nor shall I consider myself false to my vow until, abandoning my soul to vulgar cares, I content myself with the material aims which suffice to worldly men. Till then, I can repeat, *Dominus pars.* . . . Man can never be sufficiently sure of himself to swear unwavering fealty to a given system, though at the moment of his vow he hold it true. All he may do is to dedicate himself to Truth, whatsoever she be, wheresoever she lead him, no matter what the sacrifice she may demand."

PART II

CHAPTER I

NEW IDEAS

IN the first days of November 1845 Ernest Renan entered on his duties at M. Crouzet's school. They were not stimulating, they were not inspiring, but they left him his whole day free for work. During some two hours, of an evening, he superintended the studies of seven youths who followed the classes of the Lycée Henri IV. In return, without diminishing his sister's little store, he received a place at table and a small room to himself. His wants were supplied, his liberty was complete, his leisure was ample; save for his state of mind—but that is everything!—he might have been happy. Alas, he was dull and sad. The world, in his eyes, appeared terribly mediocre: a desert, tediously overpopulate, a shabby wilderness of fifth-rate souls. He felt numb and shaken as one who has had a great fall. A month ago he had been almost a priest, belonging by implication to a superior order. He had been appointed professor

in the Archbishop's College. He had been recognised as a Semitic scholar. And behold, he
was little better than an usher in M. Crouzet's
school.

For more than two months he kept his situation a secret from his mother. By a pious
fraud he continued to "paint the future," to speak
of Stanislas. But too many persons counted
on Mme. Renan's influence over her devoted
boy for his position to remain a secret. Poor
loving woman, she did not attempt to persuade
him! She wrote him heart-broken letters. He,
her delicate lad, her pride, her darling, to think
he was "on the streets!" for so she phrased it.
"You know, dear, even a mouse in your room
used to keep you awake. You were never used
to hardship!

> " O Joseph, mon aimable
>   Fils affable,
> Les bêtes t'ont dévoré!"

In those first dull November days at M.
Crouzet's school, something of the melancholy
which had tarnished all things for the young
seminarist of St Nicholas hung again over Ernest
Renan, and menaced him with that creeping
nostalgia so deadly to the Breton. His letters
to Henriette are steeped in disappointment. . . .

"Now that I see them at close quarters, men are less refined, less intellectual than I had imagined them. . . . I feel lost in this cold world, incurious of the Divine. . . . Since Christianity is not true, nothing interests me or appears worth my attention." What was the use of striving and struggling in this unimportant throng of mortals? "*J'aime mieux ne pas mentir et caresser ma petite pensée,*" he wrote to the Abbé Cognat in a phrase too charming to translate.

Renan had no longer any hope of regaining his faith. . . . Faith is a sentiment, and, once lost, there is no regaining it by evidence. . . . Doubt is an act of reason in which evidence is everything. Once we judge religious history by the ordinary rules of scientific criticism, the authenticity of Catholic tradition can no longer compel our assent. Renan continued to read the Scriptures. But the Bible, read as any other book, appears merely a collection of Oriental masterpieces, beautiful as poetry, valuable as history, but holding no peculiar promise for our souls. He looked into the empty heavens, saw no Christ on His throne there, and brooded with an obstinacy which had a sort of pleasure in it over the completeness of his desolation.

This *delectatio morosa* is dangerous to a con-

templative temperament.   That way, if not madness, melancholia lies ; the disease is potential in
many Celtic constitutions.   For some weeks,
Ernest Renan, so like his mother, felt his father's
dull and sluggish blood stir ominously at his
heart.   But a fortunate circumstance shattered
his lethargy.   A new friendship absorbed him.
The oldest of his pupils, a young M. Berthelot,
some eighteen years of age, was studying advanced mathematics and philosophy at Henri IV.
They lodged on the same landing.

" It was in November 1845 that I first set eyes
on Ernest Renan.   He was four years older than
I, but he had, perhaps, even less experience of
life—if such a term may be used of young men,
the one eighteen, the other two-and-twenty.   He
had just left the Seminary—not without some
vague inclination towards a possible resumption
of the sacerdotal cloth.   His gentle, serious bearing, his taste for things intellectual and moral,
pleased me at once, and we became friends." [1]

"We had the same religion," says Renan
simply.[2]   "And that religion was the worship of
Truth."

Truth is a diamond of many facets, and the

---

[1] *Correspondance Berthelot—Renan.   Revue de Paris :* 15 Juillet
1897.
[2] *Discours et Conférences,* p. 231.

young men had seen her at different angles.
Each knew most things the other did not know.
Renan was already expert in theology, philosophy,
philology and history. But young Berthelot revealed to him a new world of vaster vistas and
more precise perspectives :—the magnificent certi-
tudes of physical and natural science. Forty years
after those first conversations in their attics of the
Rue des Deux Eglises, fragments and echoes of
those midnight marvels linger still in the mind of
Renan.

"How infinitely the atomic theories of the
chemist and crystallographer surpass that vague
notion of Matter, which verifies scholastic philosophy ! . . .[1]

"Think of knowing that our earth is a ball
some three thousand leagues in diameter . . .
that the sun, up there, is thirty-eight millions
of leagues away, and that it is one million
five hundred thousand times larger than the
earth !"[2]

If Spinoza was a God - intoxicated man,
Renan was a man intoxicated by the splendour
of the universe ! There are stars whose
light falls through space ten thousand years
before it reaches us, falling at the rate of over

[1] *Discours et Conférences*, p. 16.
[2] *Feuilles Détachées*, p. 156.

thirty millions of leagues in seven minutes!
There are suns, larger than ours, and perhaps
whole solar systems, in the formless white blurs
that film the skies on cloudless nights. The
heavens proclaim, indeed, the glory of the
Eternal; and Renan knew how great a tempta-
tion Job resisted when he cried, " I have seen the
moon advance in her majesty, O God, and I
have not bowed the knee!"

As the last shreds of his faith fell from before
him, lo! in their place he discovered the whole
unspeakable mystery of the Cosmos.   So, with the
first elements of astronomy and physics, Renan
learned that passionate devotion to the universe
which engrosses the whole mind, and makes all
private sorrow a thing of slight account.   Already
he might have exclaimed with Marcus Aurelius,
" All that suiteth thee, O Cosmos, suiteth me!"
He was in very truth a " citizen of the great
city," a conscient atom of the whole.   The world
was too vast, our span of years too short, the
sum of science attainable too tremendous, for life,
however sad, to be adjudged a failure.   Yes, in
1846 he was already the Renan who, years later,
wrote of Amiel: "The man who has time to
keep a private diary has never understood the
immensity of the universe.   There is so much
to learn!   In face of this colossal piece of work

how can we stop to consume our own hearts, to
doubt, to repine? . . . My friend M. Berthelot
would have his hands full, had he a hundred
consecutive lives, nor find in any one of them
the time to write about himself! . . . Everything
has to be done, or done all over again, in natural
and social science. When we feel ourselves
called to labour at this infinite task, we are too
busy to pause and brood over the little private
melancholies we may fall in with by the way."[1]
. . . "When I think of the unique pair of friends
we were," he says elsewhere, "I see before me
two young priests in their surplices, walking arm
in arm. We should have blushed to have asked
each other a favour, or even a piece of advice.
Neither of us was greatly occupied with himself,
and neither of us was greatly occupied with the
other. Our friendship consisted in what we
learned together."[2]

Indeed they learned many things together, but
they learned many things apart. As time went
on M. Berthelot was drawn more and more
exclusively into the sphere of physics, and especially of chemistry, as we all know, to our admira-
tion. Semitic philology continued to engross
M. Renan. He wrote to his sister: "I have

[1] *Feuilles Détachées*, p. 359.
[2] *Souvenirs*, p. 339.

so many new and just ideas! I am throwing
all my heart into my work—all I know and all
I am—and I have the instinct of success."

His canvas was the series of lectures which he
had delivered the preceding year at St Sulpice,
and which the Abbé Le Hir strongly urged him
to publish. The book was to be a Hebrew
grammar. But, in the hands of this ardent
young thinker, philology became a new instrument of psychology. For the character of a
nation is transfixed in its language, and a Hebrew
grammar is a diagram of the Semitic soul. In
the speech of the Jew or the Arab, as in his
nature, you will find something irreducible and
stubborn, a dignified simplicity, a non-existence
of the finer shades; a something monotonous,
which recalls the desert in its immense unifor-
mity. So theorised young M. Renan, in that
general history of Semitic languages which was
to introduce him to the world of science.

The first sketch of this important work,
presented in manuscript to the Academy of Inscriptions in 1847, by a young man of four-and-
twenty, a pupil-teacher in a school for boys,
obtained the Prix Volney, one of the most
important distinctions awarded by the Institute
of France.

Thus, barely two years after leaving St
Sulpice, Renan saw a new career open before
him. He continued to pass his University examinations : he was successively Bachelier and
Licencié. In 1847 he took his degree as Agrégé
de Philosophie, that is to say, Fellow of the University, and, in consequence, he was offered the Professorship of Philosophy in the Lycée of Vendome.
Here, and later, — during the long vacation at
St Malo,—Renan occupied his leisure by a thesis
on Averroës which was to procure him his doctor's
degree. Half convinced by so much success, his
mother let herself accept some consolation. Her
" fils affable " was still her " fils affable " : amiable,
studious, gifted, as of old. He had come back to
live with her. His grave morality seemed almost
orthodox. No scandal had attended his secession
from the priesthood. " My mother shows the
truest liberality of mind," Renan wrote to M.
Berthelot in 1847 ; "she fully approves my system,
which is never to express, by word or deed, either
affection or antipathy for the profession which
might have been my own. I soon brought her to
see my point of view. And indeed we have many
a piquant conversation on this head." But despite
the charm of home, despite his native air, Renan
was not happy in the narrow provincial circle

which he had re-entered. He missed the intellectual stimulus of Paris. He was glad when a small temporary appointment,—as assistant master in the Lycée of Versailles—permitted him to return to the capital and resume his interrupted studies.

CHAPTER II

1848

THE father of M. Berthelot was a doctor, an intellectual man, above all, a benevolent man. His practice was in a poor neighbourhood; of modest origin himself, he was interested in many philanthropic schemes. He was a firm Republican. "The first I had seen," wrote Renan, who barely could remember his father and his uncles. Opposed to the bourgeois spirit of the Monarchy of July, an enthusiastic believer in the Socialist transformation of society, Dr Berthelot influenced his son and, through him, the ever-impressionable Ernest Renan. . . . Yet all through the beginning of '48, immersed in his studies, the young scholar had listened to his friend's gospel with a somewhat vacant ear. He was engrossed by an essay on the study of Greek in Mediæval Europe, which appeared to him more immediately important. In all things, always, he found it hard to take a side. He distrusted extremes. His sense of the relativity of appearances debarred him from a passionate conviction in politics no less than in religion. Moreover, if he was by opinion a Liberal, by temperament Renan was Conservative. A natural love for the Past, a natural dread of innovation, hampered him in the sphere of political reform :

"I shall never break many lances for this sort of thing," he wrote to M. Berthelot, in September 1847.

Then the Revolution broke out in February. The King and his family went into exile. There was a riot in May. One morning Ernest Renan had to climb a barricade in order to reach the College of France. He climbed it and arrived in due time at the Sanscrit lecture-room ; but there was no lecture that day, and behold ! the College was full of soldiers ! The young scholar sighed and continued his walk, in order to study Sanscrit at M. Burnouf's private house. Civil war reddened the streets in June. Ernest Renan awoke in earnest and turned all his mind to the problems of Socialism.

I know no page in Flaubert's *Education Sentimentale* which gives a more vivid picture of a political massacre than we find in some of Renan's letters to his absent sister. The dreamer, startled from his dream, sees the dreadful reality before him with a horrified acuteness.

25th June 1848.

" Frightful sight ! The whole day we heard
nothing but the whistling of bullets and the clang
of the tocsin. . . ."

26th June.

" The evening and last night were worse than
ever. There was a massacre at the Gate of St
Jacques, another at the Fontainebleau Gate. I
spare you details. The St Bartholomew offers
nothing like them. There must be in human
nature something naturally cannibal which bursts
out at certain moments. As for me, I would
willingly have fought with the Garde Nationale
until, in their turn, the guards became the
murderers. No doubt they are guilty, these
poor mad insurrectionaries who shed their blood
and know not what they ask—but are they not
guiltier who, by system, have deadened in them
every human feeling ? "

1st July.

" The storm is over. If in such a state of
things it were permissible to appeal to the artistic
sense, I would call the Paris of these last days
the strangest, the most indescribable of great
sights. A few hours after the fighting was over I
visited the field of the combat. Unless you

have witnessed such a thing, my dear, you cannot
imagine the great scenes of humanity. In the
Rue St Martin, in the Rue St Antoine, and in
the Rue St Jacques, between the Panthéon and
the Quays, there was not a single house but was
riddled with cannon-ball. Some of them were
perforated to sheer open work! The fronts of
the houses, all the windows, were pierced through
and through with bullets—wide streaks of blood,
broken and abandoned guns, marked the places
where the fight had been the fiercest. Built with
a marvellous art, and constructed, not as they
used to be with heaps of cobblestone, but with
the large flagstones of the footpath, the barricades,
with their projecting and retreating angles, had a
look of fortresses. There was one every fifty
paces. The Place de la Bastille was the most
frightful chaos : all the trees cut down or bent
and twisted by the cannon balls ; on one side
whole houses demolished or still in flames ; on
another, veritable towers of defence, built out of
beams of timber, overturned carriages, and heaps
of stones. In the middle of all that, a crowd,
dizzy and half out of its mind ; soldiers worn out
with fatigue, asleep on the pavement, almost
under the feet of the people. The rage of the
vanquished disguised under an affected calm ; the
disorder of the conquerors opening a path through

the demolished barricades—the public pity craving
alms and lint for the wounded ; all combined in
a spectacle of the sublimest originality, in which
the whole gamut of humanity was heard in
an admirable discord : man, face to face with
man, naked, without disguise, with nothing but
his primitive instincts."

16th July.

" Horror of exact reprisals ! I am always for
the massacred, even though they be guilty. The
National Guard has been guilty of atrocities I
scarcely dare recount.

" After the battle was over, posted on the
terrace of the Ecole des Mines, they amused
themselves by " potting " at their leisure, as a
form of recreation, the passers-by in the adjacent
streets, where the thoroughfare was still open.
That may have been the last flicker of the fury
of the fray. But what is awful to think of, is the
hecatomb of prisoners sacrificed several days later.
During whole afternoons I have heard the ceaseless firing in the Luxembourg Gardens—and yet
the fighting was over ! The sound and the
thoughts it suggested, exasperated me to such
a degree that I determined to see for myself, so I
went and called on one of my friends whose
windows overlook the gardens. It was too true.

If I did not see the murderers with my own eyes,
I saw what was worse, what I never can forget,
and what, if I did not try to lift myself above
personal sentiments, would leave in my soul an
everlasting hate. . . . The unhappy prisoners
were packed in the garrets of the Palace, under
the leads, in the stifling heat of the roof. Every
now and then one of them would thrust his head
out of the dormer window, for a breath of air.
Each head served as a target for the soldiers
in the garden below—they never missed their
aim! After that, I say the middle class is
capable of the massacres of the Terror!"

1st July.

" I am not a Socialist. I am convinced that
none of the theories of the hour is destined to
triumph, *in its actual form.* A system—a narrow, a
partial thing by its very essence—can never realise
itself. The system is a burgeon which must
burst its sheath in order to become a truth,
universally recognised, universally applied. . . .
I am a Progressist, that is all. . . . I persist in
believing that from petty passion to petty passion,
from personal ambition to personal ambition,
through misfortune, through crime and bloodshed,
we are none the less in the act of a great *transformation* for the greater good of humanity."

16th July.

" The great births of humanity should be seen
from afar. We see the apparition of Christianity
as something exclusively pure, sacred, and supernatural. . . . And yet what sects, how mad,
monstrous, and immoral !—accompanied, and were
even confounded with that white and beautiful
doctrine ! . . . We also have our gnostics ! " . . .

2nd August.

" Adieu, dear, excellent Henriette ; think often
of your brother. Never despair of France ! "[1]

I know no more curious moment of psychology
than the book in which Renan attempted to
answer the problems posed by the movement of
1848. The immense volume is as young as a
primrose, full of the joy of life, full of energy,
charity, hope — above all, full of faith. The
crowded, living, voluntary pages stretch out their
hundred arms to the future like some monstrous
Indian god, who needs innumerable hands to
bestow with and to beckon, to bless with and
to curse, and in whom the vital principle is too
abundant for symmetry or grace. *L'Avenir de
la Science*, is our young priest's first sermon,
heavier, more crammed with matter than those

[1] *Lettres de* 48. Revue de Paris, 15 Avril 1896.

we are accustomed to from his golden lips ; full,
not only of his own ideas but of the theories of his
time and his environment.   The multiple, hetero-
geneous masterpiece takes for its text the mystic
words of the gospel, *Unum est necessarium.*   But
this one thing needful is the Infinite—the Ideal,
identic in its essence, whatever be the form in which
it appears to us:—philosophy, science, poetry, art,
moral beauty, moral strength, or mere natural
loveliness, no less divine.   To recombine these
different elements—to trace these divergent rays
to their common centre, which is God, should be
the chief end of knowledge.   The future of
science is a new religion, to be founded, not
on abstract reasoning, not on any pretended
revelation from on high, but on the most
patient, the most critical, the minutest study
of all the material profusely strewn around
us.   Penetrate matter to find the secret soul in
it !   The study of science is still the service
of God.   Such is the teaching of *L'Avenir de
la Science.*

"I am convinced there is a science of the
Origin of Man which will be constructed one
day, not from mere ratiocination and hypothesis,
but from the results of scientific research.   He
who shall contribute to the solving of this problem
—though his test be imperfect, will do more for

true philosophy than he had achieved by fifty years of metaphysics."

Even while Renan was writing these lines a young naturalist of much the same way of thinking was classing his specimens and comparing his notes. Some ten years later, we read the *Origin of Species.* A reaction against the vague and void official spiritualism of his day, inclined philosophy to draw its conclusions from the exact results of science. The tide has now turned so far in this direction that we forget the originality, in 1848, of doctrines which at present appear the merest common-sense. In 1897 all our young philosophers are historians, or philologists, or physiologists, or students of natural or social science. But, fifty years ago, Philosophy was much too great a lady to do any useful work at all. She broidered her metaphysics in an ivory tower among the clouds.

"Believe me," said Renan, "your true philosopher is the philologist, the student of myths, the critic of social constitutions. By the subtle study of speech we remount the stream of time till we reach almost the source, till we come within hail of primitive man. By comparative grammar we touch our first ancestors ; by comparative mythology we understand their soul, by social science we watch their development.

Every speech, every myth or legend, every form of social organisation from the humblest to the most august, ought to be compared and classified. The man who could thus evoke the origins of Christianity would write the most important book of the century. How I envy it him! Should I live and do well, I mean that book to be the task of my maturity."[1]

Science is thus an instrument of religion, nay, more, a religion in herself, modest but veracious, never going back from her word. The faith of the chosen few, must she remain incommunicable to the mass? How can a religion exclude nine-tenths of mankind? If intellectual culture were but a grace the more, but an added enjoyment, it might well remain the privilege of the elect, for man has no right to happiness. But once we admit that science is a religion—a temple where faith and truth join hands—how shall we forbid the threshold to those who chiefly need a religion? Shall we look upon the poor barbarians as a necessary refuse of waste matter? Shall we consider only them human who know? " I have seen the massacres of June. I have repulsed in my own heart the instinctive wish that the barbarians might perish. Shame on such a thought! There must be no more barbarians!

[1] *Avenir*, p. 278.

" Yet it is not easy to see how the many are to be induced to work out their own salvation. How shall we make a turbulent majority choose the better part when, as a matter of fact, it does not prefer it, thinks it tiresome, prefers the pothouse and the barricade? The ancients had convenient means to this end : augurs, oracles, Egerias, who arranged the truth in a way understanded of the people. Others have had recourse to armies. . . . It is very clear that Science will none of these. It is much less clear, however, by what miracle she is to descend upon and illuminate the recalcitrant mass of the ignorant. . . .

" Above all let us never dream that Science must descend to the level of people. A cheap science, an easy science, a popular science, is the most useless of catch-words. Science must be serious, difficult, comprehensible only to her own adepts, in her more abstruse and secret recesses. But by the diffusion of a sound elementary instruction all may be made capable of understanding the value and the gist of these researches—all may follow them in their outer circuit ; all may be set upon the sacred track. If you object that to attain such cultivation, the working class must receive more money for less work, in order to secure the time for study, I reply : so be it ! Let us simplify our lives. I have no objection to

the socialistic phalanstery, nor even to a salutary
reign of terror. These do not interfere with
Science. The artless life of a community where
none would be rich or poor may even be favourable to her development, Genius lives on simple
things, and Spinoza contemplated the divine
substance in no palace while he polished the
lenses which brought him bread. Democracy has
no terror for Science. Let us all be brothers, in
truth, in simplicity, in generous and confident
human sympathy."

Such, in effect, is the gospel which Ernest
Renan caught amid the gun smoke and the
ominous fusillades of 1848. It is easy to see
how much of these theories is natural to the
author, the result of his real convictions and his
peculiar temperament, and how much is due to
the influence of the *milieu* and the contagion of an
epidemic enthusiasm. All Renan's later work is
based on that psychological interpretation of facts
obtained by a patient scientific method which he
advocates in his earliest book. His most fantastic
philosophy has ever a solid piece of sober erudition at the base. He often reads too much into
his text, between the lines, but he starts from his
text, and never evolves out of his own brain a
system independent of historic proofs. He applies
to the history of religion and to the problems of

exegesis, the experimental method of a student in physics or natural history. Thus, in all essentials, the Renan of the *Avenir de la Science*, is already Renan. True, the Renan of the future was to be no democrat. But his turn of mind, infinitely aristocratic, infinitely jealous of the rights of the minority, was never subject to the powers that be. The aristocracy which Renan commended was an aristocracy of personal merit, an upper house of virtue and intelligence. Spinoza and the fishermen of Galilee were the high barons of his heraldry. It is impossible to read the tender, human, fraternal pages of the *Apostles* and *St Paul* without perceiving how much of the great dream of '48 lingered in the mind of Renan. The day was to dawn when, mournfully, he was to admit that the barbarians are, in truth, a necessary refuse. But his barbarians were not merely the unpossessing classes : they were the selfish, the dull, the mean, the narrow, in every class, high or low, rich or poor, one with another.

L'Avenir de la Science is an example of the subjective quality of Renan's imagination. He has sympathy in abundance—the subtlest, the most penetrating, the most sensitive of any writer of his time—but he has not a particle of dramatic imagination. He interprets all things by himself. If he desire to save Society, he will adjure Society

to quit the seminary, turn philologist, and set
itself to study the origins of Christianity. In the
Avenir de la Science, Renan projects his own
sensibility and his own experience into Contemporary Society, just as later on he was to project
them into Jesus Christ and Marcus Aurelius. No
man ever lived more resolutely in the whole; but
in the whole, as he sees it, he puts a reflection of
himself. He has the extraordinary gift, attributed
by physicians to certain nervous patients, of ex-
teriorising his own sensibility.

By the time Renan had finished his book, '48
was over, the fever of democracy had passed : the
young author could only regard his socialistic projects as curious examples of the mythopoetic
faculty. No doubt they interested him from this
point of view also. Every mode and phase of his
own and the world's development impassioned his
eager intelligence. It was all matter for study.
What though one star fell out of the myriads
in heaven? What though your perfect democracy proved a poet's day dream? The universe
teemed with other problems, other mysteries,
equally important, equally engrossing.

In 1849, M. Renan obtained from the French
Government one of those travelling scholarships
which, across the Channel, are dignified by the
name of missions. He was to seek in the

libraries of Italy certain documents required by
the Academy of Inscriptions for its *Histoire
Littéraire de la France;* he was also to complete his own thesis on Averroës. For eight
months Ernest Renan remained in the Peninsula.
Suddenly freed from the bracing influence of
his environment in Paris, Renan rapidly regained
his natural bent : dreamy, idealizing, poetic. More
than once his letters from Rome must have exasperated his democratic correspondent.[1] There is so
much religion in them, so much art, vague piety,
sentiment reflected from the Roman landscape !
" Tell me less about the monuments and more
about the condition of the people " answers, in
substance, Marcel Berthelot. In vaim ; Renan
has fallen under the sway of the Past.

" This journey had the most remarkable influence on my mind. I knew nothing of Art, and
lo ! I beheld her, radiant and full of consolations.
A faëry enchantress seemed to whisper me the
words which the Church, in her hymn, says to
the wood of the Cross :—

> " ' Flecte ramos, arbor alta,
> Tensa laxa viscera,
> Et rigor lentescat ille
> Quem dedit nativitas.'

A sort of soft breeze relaxed my native rigour.

---

[1] *Correspondance Renan-Berthelot.* Revue de Paris, 1 Août 1897.

Almost all my illusions of 1848 dropped from me, for I saw they were impossible. I recognised the fatal necessities of human society, I resigned myself to a condition of the creation in which a great deal of evil serves to produce a little good, where a drop of exquisite aroma is distilled from an enormous *caput mortuum* of refuse."

Yet, whilst admitting the absurdity of yesterday's chimera, Renan did not cease to follow the ever beckoning ideal. The Infinite remained the eternal guide. And on the ledger of the Monastery of Monte Cassino he wrote in 1850 :—

" *Unum est necessarium ; Maria elegit optimam partem.*"

CHAPTER III

THE VALE OF GRACE

THE disenchantment which followed 1848 combined with the divine spectacle of Italy to turn the mind of Renan from the future towards the past. He saw no longer in his dreams a socialistic phalanstery with its Spinoza occupied in an optician's work-room. His fancy preferred to evoke some steep small Umbrian town with Etruscan walls and Roman ruins, with mediæval towers set high above Renaissance palaces and the overladen Jesuit churches of the Catholic Revival. Here was food for the mind : the past is so poetic ! We imagine the future so flat and full of prose ! The Celt especially is open to the magical pathos of historic memories, and, now that once Ernest Renan had unsealed his hearing to that siren-song, the music of the barricades might pipe to him in vain !

Impressionable to excess, Renan, while guarding his will fixed on one steadfast aim, changed the colour of his thoughts according to the atmosphere he dwelt in. Imagine a chameleon, progressing unswervingly in one direction, but sometimes blue, sometimes rose, sometimes green, in the course of his invariable traject ! Such is Renan, the bizarre and eminently Celtic fusion of a constant mind with a sensitive temperament. Among the marvels of the Sabine Hills, the utilitarian ideal which yesterday he had invoked, appeared odious to him. He continued to serve Truth and Science—but no longer in the precincts of Democracy. Rough-shod, iron goddess, might her feet never tread the Seven Hills !

" As for me, it is with something akin to terror that I face the day when life shall penetrate anew that sublime heap of ruins which is Rome ! I cannot conceive her other than she is : a museum of dilapidated majesties, a tryst for the exiles of our work-a-day world, a meeting-place for dethroned monarchs, disenchanted statesmen, and sceptical philosophers weary of their kind. Should the fatal level of modern common-place threaten this mass of sacred relics, I would fain the priests and the monks of Rome were paid to maintain within her ruins their customary melancholy and squalor, and to preserve all round about them fever and the desert." [1]

Renan's democracy had been a short brain-

---

[1] *E. ais de morale et de Critique,* p. 259.

fever. It had passed: the *coup d'état* disgusted him once for all with the lower classes. The development of his ideas made it easy for certain of his friends to dissuade him from the publication of *L'Avenir de la Science*. Although already in July 1849 a chapter of the book had been printed in a review, with the mention: "to appear in a few weeks," the volume did not see the light, in fact, until 1890—less out of date than it would have been in the first flush of that reaction which forms the morrow of every revolution. Renan had been the first to suspect the inopportunity of yesterday's gospel. He was no longer under the exclusive influence of the Berthelots. On literary matters, he consulted Augustin Thierry — his mentor in letters—and M. de Sacy : each of them advised him to reserve his great work—to dispose of it page by page, chapter by chapter, in the form of essays and reviews ; but not to overwhelm the public with his whole stock of unseasonable riches.

Thus, in five years, Renan had lost two ideals —Christianity and Socialism. Despite his robust faith in the future of Science, the present world began to wear a disenchanted aspect. Our young fanatic of yesterday was in some danger of becoming one of those "sceptical philosophers, weary of their kind" for whom the Eternal City

appeared so convenient a limbo. If we could
suppose a special Providence designed to watch
over so notorious a heretic, now was the moment
for its intervention. And lo! his sister, having
finished her ten years' engagement in Poland,
summoned Ernest to meet her in Berlin. And
Renan encountered his Egeria.

"When we meet again, my dear, we shall
hardly recognise each other," Renan had written
to his sister years before. And after ten years
they met. The slim young woman of nine and
twenty, gracious of aspect, who had bidden farewell to her brother in the seminary parlour, was
grown into a woman of forty, plain in the face,
prematurely aged and lined by the hard winters
of Poland. The girlish lightness had departed
from her figure; an affection of the larynx
threatened the sweetness of her voice. In air
and dress Mademoiselle Renan affected an elderly
fashion which nothing in her looks belied. Her
brother glanced at her, realised the sad change,—
and worshipped his austere Egeria as a second
mother, the comforting mother of his mind. She,
on the other hand, can have seen small trace of
the ungainly provincial seminarist she had left
in the travelled young philosopher of seven and
twenty who stood before her. For a moment
they were strangers in each other's eyes —

but they were intimate to the marrow of the mind.

Henriette returned to Paris with Ernest. She had lost her youth and her health in Poland, but she had paid off her father's debts, redeemed the mortgage on her mother's property, established her brother in the way he should go, and a little purse of savings remained to set up house with. They were to live together. Each had long dreamed this dream, and five years before Ernest had written—"We shall be so happy, dear! I am easy-tempered and gentle. You will let me live the serious simple life I love, and I will tell you all I think and all I feel. We shall have our friends too—refined and elect spirits—who will beautify our life."

They chose a small apartment near the Val-de-Grace, with windows looking over the garden of the Carmelite Nuns. There was room for them and their books ; place for M. Berthelot to sit and discuss with them all things under the sun ; a seat for such of Ernest Renan's masters as would honour his home. Henriette had few friends and did not desire to enlarge her acquaintance. She had Ernest and that was enough.

Ernest was absent a part of every day at the National Library : he had been appointed to a small charge of Sub-Librarian. His salary, with Henriette's savings, sufficed for their daily wants. While her brother was away the devoted sister copied out his manuscripts for him, made long abstracts from volumes needed for his work, corrected his proofs, took notes which might be of use to him, compulsed a mass of documents, verified dates and authorities. For amusement she looked out of the window at the nuns in their convent garden, or waited for Ernest's return. . . . Anxious pleasure of waiting, of listening for a glad step on the stair— and then the smile we expected, and the eager budget of the day's events !

In the evening, Ernest settled to his writing. " She had the greatest respect for my work. I have seen her sit by my side for hours of an evening, scarcely breathing lest she should interrupt my labours. Yet she loved to have me in her sight, and the door between our two rooms stood ever open. Her affection had become something so ripe and so discreet that the sweet communion of our thoughts was sufficient for her. Her heart,—jealous, exacting, as it was —demanded but a few minutes a day, since she alone was loved. Thanks to her strict economy, on our singularly limited resources she kept a house in which nothing was lacking and which could boast its own austere charm. . . .

She was an incomparable secretary. Her delicate censure discovered negligences and brusqueries which I had overlooked. It was she who persuaded me that every shade of thought can be expressed in a correct and simple style, that violent images and new-coined expressions betray either misplaced pretensions or ignorance of the real wealth at our disposal. Hence a profound change in the manner of my writing. I accustomed myself to reckon in advance on her remarks—hazarding many a brilliant passage to watch its effect upon her, whilst decided to sacrifice it if she observed it with disfavour." [1]

Henriette examined not only the manner but the matter. Her simple rectitude was disconcerted by Ernest's recurrent irony. " I had never suffered, and a discreet smile provoked by the weakness or the vanity of man, seemed a sort of philosophy." Many a winged shaft was offered on her shrine.

Fine writing, irony, and a certain abstract vagueness in spiritual matters ; such were the qualities which Henriette was anxious to discipline and chasten in her gifted brother's writings. The tender inquisitress was not satisfied until all was pure, exact, discreet, and true. She said to her brother, " Be thou perfect ! "

[1] *Ma sœur Henriette*, p. 36.

And a dash of mockery, a trace of vanity, the least little air of disdain, or flaunt of self-satisfaction, however pretty in itself, was a flaw in the absolute clear beauty she desired. Most of all, she sought to cultivate in him the habit of veracity, a habit the seminary had not inculcated, it appears. " I have never told a lie since 1851," wrote Ernest many years after her death.

Her efforts were seconded by Ernest's friends —by Augustin Thierry, who in 1851 introduced the young writer to the *Revue des Deux Mondes ;* by M. de Sacy, who admitted him on to the staff of the *Débats.* " It was these two organs," said M. Renan in 1890, " who taught me how to write, that is to say, how to limit myself, how constantly to rub the angles off my ideas, how to keep a watchful eye on my defects."[1]   The extraordinary absence of vanity which characterised Renan in his youth enabled him to profit by all this good advice without any juvenile soreness of feeling.   He was right.   Between the *Avenir de la Science,* written in 1848 and 1849, and the essays contributed to the *Revue des Deux Mondes* and the *Débats,* in the years immediately following 1851, there is fixed the abyss which divides work of fervent and interesting promise

Preface to *Avenir.*

from the peculiar ripe perfection of a great writer. Renan's genius was to grow freer and fuller, at once more human and more fantastic, more audacious and more penetrating. Henceforth it will lose rather than gain in moral grace, in a certain exquisite gravity and elegance of spirit. And, perhaps, never again was the historian of religions so religious.

In Renan's delicate philosophy, made up of semi-tones and demi-tints, piety had out-lived faith. In 1856, he no longer believes in any of the myriad forms of the one informing soul. (πολλὰ ὀνόματα Μορφὴ μία.) But that essential idea of Religion, peculiar and necessary to human kind, he asserts to be immortal and destined to an infinite development. Shall the exquisite herald-angel remain chained, trammelled, wounded, dwarfed perchance, by fetters of our mortal forging? To strike off those fetters, thought Renan, was good knight's service. Set Religion free, let her move and grow, let her guide us unenslaved, unim-prisoned. The refusal to adhere to a definite form of worship may be an act of faith in the future of Religion.

Thanks to Ernest's genius and Henriette's incessant vigilance, nothing in these early essays suggested the beginner, nor even the young man. They were rounded with a golden maturity.

The intrepidity of their conception was veiled
by a becoming reserve of phrase: the oracle
evidently wished to awake but not to startle
his audience.   They combine a soaring liberty of
spirit with an exquisite candour.   A great charm
in these essays is that, so various in their subjects
and their treatment, they are still invariable in
their aim.   United they form not an anthology,
but a book.   There is a link between them all—
whether they treat of the historians of Jesus, the
imitation of Christ, the lives of the Saints, or of
Calvin, or Mahomet, or the Prophets of Israel,
or of antique myths, or of the school of Hegel,
or whether they delicately flagellate the vulgarities
of American Protestantism.   The author studies
one by one these religious ideals, not dogmatically,
but historically ; he penetrates each movement, and
tries to resume it in a typical figure, a sort of ideal
representative ; and this man he then evokes in
his habit as he lived, with every detail of his most
intimate originality.   The portrait is singularly
living, whether or no it be singularly like. . . . On
this latter head I would reserve my opinion, ominously enlightened by a passage in one of Renan's
letters to M. l'Abbé Cognat. . . .

" God forgive me for loving Ronge and Czersky
if they be misleading spirits !   For what I love
in them—as in all other men to whom I dedicate

my enthusiasm—is a certain beautiful moral image of them which I create within myself. It is my own ideal which I love in them. Now, as to whether they really resemble this image? That appears to me, I admit, a matter of slight importance."

Imaginative, suggestive, subtle, Renan's essays as they appeared one by one in the early years of the Fifties, attracted more attention than the brother and sister dreamed of in their dear seclusion.

"What was my surprise when, one morning, a stranger of pleasant and intelligent appearance entered my attic. He complimented me on certain articles of mine which had appeared in the Reviews, and offered to unite them in a volume. Thereupon he produced a stamped document stipulating terms which I thought astonishingly generous, so much so that when he asked if all my future works should be comprised in the treaty, I consented."[1]   The visitor was M. Michel Lévy, the then rising publisher, whose fortune Renan was to help to make; and the book, the delicious *Etudes d'Histoire Religieuse* immediately established him in the first rank of literature, if not of popular success. Published on the 20th of March 1857, the *Etudes d'Histoire*

[1] *Souvenirs*, 385.

Religieuse were succeeded on the 6th of June
1859, by the *Essais de Morale et de Critique*.
Nor did Renan neglect the austerer courts of
Science.   In 1855 he had finally given to
the world the *General History of Semitic
Languages*, which, while still unpublished, had
won the Volney Prize some eight years before.
This book opened to the author the gates of the
Institute.   Uncontested master of Semitic philo-
logy in France, Renan was elected, in 1856, a
Member of the Academy of Inscriptions and
Belles Lettres.

Meanwhile, in 1852, Renan had published the
work on *Averroës*, which brought him not only
his doctor's degree, but his first reputation as a
thinker.   In *Averroës* the critic demonstrates
the sterilising effect of orthodoxy on a noble and
beautiful philosophy.   Greek science, adopted by
the Arab thinkers, fixed and crystallised by them
into a dogma, becomes thenceforth a thing incapable of development or fecundity.   To live
and grow, a thing must pass from the category
of *esse* into the category of *fieri*.   Otherwise
routine and dogmatism rust out the vital principle
in even the greatest ideas ; even as a pool of the
purest water, set apart from the natural current of
streams or the running rains of heaven, will
stale and grow stagnant.

The interest of philosophic history lies rather
in the picture it gives us of the growth of the
human mind, than in the theories which it
exhumes from bygone systems. The strange
development of Greek science by a civilisation
entirely alien to that of Greece interested the
historic curiosity of Renan. Aristotle among
the Arabs! So we might imagine Pekin to adopt
the theories of Darwin and Pasteur, commentat-
ing them during centuries in a spirit of pure
Chinese orthodoxy. The result would probably be
of no mortal value—it would be piquant and unusual; it would represent an infrequent combination; it would have a value of its own in the
eyes of the disinterested critic of the universe,
curious of moral rarities. It would be interesting and useful to see in what unlikely back-waters
the Stream of Life can meander when the main
current is blocked. . . . The Arabs took the
philosophy of Aristotle from the Syrian Christians, who had it from the pagan Greeks. The
Mahommedan Arabs bequeathed it to the Spanish
Jews, who passed it on to the Catholic doctors
of the Middle Ages and Aristotle ended as a
scholastic dogmatist in the Sorbonne! Translated, interpreted, and falsified in a dozen different
senses, the intellectual curiosity of Greece contrived in these strange elements, if not to grow,

if not to produce, at least to languish in a sort of earthly limbo. *Die Wahrheit magt Niemand verbrennen*, sang Mechtild of Magdeburg, who, in her different degree, was another child of Aristotle.

But not merely the curiosity of the man of science attracted Renan to this subject. The strongest bent of his genius inclined him to consider, above all, the origins of things. He loved the delicate, rooty fibres as others love the flowers or the fruits; and half of his secret was his extraordinary faculty for seeing underground. The scholastic philosophy of the thirteenth century is only to be understood by a thorough knowledge of the principles of Jewish and Arab thought. When Renan did not understand a phenomenon, an imperious instinct bade him seek its source. His interpretation of Catholic scholasticism led him first of all to study Averroës, even as later on it led him to study the Early Church, and thence the Origins of Christianity, whence he delved yet further back into the Origins of Judaism. *Averroës* is the first link in a chain which Renan was to spend his life in forging.

CHAPTER IV

THE MORAL PHILOSOPHER

IF we hold with Averroës that all men are the transient expressions of one enduring soul, we find small difficulty in explaining how the noblest minds of a given generation arrive, unknown to each other, and simultaneously, at a like result. While Renan was painfully deducing from documents and inflections a new psychology, a young classical master at Nevers, named Hippolyte Taine, was writing to his friends :—

"Free psychology is a magnificent science founded on the philosophy of history . . . we must make of history an exact science. . . . I take refuge from the present in reading the Germans."[1]

Taine met Renan, five years his senior, in the offices of the great Liberal reviews. Save in the fundamental independence and unworldliness of their natures, no men could be more different.

[1] See, in M. Gabriel Monod's charming and valuable volume *Renan, Taine, Michelet*, the previously unpublished letters of Taine.

The genius of Taine was absolute, positive, vivid to the verge of harshness, apt to mass and class the confusion of things in a series of brilliant syntheses : above all things he was a logician. Renan,—subtle, complex and elusive, a historian and, above all, an analyst,—was for ever dividing and sub-dividing the prism of the universe into an immeasurable sequence of minor shades ; was for ever attenuating his keen and often audacious analysis by a style serene and limpid beyond comparison.   But a like idea of Truth and Liberty animated their souls.   Equally admirable, equally eminent, Renan and Taine were as the two eyes of the generation which came to its maturity towards 1860.

The children of a later day can form no idea of the repression which followed '48, of those gloomy years in which thought was fettered, freedom stifled, in which a political and orthodox inquisition controlled the university and the press of a liberal nation.   The fusillades of the Luxem·bourg were less detestable than the intellectual tyranny of the Empire of the Fifties.   A government in reaction against armed insurrection has some excuse for excessive reprisals ; it may be right in maintaining order even by a flagrant retaliation ; but it is an error to believe that the premeditated dwarfing of a nation's intelligence can ever be the guarantee of peace. Adversity, however, steels the obstinate; the Liberal party continued its opposition, aware that no ministry, however tyrannous, can destroy the mind of a nation. When the main channel is blocked, intelligence finds new outlets. The university, the public schools, letters, the press, were constrained by an iron censure, subject to exile, prison, suspension, daily fines. Yet journalism had never been more brilliant than under the Second Empire. Beulé contrived to outrage the Government with impunity in writing the history of Augustus. Rogeard bewailed the illiberal "Liberty of December" — *libertas Decembris*, as Horace puts it — and the censor dared not seize the allusion to the *coup d'état*.

France, in the Fifties, had at least one religion which was not a mere lip-service, and that was the doctrine of Liberalism. The little office of the *Débats*, with its red-tiled floor, and its two shabby ink-stained tables, was a sort of temple of the faith. There statesmen, financiers, scholars, artists, men of letters, met on a footing of ease and equality, the result of their sincere devotion to an aim outside themselves which made rank, fortune, influence, details of no importance. MM. de Sacy, Laboulaye, Prévost Paradol, John Lemoinne, the Bertins, were the priests of this austere Chapel ;

H

and its creed was freedom, the rights of citizens, justice, and a ceaseless aspiration towards a nobler order of things. "Liberalism," wrote Renan more than once, "Liberalism represents for me the formula of the highest human development;" and the doctrine of the *Débats* was, in fact, at bottom, much the doctrine of the Hebrew prophets. The task of preaching it was attended by almost insurmountable difficulties. The censor was swift to punish and to suppress any independent expression of political opinion. So the leading articles in the first columns were models of discretion. The life of the journal passed into the "Varieties"—into studies on moral and social questions or purely literary articles, and the intelligent reader turned to the third page where he read, between the lines of an essay or a review, all that the political editor was obliged to leave unsaid. A notice by Prévost Paradol, a piece of Roman History by Cuvillier-Fleury, an article by Ernest Renan were sure, in their subtle opposition, of an attentive public.

It was easy for a philosopher to serve the Opposition simply by upholding the banner of an austere Ideal. The staff of the *Débats*, like the staff of the *Edinburgh Review*, was content to "cultivate Literature upon a little oatmeal." The traditions of the place were

all of a certain Jansenist severity. Luxury,
display,—objects of elaborate mechanical construction, even,—were suspect in the eyes of
the *Débats*. To own more than a million or
so (of francs *bien entendu*) appeared in very poor
taste. The immense expenses of the Empire,
the impetus given to industry, the heightened
standard of universal comfort, were signs of the
times regarded as distinctly ominous by these
eulogists of days gone by. They spoke of the
improvements of the Baron Haussmann with a
dash of contempt in a great deal of disfavour.
" I would give all your steamboats for an Æneid,"
exclaimed M. de Sacy. The Government was
as generous in public works as it was illiberal in
public instruction. Vast sums were spent on
the extension of railways, the establishment of
the telegraph, on industrial exhibitions, on the
organisation of savings banks. " There was
some good in the Empire after all ! " cry we of
a later date, as we read the formidable list of
Imperial improvements. " No good ! " cried the
stern young prophet of the *Débats*. " What
material progress can compensate a moral de-
cadence ? Will a steam traction engine make a
man happy ? Will a universal exhibition make
him nobler or better ? In taking the triumphs
of mechanical ingenuity for the sign of an ad-

vanced civilisation, you mistake the mere accident
for the essential." So taught Renan in France
throughout the Fifties ; while, curiously enough,
in England, John Ruskin was fulminating a similar
gospel against the gross, the palpable, ideal of
the age.

Renan discredited the advantages of tyranny,
and showed how despotism, to make itself acceptable, invariably persuades Society of its talents as
a steward : "Bow down before me, and I will give
ye cent for cent." But what shall it profit a man
if he gain the whole world and lose his own soul ?
Nothing is less important than prosperity. Man
is not born to be prosperous, but to realise, in a
little vanguard of chosen spirits, an ideal superior
to the ideal of yesterday. The bulk of humanity
lives by proxy ; only the few can attain a complete development. Millions live and die in order
to produce a rare *élite*. The true glory of
Holland, for instance, is to have brought forth
princes like William of Orange, painters like
Rembrandt, thinkers like Spinoza—not to have
the best pastures in Europe and a high standard
of comfort. Once we put the accent on prosperity,
we introduce into our midst envy, ambition, and
all their baleful sequel. The really noble society
is that in which each man is content with the
station into which he is born. The really noble

nation is that which yields the greatest sum of disinterestedness, of self-sacrifice, that in which men most live for one another : the society whose workmen are proud of the magnificence of their prince, whose princes are solicitous for the needs of the poor, whose laymen are sustained by the prayers of the nun, whose priests rejoice in the courage of the soldier, whose scholars profit by the labours of the humble, whose harvesters feel that, in their sphere, they too collaborate in the great moral masterpiece which is a nation firmly welded in an indestructible solidarity of soul. Duty is the foundation of such a society, and the satisfaction in duty accomplished the private joy of every citizen—a joy deeper than any man can owe to the mere diffusion of material abundance.

So runs the epistle of Renan to his contemporaries. In consequence of the storm raised by his essay on the historians of Jesus, published in the *Etudes d'Histoire Religieuse*, he had turned for a while from his chosen path of religious history to the neighbouring track of moral philosophy. The frivolity of the society of his age made him pause in the destruction of an illusion which was, perhaps, a restraint and an ideal. The morality of the average man is in fact generally a consequence of his piety; let us therefore respect that piety. Let us direct it. Whether or no

Christianity be true, this philosopher was persuaded of the existence of good and evil.

"An impenetrable veil screens from us the secret of this strange world whose reality convinces and oppresses us. Philosophy and Science pursue for ever, and ever in vain, the formula of this proteus whom no reason limits and no tongue expresses. But there is one indubitable foundation, which scepticism shall not shake, where man may find, until the end of time, a foothold firm amid the uncertainties around him : Good is good, evil is evil."

Good is good, evil is evil, and, above all things, truth is truth:—"Whatever system we adopt to explain man and the world, we cannot deny that the problems they arouse are infinitely curious, infinitely attaching, and worthy of the most patient investigation. And even if virtue were but a snare, laid for the noblest, if hope were a dream, beauty an illusion, humanity a vain tumult, the pure research of truth would still preserve its charm ! For even if we suppose the world to be the nightmare of a fevered divinity, or an accidental bubble on the surface of nothingness, yet are we invincibly impelled to wring its secret from it. Whatever we may think of the universe, it remains a spectacle which rivets our attention. In the life of St Thomas Aquinas we read that one

day Christ appeared to him and asked him
what reward he craved for his learned writings.
'Nothing but Thee, O Lord!' replied the angeli-
cal doctor.   The critic of the universe is yet more
disinterested.   If Truth should appear and address
him a like question, he would answer—'Nought
but the pursuit of thee, O Truth!'"[1]

[1] *Essais de Morale et de Critique*, p. 100.

CHAPTER V

A PORTRAIT by Henry Scheffer—the less known brother of a famous painter—shows us Renan at this time. The head is certainly idealized, but its likeness to the sitter's charming daughter forbids us to call it a piece of flattery pure and simple. It shows a Renan strikingly unlike the gnome-like figure, the colossal leonine head, the radiant ugliness of the affable Academician we remember. Neither the strength, nor the humour, nor the disenchanted benignant smile we knew are here. This is a serious elegiac young man, a Hamlet,—nay, too gentle and unsuspicious for a Hamlet,—almost a Good Shepherd. The cheeks and jaw have not yet taken on those formidable proportions which made the sinuous lips appear yet more delicate. All the features are larger, the heavy nose, the mouth, especially the eyes—charming, in this portrait, in their smiling melancholy. The oval of the face appears not only slighter but longer. The *ensemble*

is striking, touching, even handsome. The
relentless idealism of the painter has attenuated
the quaint awkwardness of the model, whose
small stature, heavy sloping shoulders, huge head,
and short arms can never have presented this distinguished appearance. Renan was well aware of
his deficiencies. Many a line in his earlier essays
informs us of his bashfulness in society. His
priest's education and the long habit of solitude
had left him awkward, silent, reserved. He could
discourse brilliantly on elevated subjects, but he
did not know how, at the right moment, to say
the usual thing. He was always utterly devoid of
the give-and-take of the ready talker. Thus he
oscillated between an inspired monologue and a
heavy silence, while he wondered how intelligent
persons could be so fired by the common-place,
" so interested in what does not ennoble." He
felt painfully his uncouth exterior, and perhaps
still more painfully, though with a certain pride,
that mark of the priest on his forehead, which,
as he thought, was clearly legible, destining him
to eternal solitude in the pursuit of the ideal. Sir
M. Grant Duff, who met him first in 1859, gives us
a more flattered version of the same character :—

"His manner had that charming gentleness
which is characteristic of the best of the Catholic
clergy. His conversation was very copious and

limpid, not dealing much in epigram or anecdote, but very easy and very informing."

It was towards 1855, I think, that Renan made the acquaintance of Ary Scheffer. The pure idealism of the Dutch painter's art, the liberality of his religious feeling, the generous and lofty temper of his mind, were such as to fire the young *savant's* enthusiasm. By his new friend's hearth, he found that household warmth, that simple and yet intellectual geniality which were all that was needed to thaw his chill timidities. M. Scheffer's house had not been the home it became to Ernest Renan were there no women by the hearth. He had a niece and a daughter. Some thirty-five years later I was privileged to count the former among my dearest friends..

When I knew her Madame Renan was an ageing woman, her figure grown to a great size, the shape of her face something altered by the habit of difficult breathing : she had a heart complaint. But, at sixty, her bright blue eyes, with their look of witty innocence, her clear skin, her abundant chestnut hair, her delightful smile with its winning unassailable youth, sufficed to remind us of the attractions of her girlhood. Her early portraits show a slim light grace, a pure oval of cheek and brow, with the same air of merry goodness which made her face so charming in age.

As clever as she was pretty, as kind as she was wise, the friends of her girlhood used to call her Minerva ; but imagine the most modest, the most amiable fireside divinity, prescient for others, wise with no thought of her own advancement. Lively, gay, active, sweet-tempered, capable, discreet,— Cornélie Scheffer was the ideal helpmate. Really gifted, she soon discovered the intellectual superiority of her uncle's friend. Imagine his delight to find this charming maiden, not only acquainted, but deeply imbued, with his own writings, and able to talk with him not merely as an admirer, but as an intelligent companion. Little by little her influence on her new friend became only second to that of Henriette, and inclined him ever more and more to the standpoint of the artist, of the man of feeling, as opposed to the pure scholar's point of view. I suppose M. Ary Scheffer saw how things were drifting. Often Madame Renan has told me of a ride she took with her uncle on the sands near Scheveningen— I suppose in the autumn of 1855. They were talking of the future—of other people's future. Suddenly he wheeled round his horse, confronted her, and said—"You, my dear, you ought to marry the most intelligent man I know." Neither said any more ; they broke into a gallop, and continued their thoughts in silence.

But Mademoiselle Renan, in her dear seclusion, laid no great stress on this intimacy with the Scheffers. Long before she had proposed to Ernest what she had considered a suitable alliance. He had refused ; the years glided on ; and the tender, jealous sister, so happy in her double solitude, had come to count upon her brother as exclusively her own for ever. He, on the other hand, relied on her sympathy for a confession which his reserve continually put off. And one day he awoke to find himself condemned to break the heart of one of the two women he loved best in all the world.

In pages of a penetrating beauty, Ernest Renan himself has told the heart-wrung modest tragedy. Who shall repeat the words which a sacred emotion has let escape from the lips of a master ? Henriette Renan could not, would not, at first accept the bitter cup. And one day her brother, forced to choose between two affections, decided for that which seemed most like a duty. He bade farewell, an eternal farewell, to the young girl he loved. At night-fall, he went home ; entered quietly the little study, henceforth desolate, and told his sister of his sacrifice. Thus set face to face with a generosity superior to her own, all that was noble, all that was the infallible protectress, revived in Henriette and forbade the

sacrifice. The next morning early she went to
M. Scheffer's house; asked for her young rival,
sought and found her peace. The two women
wept long in each other's arms; but they bid
each other *au revoir!* with glad faces. In those
hours of shaken tears their sisterhood had begun.

But not yet, if ever, was the demon of tender
jealousy allayed. The first years of Madame
Renan's married life were filled with a difficult and
tormented happiness. The young wife, brought
up with all the triple liberty of a cosmopolitan,
Protestant, and artistic home, must often have felt
the provincial reclusion of the Renans' house
weigh upon her spirits. For she was not mistress
there. The Minerva of Ary Scheffer's studio never
complained of the subordinate position allotted
her by her own conventual hearth. Her husband, accustomed all his life long to look up to
Henriette and obey her, thought it quite natural
that his young wife should obey her too. And
the exquisite, the devoted, the noble Henriette
was sometimes a jealous divinity.

The birth of a son lit a warmer glow at their
fireside. Henriette adored her nephew, and this
great new interest reconciled her to her brother's
marriage. Melancholy, tearful, anxious, she remained; ever susceptible, easily wounded; but a
real affection for Ary's mother knit her at last

to her sister-in-law. In 1860 they were still closer drawn together by the loss of a little girl, Ernestine, passionately beloved by her father, who consecrated to this baby soul an exquisite *In Memoriam*, still unpublished.—Little Ernestine, who lived nine months, was never forgotten ;— often has Madame Renan recalled to me a loss still recent to her faithful love ; and Henriette Renan in her last illness spoke many a time to Ernest of their "little flower."—Meanwhile old Madame Renan had joined the family circle. The witty, voluble little old woman had much more in common with her daughter - in - law than with her daughter. At heart, she had never forgiven Henriette her plain face ; and she, at least, knew the value of youth, charm, beauty, and vivacity in a woman. Her presence made things go smoothly. Her son adored her, admired her, no less than in the old days at Tréguier. Every afternoon at dusk he was wont to spend an hour in her room, lit only by the gas lamps in the street. And she would discourse to him of Tréguier and Lannion as they were before the Revolution, of her own early youth, and of a vanished Brittany. More than twenty years later, these talks in the twilight were to receive an immortal setting in Renan's *Souvenirs d'Enfance et de Jeunesse.*

In 1858 Ary Scheffer died, and Renan lost in him not only a near related friend but a collaborator. Ary Scheffer's last design had been made to illustrate his nephew-in-law's translation of the *Book of Job*. The volume appeared, without the promised illustrations, in 1859. And thus Renan began his version of the Bible, choosing by a sort of instinct the great hymn of doubt and despair, the terrible dialogue of an irresponsible God who mocks at justice, and of a baffled and ignorant humanity. In the following year he brought forth his second book—" The Song of Songs," the triumphant pæan of Profane Love. More than twenty years later, he was to give us *Ecclesiastes*, the last word of scepticism, the last ironical smile-and-sigh of the pessimist convinced that man shall never triumph over fate. Strange scriptures these. In the Bible, according to Ernest Renan, there is neither a prayer nor a psalm. Renan's translation of *The Song of Songs* is a masterpiece of ingenious scholarship, and one may say that only those who have read this charming version can appreciate all the beauty, freshness, and candour of the exquisite little Hebrew morality-play.

In 1857 Quatremère had died, and since then there was a Chair vacant at the College of France—the Chair of Hebrew and Syro-

Chaldaic languages — the place which Renan had desired consistently, and to which every succeeding volume showed his title clearer.

The Professors of the College of France are named by the Minister of Public Instruction from two lists, the one drawn up by the College itself, the other by the Academy of Inscriptions. These lists are almost always identical. Certainly the name of Ernest Renan would have headed either. But month after month, year after year, dragged on ; the Chair of Hebrew remained vacant ; the Minister never asked for the lists. The Professorship of Hebrew at the College of France is, in point of fact, a Chair of Biblical exegesis. The Catholic party, all-powerful in the first years of the Spanish Empress's influence, had devised this means of reducing a renegade to silence. Renan waited, and continued his duties as one of the sub-librarians at the Bibliothèque Impériale. He knew his time would come. When, in 1861, overtures were made to him, to discover if he would accept another Chair at the College of France, he replied, No. He meant yet to fill the seat of Quatremère.

CHAPTER VI

MEANWHILE the Empire prospered and became mellower in its prosperity. The laurels of the Crimea hid, in some measure, the blood stains of the Deux-Décembre. Men began to speak well of a Government which secured a triumph abroad and magnificence at home. When Napoleon III. declared war against Austria in favour of Italian independence, the usurper appeared the champion of liberty, and the popular enthusiasm knew no bounds. And, in fact, at heart, Louis-Napoleon, curious of all things, convinced of none, inclined as much to democracy as to any other popular idol. Like one of those late Roman Emperors, in whose private oratory there was a place for Isis and a place for Abraham, his eclectic mind gave a fragmentary worship to the idea of Freedom. Personally, he was liberal in his views, though a wave of conservative opinion had brought him to the throne. But while he began to disassociate his influence from the tyranny of his Ministers,

I   129

he kept them in power.   He attempted to realise
democratic projects by the aid of the repressers
of '48.   He and his Government pulled in
different directions—the tension reassured him :
in that way he was sure of not going too far.

On the 15th August 1859, the Emperor proclaimed a general amnesty for all political offences.
Of the six thousand exiles of December, many
refused the Emperor's pardon.

> " Si l'on n'est plus que mille, eh bien ! j'en suis. Si même
> Ils ne sont plus que cent, je brave encor Sylla !
> S'il en demeure dix, je serai le dixième
> Et s'il n'en reste qu'un, je serai celui-là ! "

So sang Victor Hugo, and many took up the
echo.   Others were dead in banishment, but
many returned.   Nothing succeeds like success,
as we all know, and the empire appeared a great
success.   One after the other, great names began
to slip from the ranks of the Liberals and to
appear on the horizon of the Court.   Soon genius
became a frequent guest at Compiègne.   The
Emperor's marriage had drawn Mérimée into
his circle ; Sainte-Beuve, Nisard, Gautier, Emile
Augier followed suit.   And the Empire, in
admitting these great men, was modified by
their influence, became eager to patronise art
and letters, to further the pursuits of Science.
The Emperor himself was a sort of a scholar,

a kind of an author, a hanger-on of Clio.
Hesitatingly, doubtfully, though he still clung
to his guides of yesterday, he began to
follow, with one step back for every two steps
forward, the brilliant phalanx that showed a
better way.

Curious, indulgent, Renan watched this new
departure with a sort of benign amusement, but
made no advances. He, at least, never changed
his political position. Liberal in 1848, Liberal
in 1851, he was no less Liberal in 1860, when
Liberalism had become a sort of fashion. Yet,
when in the month of May 1860, the Emperor
made a feeble advance to the man he had injured,
offered to send him on an archæological mission
to Phœnicia, Renan immediately accepted. Some
of his old friends wondered. " The feud between
the Government and the intellect of France
was then so bitter that many persons of great
merit would not have accepted even a scientific
mission at its hands ; " so Sir M. Grant Duff
has well observed. Renan had no such scruple.
Henriette, moreover, urged him to undertake an
expedition which implied no political adherence
to the Government, no personal advancement,—·
which took him from what still remained the
scene of his ambitions, merely to further the
gain of Science. And it was arranged that she

should accompany him as secretary, as accountant, as steward of his resources.

The arrangements for their departure were not yet completed when the Druses fell on the Christians of Mount Lebanon, and massacred them in a Holy War. The Second Empire, however illiberal at home, was more than generous in its foreign policy. Napoleon immediately decided to protect the unfortunate Maronites. The vessel which carried M. Renan and his sister to Beyrouth was one of those which transported a French division to Syria. Renan, in his candid absorption in the ends of Science, appears to have accepted the whole affair—massacres, Turkish incapacity, French army *partant pour la Syrie*, &c.,—as providentially combined in the interests of archæology: "The presence of our soldiers on the spot was a most favourable element in my design. Thereby my excavations were singularly simplified—they were made by the soldiers. Thus my mission to Phœnicia took that place in the Syrian Expedition, which the French army, in its noble preoccupation with the things of the mind, has ever loved to accord to Science in her more distant ventures."[1]

The blood of the Maronites was scarcely dry on the sand when the Renans reached the Syrian

[1] *Mission de Phénicie*, Ière Livraison, p. 2.

shore. Thus they saw the East at once in the
squalor and horror of Moslem misrule, and in
all the glory of its past. They landed at Beyrouth, and at once began their excavations at
Byblos. Ancient Phœnicia, as the reader may
remember, comprised that strip of Syrian coast
—some thirty miles wide at largest, but nearly
thrice as long—which runs between the Mediterranean shore and the range of Lebanon. There
stand Azad and Marath, Tyre and Sidon, the
Byblos of Adonis—memorable names! Ports,
whence the Canaanitish traders put forth to carry
cedarwood to Solomon, and purple from Tyre,
and, from Sidon, the famous wares of Artas the
glassmaker; ports whence they sped to Greece,
Spain, Africa, Italy, founding Carthage, founding
Cadiz, building harbours and stations until they
made the Mediterranean a mere Phœnician lake.
In their boats, with their bales, these hardy
traders carried knowledge : but for their alphabet,
where were all our science? But in art these
English of the East were less happy. Colossal,
irregular, impressive, their strange dome of Amrit,
guarded by its lions, is almost their only masterpiece. For the best part, their monuments are
a half-barbaric reminiscence of Egypt or of
Greece, coarsely wrought, overloaded by plaques
of metal ornament.

If the sarcophagi which the Renans unearthed
at Byblos, showed no happy marvel of design—if
they were but honourable examples of provincial
art roughly executed in the best materials,—at
least they afforded a singular pleasure to their
excavators. Brother and sister had never dreamed
of a life so free.   Here they sat, on this beautiful
border of the Holy Land, commanding their little
camp, discovering the secret of antiquity.   Care
and poverty had dogged their youth : for Ernest
the dull hours of the usher, or the dusty fatigues
of the sub-librarian ; for Henriette, exile and
dependence amid plain after plain of sand and
snow, endless forests of foreign pines.   And now,
united, the great cities of Phœnicia lay at their
feet, and over the last blue mountain rim, Palestine !   A new energy, a light of youth, animated
them both.   Henriette, the recluse of the Val-de-
Grace, would spend ten hours at a stretch on
horseback, nor speak of fatigue.

The autumn in Syria is long and full of charm.
All the rocks of the gorges of Lebanon are
wreathed with cyclamen.   The plains towards
Amrit are blue and red with flowers.   From the
heights of the mountains, which rise here, tier
upon tier, in a quadruple range, the eye glances
across chasms and forests, towards a sea more
brilliant than the freshest blossoms.   Cascades

and torrents, clear as crystal, cool as ice, leap
from their rocky sources, and dash down the sun-
baked mountain-side, filling the hot air with the
sparkle of their spray. A spectacle so extraordinary forced itself upon the long slow gaze of
Renan. His unremarking eyes at last observed
the vision of natural beauty, absorbed it, retained
it. Syria completed the work begun by Italy :
Renan was henceforth to be one of the subtlest,
one of the profoundest painters of nature. Rousseau
himself has not more exquisite tints on his palette.
And, like Jean-Jacques, he reproduces less a landscape than his own dream of a landscape floating
in some pellucid haze of sentiment through which
reality takes on a prestige more magical, an air
of mystery and remoteness, peculiar less to the
landscape than the seer.

The climate, though beautiful, is unhealthy in
its brusque alternances of heat and cold. Sometimes sudden gusts of neuralgia, terrible, appalling
to witness, would sweep over Henriette Renan,
lay her prostrate for some hours, or some days,
and she would rise up again with unabated
courage and resume their hard, happy, adven-
turous life. Seated squarely on her horse, she
skirted the precipices of Lebanon, and never
paled. Rough fare, the huts of the mountain
for shelter, constant transitions from the burning

sunshine to the sepulchral chill of the gorges in shadow, were but as welcome episodes in a continual pleasure. At Tyre, the high pavilion she occupied was rocked by the winds. The spectacle of their little camp, lost in the desert, filled her at night with a religious exaltation.

In January 1861, Madame Ernest Renan came out to join them. Together they set out in the spring for Palestine. Often at night, their tent set under the shadow of Mount Carmel, or by the deep hollow of the Lake of Galilee, the travellers read the series of Pilgrims' Psalms, which Renan was to recall a few months later in writing the *Life of Jesus.*

"For those provincial families the journey to Jerusalem was a solemnity full of sweetness. Psalm after psalm records the happiness of these pilgrim households travelling together in the spring time over hill and down dale, with the sacred splendour of Jerusalem at the journey's end. 'How happy are brethren who dwell together in amity!' . . . The last stage of all, Aïn-el-Haramié, is full of charm and melancholy. Few impressions rival that of the traveller who sets his camp there at nightfall. The valley is narrow and sombre; a dark water drips from the walls of the rocks, pierced with tombs. It is, I think, the 'Vale of Tears'—the 'gorge of

dripping waters,' which is celebrated in the exquisite 83rd Psalm as one of the stations on
the way, and in which the tender sadness of
mediæval mysticism saw an image of the life of
man. Early on the morrow the caravan will
reach Jerusalem. Even to-day the thought reanimates the caravan, renders the evening short
and the travellers' slumber light."

Jerusalem, tragic, arid, barren, seemed then as
the law after the Gospel, as the letter after the
spirit, and sharpened by contrast the souvenir of
Galilean grace. In this harsh environment, the
newness, the freshness, the divine originality of
the New Testament appear more apparent still.
Ever since his year of spiritual crisis Renan had
pondered in his heart a Life of Jesus, unlike any
yet written, which, while hiding nothing of the
textual errors and apocryphs of the Gospel as
we possess it, should set in high and clear relief
the divine character, the exquisite inventions in
moral sentiment of the Founder of Christianity.
Here, in the Holy Land, that great figure never
ceased upon his inner vision. No saint in his
cell, no Crusader, was ever more fervently haunted
by Christ Jesus than this unfrocked Churchman,
this sceptical archæologist, busied with the details
of a scientific mission. In the desolate Galilee
of a Moslem rule, his mind's eye noted the

flowery Paradise described by Josephus where
the walnut and the date palm grew together.
On the abandoned lake, with its one ruined
ferry-boat, he saw the sails of Andrew and
Peter, the prosperous fishermen of old.   On the
little promontories, overgrown with tamarisk
and oleander, he followed the trace of the
very footsteps of the Son of Man.   Far to
the north the ravines of Mount Hermon are
drawn in dazzling silver against the sky.   The
horizon, at least, has not altered in these two
thousand years.

After the month of May the heat in Syria
becomes oppressive.   Galilee, deforested, deserted,
is now so naked that the caravan reckons over-
night where it shall find a spot of shade for the
mid-day meal on the morrow.   The journey
back to Beyrouth cost the travellers much
fatigue.   Mme. Ernest Renan, *enceinte*, returned to France in the course of July.   Her
husband and sister-in-law would have done well
to accompany her.   Almost every member of
the mission engaged under M. Renan in the
excavations had already fallen dangerously ill
with pestilential malaria.   And the worst heat
of the summer was to come.   But the sense of
scientific duty, always so strong in Renan,
which over and over again prompted him to a

course of action disastrous to his interests, urged him to remain on the parched and feverish Syrian coast in order to supervise the shipping of his archæological treasure, in order, also, to complete his exploration of the upper range of Lebanon. He meditated, even, an autumn excursion to Cyprus. Henriette happier, she declared, than ever she had been in her life, Henriette, satisfied to find herself still indispensable to her idol, remained with him and braved — alas too courageously! — the exhalations of a Syrian autumn.

The implacable sun of Beyrouth drove the Renans to the hills. At Ghazir they found green pastures, fresh snow from the mountains, wholesome springs, and a little house with a pergola. Here, in the utmost peace conceivable on earth, Renan began his Life of Jesus. All day long he sat in the cool shadow of his Syrian home absorbed, intoxicated by that inner dream which little by little took shape and lived before his eyes. A New Testament, a Josephus, comprised his library; but the book of the East was open before him; but the very past, familiar through a hundred texts and inscriptions, rose before him more real than the actual moment. Thrown full length on his Syrian rug, his books and papers scattered round him, he wrote hour after hour in the fervour of a veritable inspiration. Henriette was his perpetual confidant, as soon as the page was written she copied it fair. When at last the night fell, the clear, magnificent Oriental night, brother and sister rose and sought their terrace on the house roof. There they would speak at last of the day's silent work, and she would make her reflections, often profound, always pregnant with that fine, moral tact of which she had the secret. " Many of them," her brother has said, " were to me as veritable revelations."

" This book," she would say, " I shall love. Because we have done it together. And because I like it ! "

Days of earnest thought, nights of dreaming scarcely less fecund. When, in the first days of September, the Renans were compelled to return to Beyrouth the book was three parts written, and Christ on the eve of the last journey to Jerusalem.

Alas ! the soul and the body have not the same requirements. An immense moral satisfaction had not preserved the health of Henriette Renan. The cruel neuralgia from which she suffered was perhaps even aggravated by so intense a nervous strain. Yet had the *Cato* started at the date fixed, the sea winds and the air of home

might even yet have revived her. As chance
would have it, some ill-hap delayed the ship one
week. Made aware of this postponement, the
Renans started for Gebeil (Byblos), in order to
see to the shipping of two last sarcophagi, which
they had given up as untransportable. They
secured their spoil, and climbed the hill to find
shade and rest at Amschit, that Syrian village,
dear to Henriette, where they had spent together
the first few weeks of their Eastern sojourn.
Here, on the Tuesday, 17th September, Henriette
fell ill with a vague sort of intermittent fever,
accompanied by neuralgic pains. But she was
so accustomed to neuralgia! She had often
seemed more violently ill. Even on the Wednes-
day, the surgeon of the *Cato* saw no reason for
anxiety. When Ernest Renan could be spared
from the wharves of Gebeil, he sat at her side,
she uncomplaining, he undisquieted, and continued
the work they had both so deep at heart. He
had reached the chapters of the Passion. But
on the Thursday he too fell ill with the same
mysterious disease, turn by turn mortal and
trivial, which seizes on the victim, and looses
him again, as a cat plays with a mouse. Un-
happily the surgeon of the *Cato* always arrived
when his patients were in their languid intervals
of remittance. He did not know the pernicious

malaria of the Syrian coast. He foresaw no
serious consequences. But on Saturday morning
M. Renan, when he dragged himself from his
couch in the sitting-room to his sister's side,
meaning to work beside her at his *Life of Jesus*,
was terrified by a new feature of the malady
—the heart appeared affected. He dispatched
a brief note to the surgeon of the *Cato*. He
had time to remark the Maronite peasants
passing his window on their way to church, and
in this foreign half-savage country, the familiar
sight filled him with a feeling of utter desolation
and helplessness which he has since recorded.
Then he himself fell down unconscious among
his scattered books and papers.

When, at nightfall, the French doctor arrived
at Amschit, he found brother and sister, both
apparently dead, laid out upon the carpet of
the little *salon*, watched over by Antoun, their
Syrian man-servant. The ship surgeon, dumb-
foundered by this strange neuralgia, apparently
of an irregular, fatal sort, retreated hastily to
Beyrouth in search of more experienced advice.
Later in the day the French commandant and
the French doctors, seriously alarmed, climbed
the steep road to Amschit. When they arrived,
the unconscious bodies of Ernest and Henriette
Renan had been transported from their rooms to

the large reception-room of Zakhia, their wealthy
Maronite host. There they lay, stretched out
on the floor, the family of the worthy Zakhia
grouped around them, wailing them as dead. It
was a scene of a poignant barbaric melancholy.

Henriette Renan never recovered consciousness.
She died on the Tuesday morning. Her brother
awoke from his long swoon about an hour before
she expired. But he awoke to a troubled dream
of things, clearly aware of nothing; and Henriette died without his hand in hers. For days
after he babbled of green fields, imagining that
he was resting with his sister by the springs of
the river Adonis, under the great walnuts that
stand above the waterfall. She was seated
beside him in the deep grass; he held to her
lips a cup of ice-cold water. When he stirred
in his dream it was to ask, " How is my sister? "
They answered, " Very ill! " He smiled, and
fell again to dreaming. When at last they said,
" She is dead," he barely understood. No
merciful silence was possible, for the *Cato* was
waiting in harbour, and so soon as the invalid
could bear the journey, he was put in a litter
and carried seaward. Henriette he left behind
him. She sleeps in the vault of Zakhia, under
the palms of Amschit; distant, in death as in
life, from the Breton land she loved so well.

As a dream within a dream, there remained to haunt her brother the thought that Henriette had been spirited away from him alive, buried in the caverns of Lebanon while still in her living trance. For the likeness of that swoon to the last sleep filled him with fearful apprehensions, and he had never looked on Henriette's dead face. Even the presence of four French doctors at her deathbed could not entirely reassure him. And nearly twenty years after, in the *Dream of Leoline*, he speaks out this inner anguish: " Ah, see, her eyes open! Her long white hand moves out of the coffin. Her face is pale as of old, and her eyes swim in tears. Come, kiss me! Dear, I have so much to tell thee! How many years have passed since thy mortal fever. How weary thou must be with the long journey from thy grave. God knows that in all my joys I have never ceased to long for thy presence; not one happy moment but I would have shared it with thee! Ah, white shadow, open thine eyes, though it be for a quarter of an hour; only one quarter of an hour in which to weep with thee, and expiate my faults towards thee, or suffer thy pious reproaches. O, pierced heart, how hast thou made me suffer! For so many hours, bitter and sweet, give me at least a glance."

There is no grief so terrible as to feel that,

however innocently, we have abandoned our dearest
in their hour of need. It is the grief of Peter.
Renan never forgot that his sister died alone.
For many years, she, at least, did not forsake
him ; for those whom we lose by death do not
quit us all at once. All the company of true
mourners may echo the words of Hippolytus,
μεῖζω βροτείας προσπισὼν ὁμιλίας . . . κλύων μὲν αυδῆν, ὁμμα
δ'οὐχ ὁρῶν τὸ σόν. We feel an irresistible ægis above
us. An inner presence is more penetrating and
more intimate than we ever knew it, for the dead
speak to us now from within. Our continual
meditation on a vanished object recreates it in
ourselves. We grow like the dead we adore ;
their spirit finds a home in us, and appears to use
us and direct us at its will. But in the end our
natural personality reasserts itself ; only very few
souls are transformed into the image they recall.
Renan's character, so sensitive, so impressionable,
had none the less a ground-work of singular *un-
modifiableness;* even the kindred spirit of Henriette,
so like his own, could not permanently change
that stubborn essence. . . . Time passes ; the
dead remain as dear ; but their influence per-
vades us less and less, shrinks gradually back to
its own centre, leaves us—as the fields are left on
the retiring of a flood—fertilized, no doubt, and
richer, but the same as before, land and not

water, ourselves and not another, for the rest
of our time. . . . Even Love-in-Death cannot
create a new spirit within us.

So great, however, was the influence of Henriette,
that, for years afterwards, not only her brother
acted as she would have bid him act, but—far
rarer triumph of love !—he thought as she would
have bid him think, in all seriousness, in all
tenderness, with a remote and noble elevation—
checking as they rose those impulses towards
irony, towards frivolity, towards scepticism, which
Henriette had not loved.

PART III

CHAPTER I

THE COLLEGE OF FRANCE

WITH half his heart in the mysterious kingdom of the dead, and himself still pallid
with the reflection of that unseen world, Renan
set himself to finish his *Life of Jesus*—the book
which Henriette had loved, "because we wrote
it together." Never had the problems of religion
appeared so all-important in his eyes ; never had
he felt nearer to that infinite and eternal energy
which beats at the heart of things : One in All.
"The loss of my brave companion attached me
closer than ever to studies which had cost so
dear. . . . I have looked Death in the face.
The pygmy cares which eat our lives away are
henceforth meaningless to me. I have brought
back from the threshold of the infinite a livelier
faith than I ever knew in the superior reality of
the world of the Ideal. It alone exists : the
physical world appears to exist. . . . The
older I grow, the dearer I have at heart the one
problem which ever keeps its profound significance, its enchanting novelty. The Infinite sur-

rounds us, overlaps us, and haunts us. Bubbles on the surface of existence, we feel a mysterious kinship with our Father the Abyss. God is revealed, by no miracle, but in our hearts whence, as St Paul has said, an unutterable moaning goes up to Him without ceasing. And this sentiment of our obscure relationship to the universe, of our Divine descendance, graven in fire in every human heart, is the source of all virtue, the reason we love, and the one thing that makes our life worth living. Jesus is, in my eyes, the greatest of men, because He developed this dim feeling with an unprecedented, an unsurpassable power. His religion holds the secret of the future. . . . To transport religion beyond the supernatural —to separate the ever-triumphant cause of ·Faith from the vain forlorn hope of the Miraculous, is to render a service to them that believe. Religion is necessary—as eternal as poetry or love : Religion will survive the destruction of all her illusions. I say it with confidence : the day will come when I shall have the sympathy of really religious souls." [1]

Henriette had said : write the Life of Jesus. Henriette had also said : maintain your candidature to the Chair of Hebrew and accept no other chair. Behold, her least utterance had now

[1] *Questions Contemporaines,* 195 . . . 237 . . . 232 . . . 235.

become oracular.   As Renan himself wrote to the Professors of the College of France :—" I saw an imperative revelation in the counsel of a beloved person who appeared to me haloed in the sacred aureole of death."   Ah, why was Henriette not by his side !   She would have bid him keep distinct these two noble ambitions—bid him speak of Jesus in his book, analyse Semitic philology at the College of France.   But at bottom, for all his airs of indecision, Renan burned to give a reason for the faith that was in him.

At last, after nearly five years of silence, the Minister of Public Instruction demanded the lists from the College of France and the Academy of Inscriptions.   Renan's name headed either.   And a decree of the 11th January 1862, proclaimed him Professor of Hebrew at the College of France.

This election was passionately unpopular among the Catholics, and for due cause : the Chair of Hebrew being in fact a chair of Biblical criti-cism as we have said.   But it was also, oddly enough, unpopular among the students of the Latin Quarter, indignant that Renan, *their* Renan, should have accepted office at the Emperor's hands.   Was he going to turn his coat ?   At the mere idea they were all ready to shout with Robert Browning—

" Just for a handful of silver he left us."

It was clear there would be at his opening lecture what the Latin Quarter loves to call a *Chahut*. Renan's opinions were known. If the Church was conspicuous by her absence, the young Catholic party was there *en masse* to avenge her. And the Liberal students were no less suspicious and defiant. The University, not wholly sympathetic to this unfrocked Seminarist of supposed Radical opinions ; the world of fashion, attracted by Renan's literary renown, helped to throng the hall. The lecturer appeared, his head in a dream, his mind full of Henriette, so cruelly absent, of the Life of Jesus, of his old dreams at last come true. He was barely aware of the various causes of offence which he had given. He just glanced at the amphitheatre crammed from floor to ceiling—at the students, clinging in clusters to the window ledges, shouting news of the lecture to the crowd, black in the street. . . . I have heard it all described so vividly that it seems to me I, too, was there !

Then he began a parallel between the Semite and the Aryan. Anti-semitism was not yet a fashion ; there was nothing here to rail at. The face of the audience fell : was it this they had come out into the wilderness to hear ? The lecturer continued — " The Political Idea is Aryan. The French Revolution, for instance, may often have compromised Liberty, but " . . . (Here the Latin Quarter saw its opportunity.)

"Respect the Revolution, sir!" thundered from a hundred throats. A quarter of an hour later an audacious comparison of King David to an "energetic Captain of Adventure" threw a bomb into the Catholic camp. By this time the Liberal students were aware that the lecturer was still *their* leader; one and all they became forthwith his clamorous partisans. Their support alone rendered the delivery of the lecture possible.

Was it well? Better perhaps if, at the outset, an unjust turbulence had drowned the orator's voice. For one phrase in his speech — one sentence which nowadays any Liberal Christian would hear with tolerance, if not with approval — falling just at that impassioned moment on prejudiced ears, began a sequence of injustice, a series of misunderstandings, which were to make of the mild impartial scholar the notorious martyr of the Empire, the demigod of a Republic he only half approved. To this day, in his native place, Renan is chiefly remembered as "a great Republican" by those who have never read a line of his writings.

I can imagine Henriette's phantom mur-
muring—

"Ni cet excès d'honneur ni cette indignité !"

This was not the future she had foreseen,
illustrious yet retired ; the life of a Le Nain de
Tillemont secluded in some park of Seine-et-
Oise, whose peaceful *charmilles* are not too far
from the libraries of Paris, whose lofty grey-
panelled chambers afford space and quiet for a
voluminous research.   Such a life, irradiate with
the limpid light of Science, productive of labours
which should satisfy countless generations of
scholars, and never be profaned by the vulgarity
of fame, such a life she would approve.   She
would have found something gross in the immense celebrity which began, on that 21st of
February 1862, in the amphitheatre of the
College of France.

What a riot ! what a tumult !   Only here and
there we catch a word, half drowned in hisses
and acclamations. . . . "An incomparable Man,
whom some, struck by His exceptional mission,
call a God . . . victim of His ideal . . . deified
in His death . . . founded the Eternal Religion
of Humanity. . . . No man before Him had
reached so high a standard of perfection. . . .
For the time is come when ye shall worship

Me no longer along this mountain nor at Jerusalem, but in Spirit and in Truth."[1] St Paul did not disdain to say: "Jesus of Nazareth, a Man sent from God among ye" (Acts ii. 22). Bossuet, after him, wrote without reproach of Christ as "a man of admirable mildness." But Renan's "homme incomparable" appeared the thrown gauntlet of the defiant apostate. The Church was not slow to take it up, nor the students to defend it; the confusion grew deafening. The lecture over, Renan escaped by some back way to the house of a friend, haunted by the dread of a public ovation. The piece was played without Hamlet; the students, *en masse*, swarmed to the Rue Madame, where the Renans lived, and (true Frenchmen!) demanded, in default of their idol, a glimpse of his mother. M. Egger, who was calling at the time, harangued the crowd in terms sufficiently vague to disguise from the old lady (a devotee of Throne and Altar) the full scandal of her son's success. He need not have been at the pains. The dark, witty old face had only its most benignant smile for the turbulence of Ernest's riotous champions.

The fact remained that M. Renan's opening

[1] *Mélanges d'Histoire et de Voyages*, p. 18.

lecture had disturbed the cause of public order.
Beset by the Church, by the Empress, Napoleon
seized this excuse to suspend the young Professor
from his functions.   And Renan continued his
lectures in his private study, still, nominally,
Professor at the College of France.   But on
the 2nd of June 1864, on opening the morning paper, he saw his name.   He was trans-
ferred from his chair at the College of France
to a post of sub-librarian at the Imperial Library.
The thing came on him as a thunder-clap.
And insult was added to the injury by an
official note, observing that this new appointment was more in accordance with the dignity
of a distinguished *savant*, " at present subject
to the anomaly of receiving pay for work
which he is not permitted to perform."   Renan
had acquitted himself of his duty, exactly, if
in private.   The fund of combativeness which
every man has at heart seethed within him.
He wrote to the minister, in a mood of ferocious
irony : *Pecunia tua tecum sit.* He refused the
post of librarian, and maintained his right
to the title of Professor at the College of
France.

On the 11th of June Renan was officially
destituted.   He became one of the most popular
members of the Liberal Opposition.   Already,

in 1863, he had been invited to stand for Parliament. In March of that year he wrote to Michele Amari.[1]

" I am preparing my *Life of Jesus*, which will appear in about two months. I need not tell you on what lines it is written. The partisans of miracles will not be satisfied. I do not know what will come of it all! Between you and me, I may say that if I should be deprived of my chair at the College of France, it is probable I may be elected as one of the Members for Paris. I cannot say that I am in love with the idea. I should have preferred the free and peaceable career of Higher Education. But it is not my fault if my feet are set on another road. And, if my election take place, it would have a meaning which would fill me with satisfaction; to bring about such a declaration, I am ready for many sacrifices. All these things may be! I am playing a difficult game and I do not see the upshot."

The *Life of Jesus* appeared on the 23rd of June 1863. Before November, sixty thousand copies of it were in circulation. No such success had as yet issued from the printing presses of the century. . . . At such a moment, there was something fitting in the destitution of Ernest

[1] *Carteggio di Michele Amari*, 2 vols., Turin, 1896.

Renan.   The professor had become the artist ;
the philologist, the man of letters ; the scholar,
the politician.   Too much glory, too wide an
audience, ill befit the patient research of a
laboratory.

CHAPTER II

THE LIFE OF JESUS

THE *Life of Jesus* is naturally the first of Renan's seven volumes on the Origins of Christianity. Even more than its successors it is a work, not of erudition, not of technical exegesis, but of moral and psychological enquiry, based on historical documents. Renan was certainly familiar with the curious mosaic of Le Nain de Tillemont, he knew almost by heart the New Testament, he had read and re-read the pages of Josephus ; to this foundation, solid if restricted, he added a rare archæological capacity, an acquaintance with the monuments, moneys, and inscriptions of the first centuries of our era which, of a surety, no other religious historian possesses ; he was, moreover, a traveller, whom a year's residence in Syria had accustomed to the horizons, the races, and the character of the Holy Land : the fresh impressions of his visit colour every page ; but, above all, he was a psychologist, a man who had once believed, who had felt the pulse of his soul, with as much curiosity as anguish, during the long years in which that dear belief expired : a man to whom, even after its death, the impulse of Faith remained the holiest, and the most interesting thing in the universe. His rustic and religious origin enabled this man of science to enter into the spirit of a credulous country folk, and to analyse, without illusion, without derision, the creative process of their minds. The result is a master-piece. The pure idyll of Galilee, hardly less sacred to Renan than to the most fervent Churchman ; the Passion of Jerusalem ; the religious East ; and philosophic Greece, animating a Syrian people with the spirit of the Gospel of St John ; the dogmatic force and fervour of St Paul, supplying, as it were, channels and imperishable aqueducts for the New Source of Life which the rod of Jesus had set welling; all the great concourse of saints, martyrs, mystics, heretics, and charlatans who laboured together blindly in a Cause superior to even the noblest among them ; and the cruel consolidating force of persecution ; and Nero, the Antichrist, throwing into stronger relief the ideal perfection of Jesus : all this, grouped against a vast Mediterranean background—Syria, Antioch, Alexandria, Athens, Rome—lives and glows before us in the pages of Renan.

In the beginning there was a Life of unequalled

perfection. The origins of Christianity begin with the Life of Jesus. To write a *Life of Jesus* has been the fatality of modern theology, for the hero of a biography can only be a man. The Christ, who, at a given date, was born of Jewish stock, in the obscure village of a distant Roman protectorate ; who grew to manhood among certain Syrian peasants, whose appearance, education, and racial character he shared ; who spoke an Aramean dialect, and never knew Greek ; loses, by just so much as he gains in historic precision, the vague glory of universal Divinity. The theologian who would write the life of Jesus should compose a hymn. In such matters the Trisagion alone is really orthodox.

So early as 1838, Salvador, and towards 1860, Bunsen, had published, in their different fashions, material towards a history of the early Church. In 1840, Littré's translation of Strauss's *Life of Jesus* acquainted the French public with the speculations of Tübingen. More than to any of these, Renan owed to Herder : Herder, whose philosophy of history had helped to mould his mind. That elegant philosopher, Christian archæologist, and philologist, fully alive to the literary excellence of the text he examines,—that man of feeling and ideas, in-

L

fluenced by his age and largely influencing it,—
was a man after Renan's heart. He never understood the austere and hard-headed rationalists of
the school of Tübingen, as deficient in tact and
measure as they are rich in knowledge.

Renan's debt to Tübingen has been exaggerated. The fault and the charm of his *Life
of Jesus* is that he wrote it insufficiently prepared. The charm — because its extraordinary
spontaneity makes the book a sort of fifth Gospel
—the gospel, if you will, according to Thomas
Didymus. The pages written on the mud floor
of a Syrian cottage, with Joseph and the Gospels
for their only sponsors, keep the freshness, the
life and the beauty of their original inspiration.
Renan's *Life of Jesus* is the biography of a
divinity written by a worshipper still prostrate
before the dead body of his god, but convinced
there will be no resurrection. Its superiority
is its profound religious sentiment, its living,
vibrating atmosphere of the East, its sense of
the human personality, the *life* of Jesus.

Strauss, on the other hand, is a gnostic of
the nineteenth century. All that he touches
turns to allegory, myth, and symbol. His
Christ is an Æon—a glittering abstraction. The
aureole which the faith of the multitude has
lit around the face of Jesus blinds him to the

features which it frames. His Saviour is a logical
deduction from prophecy. We wonder why the
first Christians lived hard, and died harder, for
love of so unreal a Messiah. There is no life
in these dead bones. The dogmatic man of
science has no sense of a thing so delicate, so
fluctuating, so spontaneous, so mysterious, as the
birth of a faith.

But only a German university can produce the
sum of labour necessary to collect, control, revise
and criticise the vast material of any given history. If, when he began his *Life of Jesus*, Renan
had been better acquainted with the researches
of Strauss, Baur, Hilgenfeld, Reuss, Schwegler,
Ewald, Zeller, and other erudites, he would not
have taken a document of, we suppose, the end
of the first century for a contemporary narrative
of the life of Christ. A characteristic preference
for ideas over facts, an affinity for the man who
philosophises about events rather than for him
who simply records them, led Renan to lay the
greatest stress on the Gospel according to St
John. Later on he saw the error of his ways,
and, with the good faith he always showed, he
recast many passages of his original work : after
the thirteenth edition the difference is striking.
But something undecided, embarrassed, clings to
the work, which I consider inferior to at least

three of the volumes which were to follow it—the exquisite *Apostles*, so humane and so tender in its feeling of human brotherhood ; *St Paul*, a study in sociology and in the psychology of geography ; *Antichrist*, a magnificent historical painting.   The *Life of Jesus* contains incomparable passages, but the whole does not carry conviction.   This Christ is too Celtic, too German ; he is too much like Ernest Renan.   And the writer's attitude is not clear.   He is not a Catholic, so much is evident since he denies the divinity of Christ ; but he is also not a free-thinker, a disinterested historical student ; for his Christ is more than the founder of a great religion, he is something quite apart from, quite above and beyond such human sons of God as Moses, Mahomet, or Buddha.   Renan will none of them.   "Christianity," he declares, "has become almost the synonym of religion ; all that is attempted outside its great and fertile tradition is doomed to sterility. . . . Christ is the creator of the eternal religion of humanity."   This is limiting the future.   The divine essence has more than one manifestation, and in the million years of man's progress may reveal itself in many ways.   On the lips of an unbeliever, so absolute an affirmation is more than incongruous—even a little exasperating. And occasionally Renan reminds us of some inconsolable widower who, after the stormiest married life, waxes eloquent of the departed. If the marriage was so impossible, why these tears? But if the poor man be sincere, he will not listen to you.

Renan was sincere, and in the things of the heart there is no magic like sincerity. So heart-felt, so hopeless, his pious unbelief took the world by storm. For the world is full of men and women who once believed, and who keep green and strown with flowers the tomb of a dead ideal. Here was a man who could speak the dumb word in their hearts; a man whose lips the Eternal had touched with his fiery coal ; a man who cried no more, as we all cry—*à à domine, nescio loqui !* Genius was in the book, and sincerity, and a very tender reverence. As the Empress said to Madame Cornu, in great surprise, when at last she had read the maligned volume : " It can do no harm to believers ; to unbelievers it can only do good."

The most beautiful pages of the *Life of Jesus* open the succeeding volume, the *Apostles*, and treat of the life-after-death of our Lord. We doubt if there exist in any language more ex-quisite pages of religious psychology. Here, again, it is, from the historical point of view, unfortunate that Renan should have followed the narrative according to St John.   As was often the case, the artist in him tempted the historian, and the historian yielded.   For the version of St John is infinitely more pathetic, more probable, more lovely than the versions of the synoptic Gospels.   And doubtless the narrative was inspired by an authentic oral tradition.   But, in a question of history, a scientific historian has no right to choose a page, however beautiful, of a later writer, in place of a prosaic narrative copied from a lost recital possibly contemporary with the event described.   If Renan had been, as single-mindedly as he believed the sole servant of Truth, he would have chosen Mark or Luke for his guide in this matter.

But if we may question Renan's judgment in the criticism of his texts, we can only marvel at the extraordinary ingenuity with which he interprets them.   With all the piety of the Christian, with all the scruple of the man of science, he gives an explanation of the Resurrection which leaves no least suspicion of fraud to blur the aureole of our dearest saints, and yet sets an event, which we cannot accept as supernatural, in accordance with the normal laws of things. The vision of Mary Magdalene accomplished the necessary miracle—Christ had arisen. "In these crises of the miraculous, it is easy enough to see what another has seen. The one merit is to see before the others, for those that come after model their vision on the received type. It is the peculiarity of fine organisations to see promptly, exactly, and in the true line of things. The glory of the Resurrection belongs to Mary Magdalene. After Jesus, she, more than any other, laid the foundations of Christianity. The shadow which her delicate senses perceived—nay, created—still shelters the world. Queen and patroness of idealists, she knew, as no other has known, how to affirm her own ideal, and to force upon others the sacred vision of her passionate soul. Her great woman's assertion, 'He is risen!' is the basis of the faith of Humanity."

Beauty of the fabric, fragility of the foundation, necessity of the consoling vision, fleeting illusion of all things save the infinitely small which we measure in the hollow of our hand! And who shall say which, in the essential is truest: Life which is a dream, or the dream which may be Life? All here below is but a sign and a symbol, the sun in the heavens no less than the phantom of desire. The symbols which serve to give a form to the religious sentiment are incomplete and transitory ; but a great truth inhabits them and makes of the least of them the temple of an hour.

CHAPTER III

THE ORIGINS OF CHRISTIANITY

C HRISTIANITY is not a simple faith ; it is a profound theology, a tremendous organ-isation. The Son of Man appeared, loved the world and died, leaving a trail of light behind him. His message is contained in the dis-courses of Matthew, in the parables of Luke. But a pure religion is too ethereal a thing to subsist uncontaminate in the dense atmos-phere of reality. The work of Jesus was taken up and completed by a man of action. And this is what Renan shows us in his volume on St Paul.

His portrait of the Apostle is striking, life-like, unexpected. For hitherto, in all the great images which he loves to evoke from the recesses of the past, Renan has sought some secret kinship with his own soul. Here there is none ! St Paul is scarce a saint, not at all a poet, a sage, a dreamer, or a man of science. He was a hero of the Active Life—a missionary and a conqueror, with a fierce, tender, proselytizing soul, not averse to combat, often susceptible, sometimes jealous, capable of rancour and aggression. For once Renan has got outside himself. He calls up before us the bizarre little Jew with his halting speech, his incorrect and hurried eloquence, his bent shoulders, his pale face with the large features, his piercing eyes under their shaggy eyebrows. The vision is so vivid that we scarce have the heart to cavil at the insufficient tradition which is its only warrant : the same tradition maintains that St Paul was remarkable for his personal beauty.

St Paul, as we know, was a Pharisee and a man of some education. The fact that he spoke with fluency a Greek dialect was all-important in the propagation of Christianity, for Greek was the chief language of the Mediterranean ports, and a mere Hebrew missionary, confined to his own tongue, would have been of scant influence with the Gentiles. Paul, a Jew by birth, a Roman citizen by hereditary right, a Greek by language, was no less cosmopolitan than the world he moved in—the brilliant, variegated, incoherent world of Asia Minor : Splendid Antioch, "third city of the globe," with its temples, baths, and aqueducts, its wide streets bordered with stately columns and statues ; immense Ephesus clambering from the marshes up the sacred hills, with the shrine of Diana in its midst, and all round the clear horizons of the Asiatic plain ; Antioch, Ephesus, Corinth, vast centres of wealth and superstition, cities full of magicians and miners and flute-players, of goldsmiths and courtezans, of priests, rhetoricians, and novelists: such were the unlikely cradles of the New Idea. Renan who, in 1864, visited the whole area of the peregrinations of St Paul, has fixed with the subtlest, most vivid art, the very image of this vanished world.

" Like Socialism now - a - days, Christianity sprouted on what we call the corruption of great cities." It was a movement of the hard-pressed, intelligent, unlettered poor, who abounded in the meaner suburbs of the Mediterranean ports.

There the wandering Christian workman set up his tent, there he sowed the good seed, and then passed on. Like a travelling journeyman who leaves behind him the trace of his opinion in every wayside tavern where he has halted, in every village where he has made friends, Paul, in especial, wandered from place to place, tramping over hill or down dale, coasting from port to port, working for his bread, even while he set forth how man does not live by bread alone. At Ephesus and Corinth, assisted by Aquila and Priscilla, he set up, in some back street, a small shop for the sale of the coarse Cilician canvas which it was his trade to weave. In every town where he halted he gained converts to the Faith. Christianity was to spring in all her glory from these small clusters of fervid, illiterate, primitive persons, grouped, as a rule, round some virtuous well-to-do widow, some spiritually - minded tradesman of means. The Early Churches were narrow circles of some dozen believers. " Probably all the converts of St Paul did not number a thousand all told."

Renan's rare knowledge of the social conditions of antiquity on the Mediterranean shore has enabled him to reconstruct the double organization which was to contain Christianity, even as the hive and the wax contain the honey. The outer framework, as we may say, was the compact *Orbis* of the Roman Empire. One sole administration governed all the countries visited by the Apostles. Their propaganda would have been impossible had Asia, Macedonia, Malta, the cities of Greece and Italy, each been constituted in separate and vivacious nationalities, each with their own exclusive tradition, faith, and speech. But the Pax Romana enveloped them all in one monotony. A great dull well-being brooded over the vast Empire : the tedium of a civilization which has attained its goal and has nothing left to desire.

" If life consisted in amusing oneself by order of the Law, in eating one's ration of daily bread, in taking the regulation pleasure sadly under the eye of one's chief, then the Roman juris consults would have solved the problem of human government." But a mortal coldness breathed from this dismal prosperity : Rome offered nothing to love! Deep in man's heart is the instinct of choice. The phalanstery, however comfortable, is not the home, nor the chance desk-fellow the selected comrade. He longs for the little coterie of chosen spirits, the guild the confraternity, where he contributes, of his own free will, to the welfare of his mates and his own security. The sense of fellowship is an instinct which must be allowed for! In the lowest circles of the Roman Empire men met together in secret to satisfy this sacred prompting. The Syrian, Greek, and Jewish quarters were full of little illicit *Collegia*—Friendly Societies, Mutual Aid Societies, Burial Societies especially—condemned by the Government as possible hot-beds of disaffection, but in reality peaceful enough in their humble brotherhood. The members were all of the poorest class :

servants, porters, hucksters, old-clo' men, tinder
sellers and such like. Christianity immediately
illuminated the small *Collegia*.

And what was the ghetto but a larger, a
more complete *Collegium?* A *Collegium* whose
life and centre was the Synagogue? No gulf,
no apparent schism, as yet divided Christianity
from the Law and the prophets. The first
apostles sought their quarters in the ghetto.
There they awaited patiently the Sabbath day,
and then followed the crowding Israelites into
the square, plain structure which was less a
church than a school, a debating society. It
was the hospitable custom of Jewry to invite
the stranger within its gates to greet the brethren
with some discourse of edification. Paul and
the apostles found thus their opportunity. In
the Synagogue they preached the Gospel. In
the Synagogue they made their first converts.
In the Synagogue they aroused their earliest
persecutors.

For no people are (or *were*) so well instructed
as the Jews in the authentic dogma and tradition
of their own religion. Paul's audacious theories
roused a dozen eager voices, clamouring to con-
fute the heretic. Hence stonings, flagellations,
prison, exile. But hence also the instantaneous
bruiting abroad of Christian doctrine. The

complicated ritual of Judaism was perhaps a safeguard, it was certainly a barrier. It is impossible to imagine the world accepting a creed overcharged by so many observances. Paul proclaimed : " The Letter kills, the Spirit maketh alive." By declaring of no account the distinctions between the clean and the unclean, he admitted the Gentiles to the Faith, but he outraged Judaism. In every religion there are always more men ready to avenge a violated ritual than to accept the new life of a free spirit. Judaism, as a body, was lost to Christianity. But in exchange it gained the world. Instead of a sect of the ghetto, it became the purest worship of the civilization it renewed.

Therein was the merit of Paul. By his passionate affirmation of the broad freedom of Christ he completed and secured the work of Jesus. The history of his struggle at tremendous odds ; the sunny, breezy, joyous narration of his divine Odyssey ; the picture of the social conditions under which he laboured, is the subject of Renan's two volumes, *The Apostles*, and *St Paul.* Seldom has the master shown a science more solid, a profounder sense of the secret roots of things, a more vivid and brilliant vocation of their living image,

than in this volume which, dealing with documents and facts beyond dispute, contains nothing
to grieve the liberal Christian, much to instruct
the student, and, more to rejoice the lover of
literature.

CHAPTER IV

POLITICS

NOT for a moment was Renan's weighty mind thrown out of gear by the prodigious success of the *Life of Jesus*. He was aware that an author's popularity is almost always the result of a misunderstanding. He liked being liked, no doubt, as much as St Augustine "loved to love." Popularity was a pleasant episode. He would not let it become an aim.

Had he continued the "Origins of Christianity" in a *crescendo* of anti-clericalism, Renan would have become the idol of the market-place. He would have been to 1870 what Lamartine had been to 1848 : the *vates*, the philosopher, the chosen guide. But the unity and the dignity of Renan's life sprang from his sense of belonging to a superior order vowed to superior duties : he was the priest of Truth. Instead of contesting a Parisian circonscription, he went to Asia Minor with his wife and studied on the spot, as minutely as he had studied the civilization of Palestine and Syria, the local conditions into which were born

M   177 the Christian churches.   Then he came home and continued the *Origins of Christianity* in a mood of absolute abstraction from the passions of the hour.

The *Apostles* appeared in 1866, *St Paul* in 1869.   Renan looked up from his task at the world about him, and saw that the soul of France was disquieted within her.   At heart he was still a priest, a man set apart, elect, a member of a moral aristocracy,—and *therefore* responsible for the errors of his inferiors.   To-day, as in 1843, he thought :—

"A private life would be my happiness ; but such a life appears to me tainted by selfishness. I ought to be a priest ; for the priest is the depositary both of wisdom and good counsel ; the man of study, the man of meditation, and yet a very brother to his brethren." [1]

Renan, so far at least, was no sceptic, no mere *dilettante* indifferent to mankind.   He had the tenderest sense of fraternity, the most absolute sense of the efficacy of the Ideal ; there was balm in Gilead still !   If he believed it impossible, and perhaps unnecessary, to admit the multitude into the arcana of that temple wherein he was a servant, he accepted none the less, and indeed all the more, the claim which the ignorance

Lettres Intimes, p. 118.

of the laity laid upon him in their hours of perplexity and error. It is a mistake to say, as I have heard it said, that Renan was an ambitious man—that he desired to govern his inferiors, and to impose the triumph of his own ideas. But it is less of a mistake, I maintain, than to imagine him, as the main public of France imagines him, an idle dreamer in his ivory tower. He was, in fact, a conscientious leader of humanity, sometimes misguided, ever willing to seek a better way.

France in 1869 had reached a high degree of material prosperity. Napoleon III. had taught the French how rich they were. But the seeing eye could read the threat of disaster in the shifty brilliance of the hour. All the roots of France were exhausted in the production of one beautiful, sterile orchid, — Paris. The provinces were sapped, drained, lifeless ; neither country gentry, nor county boards, nor local interests, supplied the provincial with an existence of his own. As France only bloomed in Paris, so Paris flowered in the Court : a fast, frivolous, superficial, spendthrift Court of tinsel soldiers, of reckless beauties, of brilliant authors : a world of little theatres and universal exhibitions, of Baron Haussmanns and Cora Pearls. It was clearly time that the order of things should change.

The General Election came round in May 1869. It was then that the Liberal Opposition asked Renan to stand for Meaux. At some sacrifice of time and fortune he consented. The gods must have smiled to see Ernest Renan go a-canvassing among the wealthy corn-growers, the rich butter-merchants and cheese-mongers of the plains of Brie. Brie, by nature of its proximity to Paris, is Radical, anti-clerical, and prosperous : it sells its wares to the Capital, and takes, in exchange, some tint of Parisian ideas : but it is a Radicalism fat with grass and grain, fed to bursting with rich milk and the flesh of kine : the Radicalism of the peasant landlord : the most illiberal opinion of any party.

The vast plains were one shimmering ocean of pale green, with last year's great ricks stranded here and there, like ships, among the unbounded corn, when Ernest Renan traversed them in the spring of '69. What can he have said to the influential voters who inhabit these solid farms ? How they must have astonished each other, he and they ? I can imagine a conversation something after this fashion :—

Farmer of Brie.—"Good morning, Mister. You support the Liberal programme ? "

M. Renan.—" Yes, on the whole. . . . We can indeed imagine a superior social order in

which the individual would be remorselessly—
perhaps, indeed, willingly—sacrificed in order to
promote, in a few, the acquisition of some yet
undreamed-of good. But France appears irre-
vocably devoted to Liberty, to the happiness of
the mass, to a small, prosperous, somewhat vulgar,
affluence."

F. of B.—"Well, well! And you will vote for
the extension of the Board Schools?"

M. Renan.—"Certainly! If Science be the
chief good, what right have we to debar our
brother from it? And yet, I own, I deplore
the abolition of the unlettered class, charming in
its rural simplicity, shrewd with a mother-wit of
its own, the faithful depositary of the ideas and
fancies of our remotest forefathers. The peasant,
the priest, and the noble are the only loveable
classes! The Board Schools will replace the
peasant by a pretentious, ill-bred, self-made rustic,
infinitely more dangerous to Science, and probably
hopelessly unfitted for the sphere into which he is
born. The School Board will be the ruin of a
superior ideal. But let Justice be accomplished!
Yes, yes, my friend, I shall vote for the School
Board."

F. of B.—(Does the man think me an ass?)
"And the taxes? At least, you are firm for
cutting down the taxes?"

M. Renan.—" In part.   It is certain that, in the whole cause of history, nothing has ever rendered a government so unpopular as excessive taxation. And yet! a tax, rightly regarded, is a form of disinterestedness, a way of participating in the real life of the world.   Our poor selfish aims —all the criss-cross of rival activities which make up the struggle for our daily bread,—are as nought in the sight of the Eternal!   Our personal ambitions, our thousand little strifes, successes, and reverses are all, as we may say, consumed in the wear and tear of the universe : every day supplies the fuel of every day.   But the little fund of reserve force which makes the world go round is the devotion which we willingly give to an end outside ourselves, distilled, drop by drop, from millions of selfish lives.   Nothing is so vain, so imbecile, as selfishness : beware of selfishness!   Sometimes, I confess, I see the future of earth as a planet of idiots, each basking in his own particular ray, indifferent to all outside his well-sunned limbs.   Selfishness is the curse of great material prosperity.   And it may be that, in this vast sunlit sheet of springing corn before us, in all this panorama of grain and kine, of earth and river, the one thing which *really* exists is the tax which each yields of its increase for the general weal of the nation."

F. of B.—"Dang it, the man's gone daft!
Good morning, Mister!"

On one point, at least, M. Renan and his constituency were as one. All his electioneering
bills bore in flaming letters—"No War. No
Revolution. A War would be as disastrous as
a Revolution." The Prussians may still have
read them on the village walls round Meaux.
And on this theme M. Renan was never too
eloquent to please his hearers. He had then, as
always, the most brilliant success as a speaker.
His wit, his astonishing naturalness, the originality
and the fundamental good sense of his paradoxes,
the charm of his manner, his air of enjoying the
ideas with which the occasion inspired him, made
him irresistible as an orator. And, at bottom, his
hearers and he were of a like opinion—at least as
to the prospect of war. Among the peasants of
Brie there reigned, in 1869, the most complete
indifference to military glory. They had a
certain honest respect for freedom, but at bottom
all that they asked was that the Préfet should
meddle as little as possible in their affairs,
that the taxes should be diminished, that the
term of military service—which took so many
strong young arms from the harvest—should be
shortened as much as possible. All that they
asked was to be left free to make their own for-

tunes out of their own fields in their own way.
M. Renan looked in some wonder at these persons
incapable of a sacrifice, incapable of a general
idea. He found the farmer of Brie *un être borné*.
He wondered at this thriving rustic, " content in his
gross and trivial comfort without a thought in his
head." M. Jules Simon used to say that, when asked
if he would vote with his party, M. Renan was wont
to muse, and to reply, at last :—Sometimes ! But
though he must have appeared an extraordinary
politician, Renan's reputation was immense ;
probably his eccentricities were taken as the
hall mark of his genius. The Minister of the
Interior took great pains over this affair, and it
was not without a struggle that Ernest Renan
was defeated for the constituency of Meaux.

The tendency of the elections as a whole was
distinctly Liberal. The Empire itself at last, and
especially the Emperor, had absorbed a great deal
of the Liberal theory, and gave out as much
liberty, or thereabouts, as France at that moment
could assimilate without excess. *L'Empire Libéral*
sought to repair its wrongs towards Ernest
Renan : already in the spring of 1870, there
was some talk of reinstating him in his Chair of
Hebrew at the College of France. True, the
affair was only completed under the Ministry
of Jules Simon, on the 17th November, after

the fall of the Empire; but the first steps
towards Renan's rehabilitation were taken six
months before that catastrophe. And, in fact,
Renan had accepted the Liberal Empire. It was
part of his theory that progress comes not by
leaps and bounds, but little by little: that out
of chaos comes misrule, and out of misrule
gradually a better order. He would have
accepted the chair of Quatremère as a Liberal
victory, infinitely more important than the defeat
of Meaux.

Much in the spirit of a Merovingian Bishop,—
who, unable to chase the barbarians from Gaul,
should set himself to civilize them,—Renan not
uncheerfully assumed the moral education of the
Empire. He had no doubt of its stability; he
had touched as it were with his hands the wealth,
the solidity, the love of peace, of rural France.
The Government was certainly bad; but a
system which encouraged the endowment of
research could surely not be wholly corrupt.
On the 8th of May 1870, seven and a half
millions of Frenchmen declared themselves
satisfied with *L'Empire Libéral*. Brilliant and
hollow beyond example, France appeared destined
to show that a nation can flourish merely by the
excessive animation of its surface, as if a man,
having coughed up all his lungs, should live on

by the extraordinary breathing power of his skin.

Such health is deceptive. The Emperor himself was not deceived. The Empress said : unless we have a war, my son will not come to the throne. By a second act of high treason, by a second *Coup d'Etat*, more culpable and more disastrous even than the first, on the 19th July 1870, the Emperor declared war against Germany. Renan was at Tromsöe, in the far North of Norway, in company with the Prince Jérome-Napoléon, as innocent of apprehension as himself. "What a crime, what a fit of stark, staring madness !" he wrote to Sir Mountstuart Grant Duff.[1] "I had thought the danger of war waived for years, perhaps for ever. . . . The greatest heartache of my life followed the opening of that fatal telegram."

[1] *Sir M. G. Duff, Ernest Renan*, p. 81.

CHAPTER V

THE WAR—RENAN AS PROPHET

RENAN hastened home and joined his family at the small house near Sèvres, where he was accustomed to spend the summer. From the first he knew what to expect. A formidable discipline, an organised force at the service of a great idea, had come into contact with an incoherent mass of martial vanity and irresponsible impulse. Electrified by the mere hallucination of Napoleon's ghost, France was doomed to defeat; and, in his prophetic vision, Renan wept her defeat in tears of blood, for she suffered it at the hands of his ideal.

All his life he had dreamed of uniting France and Germany. He saw them lead the United States of Europe in the van of civilization—the one passionately alive to all that is generous, liberal, or lovely; the other proud in her hereditary strength of science and authority. Together they might head the world; and now . . . !

Behold, the nation to which Renan owed all that was best in him—the nation of Gœthe, Herder, Kant—revealed itself as a rout of drunken troopers setting fire to Bazeilles! The brutal Bavarian, the plundering Swab, the blustering Prussian, *these* were the teachers whom he had ever held up as patterns of morality and culture! No man in France, we may fairly say, suffered more in that hour than Ernest Renan; for the Franco-German war was to him as a civil war, and he saw his two countries closed in a murderous struggle.

Admirable in his freedom from party passion, Renan never let go his hold on the general relation of things. After Bazeilles, after Sedan, in the midst of his cruel experience of the hard and arbitrary spirit of Prussia, Renan still saw unobscured the ideal Germany which had formed his mind. His country in flames, the Prussians in sight of Paris, his own little house at Sèvres pillaged by his divinities, left him still convinced. Behind this evident mass of drill-sergeants, quarter-masters, heroes, and scoundrels—Goths alike—there existed none the less a superior order, an invisible senate of philosophers, men of science, scholars, jurists (men of action also), working together in the service of humanity. *These* were really Germany; and Germany being

the most adequate expression of reason, would
listen to reason.

While the Prussians were taking up their
positions at Versailles and St Cloud, Renan sat
down and wrote to David Strauss an open letter
denouncing the war as a crime against civilization,
pleading against the annexation of Alsace-Lor-
raine as a blunder in history, for Germany has
need of France as an ally against the growing
strength of Russia. The letter is eloquent and
noble. All through it echoes that love of Europe
which was Renan's true patriotism, that disinterested devotion to the future of humanity
which is his peculiar glory. But, alas! when
did prophet arrest the course of battle? Strauss
chuckled in his beard, translated his ingenuous
correspondent's pamphlet, and sold it for the
profit of the Prussian ambulances; whilst, on
the horizon, Germany wrote her answer in flames
by the arson of St Cloud.

If Renan's attitude was a failure abroad, at
home it was a scandal. Even his nearest friends
deplored the prophet's madness. An exasperated
patriotism contracted the nerves of France. It
was not precisely the moment to speak of the
chosen few, of that *élite* of reasonable humanity
the wide world over—" Neither Greek nor Barbarian, neither German or Latin "—who from an

empyrean raised above the struggles of race and country, should remain undivided in their Olympian goodwill,[1] and direct the affairs of mankind. A line in Goncourt's *Journal*, — reported with the inevitable inexactitude resulting from the incapacity of a Goncourt to comprehend a Renan, yet undeniably precious — shows us the completeness of the misunderstanding between the idealist philosopher and a defeated nation :—

"Berthelot continued his distressing revelations. When he had done, I exclaimed, 'All is over! There is nothing left save to rear a generation to avenge us!' — 'No! no!' cried Renan, starting up, with his face aflame. 'No vengeance! Perish France, rather! Perish the idea of country! Higher still is the Kingdom of Duty and Reason!'—'No! no!' yelled the whole table, 'there is nothing above one's country —nothing!' By this time Renan had left his chair and was walking round and round the table with his shambling gait, waving his little arms in the air, and quoting aloud fragments of Holy Scripture, as he muttered, 'That's the essential!'"[2]

Doubtless Isaiah appeared as odious, and no less

[1] Lettre à David Strauss, *Réf. Intellectuelle et Morale.*
[2] E. de Goncourt, *Journal,* 2nd série, 1st volume, p. 28.

grotesque, in the eyes of the Court of Jerusalem on more than one occasion.[1] Was not the reproach of old cast up against the prophets that they, sons of Israel, were friends of the Assyrian ?

What is a prophet but a popular spokesman animated by the idea of God ; inspired by the Spirit to protest against the dulness, the meanness, the cruelty or the iniquity of the times? Such, at least, and not mere visionaries and soothsayers, were the seers of Israel. Such, on his measure and degree, was Ernest Renan during the one difficult and heartbreaking year of the war. Exposed to the long agony of the siege, unpopular, without credit in the eyes of the violent factions which divided the country, Renan continued to preach his message, and to show the sacred hope of a future redeemed by the humiliations of the present. Repulsed by Germany, he sought to raise up France, to bind her sores, and renew a right spirit within her. Like his great forerunners, he called for a king in Israel ; a king to impose on his people a new discipline and a new ideal, to build their foundations on wisdom, earnestness, submission, justice. "Democracy has no discipline, and no moral ideal to impose. Children, left to their own

[1] For instance, Isaiah viii.

devices, will not educate each other." [1]   It may be that the only fruitful discipline comes from within, is not forced upon us from without, but so thought no longer the ex-Democrat of 1848. Germany still haunted him.   He would fain have reconstituted France in the image of her conqueror, as a mighty kingdom, governed by a strong provincial aristocracy, kept in respect by the fear of the throne.   " The victory of Germany was the victory of the man who is full of reverence, careful, attentive, methodical, over slapdash and hap-hazard. . . . It is the victory of Science and Reason.   But it is also the victory of the feudal idea, the victory of the historic right of kings."

Such was not the mind of the French.   There are two great tendencies in modern politics. The first, ever more and more predominant, is jealous above all of the greatest happiness of the greatest number, preoccupied by the rights of individuals and their liberty; and such, for a hundred years, has been the trend of Liberal France.   The second establishes *à priori* a providential order, sacrifices hecatombs of individuals to the attainment of certain abstract aims, and is content if the sweat of a multitude permit the nobler lives of a chosen few, and so increase,

[1] *Réforme*, &c., p. 66.

little by little, the intellectual capital of the race. Which of these twain is the true end of humanity? We may not know. The obscure soul of the universe finds, perchance, its expression in either.

At least it is certain that, on the morrow of the war, Renan was convinced of the efficacy of the aristocratic ideal. Full of fervour, he presented himself at the elections of 1871. He was again rejected. He took his defeat to heart; the sense of his uselessness in the hour of need appears to have overwhelmed him. His desperate struggle with the impossible altered the natural gentleness of his nature. Condemned to look on, impotent, he beheld the most cruel of his fears come true. The Prussians were still round Paris when, on the 18th March, '71, the capital, delirious with famine fever, broke out into the Commune. The barricades were up in the streets; blood ran in rivers; all the old mad dreams and hopes and hallucinations of '48, all the atrocity of excessive reprisals, all the endless sequel of hate and wrong, rose, like bloody froth, to the surface of the troubled nation. Renan's heart broke then, I think. The lees of a harsh disgust for life shrivelled the lips that hitherto had only spoken golden words. Like Zachary, he abandoned Juda and Israel; both had betrayed

N

him.   He shook the dust of the city from his
feet ; he broke in twain his shepherd's staff ; and
the name of the staff was Fraternity.

Beside the Thing that Is, beside the real fact—
there exists the ideal fact, which ought to have
taken place, but did not—

" Look in my face—my name is Might-have-been."

Were I writing not a biography, but a study in
absolute psychology—were I writing for a public
which could not match an ideal truth with its
obvious irrefutable counterpart—it is here, I confess, that I might place the end of Ernest Renan.
Something died in him then ; the Breton, I think.
It is sure that in his despair he would fain have
died altogether, knowing that it is sometimes well
that one man should perish to redeem the people.
" If ever I have wished to be a Senator, it was
chiefly because I saw there a fair occasion for a
violent death."   Let us then imagine him, like
his own Antistius, a victim to the strife of the
ideal with base reality.   In some Parisian street,
full of March sunshine, riddled with shot and
shell, behold him mounted on the great barricade
of beams and flagstones.   With the light of the
Sacred Mount on his face, he delivers undismayed
the message of a free spirit.   But hark, a brief

explosion, a burst of flame and smoke! Struck at once in heart and head, slain by the splinter of a Prussian obus, and by a stone thrown by the people of Paris, the prophet falls. So might have ended Ernest Renan.

CHAPTER VI

THE ÉLITE

BUT Renan did not die. He merely took the train for Versailles, a disenchanted *émigré* of the Commune. It was the end of April. The stately Park of Le Nôtre was at its rarest,—a greenness in desolation, a hope in abandonment, such as perchance the world contains not elsewhere. All through the month of May, M. Renan wandered to and fro under the tender leaves of the stately alleys, beside the straight waters full of flowering weeds, where the gummy scent of the poplar is fresh on the air. There are few lonelier spots than may be discovered in that forsaken pleasure ground : Renan made it his habitual phrontisterion. Deprived of his books, separated from his work, he mused on the melancholy of human destiny. The old thoughts that, thirty years ago, he had revolved in endless meditations under the limes of Issy, visited him again. Fragments of Herder and Hegel and Malebranche rose to his lips. 'Twas

an endless conversation between the different
lobes of his brain. An echo of this long lonely
soliloquy has been preserved to us in the *Philosophic Dialogues.*

We appreciate the violence of a storm by the
ravage which it leaves behind it. Compare this
book with *St Paul* or *The Apostles*, and you have
the measure of Renan's profound and embittered
disappointment — a disappointment which embraced not his own country only but his enemy's,
and the two main conceptions of human society ;
since the peaceful democracy of France appeared
a Commune unchained, shooting its hostages ;
while the military aristocracy of Germany was
revealed as a " handful of aristocrats, urging the
placable populations to the slaughter." Neither
these savage iconoclasts, nor those arrogant
uhlans full of oaths, were fit to be the instruments of the Ideal. What was the future of
society ? How should the kingdom of God be
brought to pass ?

Like Boethius, composing in prison his Consolations of Philosophy, amid the ruins of his
world ; like Condorcet, writing his Progress of
the Human Mind, in hiding during the Reign
of Terror ; Renan, from his avenue of Versailles,
with Paris flaming on the horizon, sent forth
his soul to seek a solution of this apparent

anarchy of things.   His *Philosophic Dialogues*
show a change of attitude rather than a change
of mind—few of us change much at bottom after
five-and-twenty.   His old ideas still guide him :—

1. God does not proceed by special provi-
dences.

2. The universe fulfils, unconscious, a divine
destiny with which, from the beginning, it was
big.

3. One day, God, as yet inarticulate, shall come
into conscious being.

4. Every disinterested effort makes for the
little residue of excellence which, for ever accumulating, goes to shape the Divine Idea.

To these leading themes he adds two predominant *motifs*, not new in his philosophy, but
developed out of all recognition.   They are :—

5. The theory of the elect ; and

6. The suggestion of Conditional Immortality ;
both of them, as a fact, an ingenious application
of the Evolutionist Theory : the Survival of
the Fittest.

In sight of the magnificent arson of Paris,
Renan assumed it improbable that the Kingdom
of God would arrive by Democracy.   In a
mood of bitter reaction he reiterates with em-
phasis a conviction which long had lain at the
back of his mind, namely, that *the masses do*

not count, are a mere bulk of raw material out
of which, drop by drop, the essence is extracted
—the rare essence, the one thing needful, which,
whether as Truth, Beauty, Self-sacrifice, or Genius,
goes to make the Ideal. Wherefore, then, cum-
ber ourselves with the education of the masses?
Let them think as they please—*if* they think.
What matter the opinions of millions of fools?
Why trouble with difficult speculations the un-
developed brains which were not made to hold
them? Is not the average man ephemeral as the
May fly, here to-day, gone to-morrow without a
trace, wholly eliminated from the Universe?
Such as these are not born to know, are not born
to have power, are not born to govern. But,
alas, they are born to transgress, to revolt, born
to immolate the Higher to the Lower, and
continually to crucify their Redeemer. If not
for their own sake, then for ours, and for the
dim-descried and distant goal of things, let us
put the masses within harness and drive them
whither we will, well within bounds, kept under a
yoke of gold and iron!

The peculiar pride of the priest rings in these
theories, and still more in what follows, sinister
with odd reminiscences of Inquisition racks and
stakes. In an extraordinary symbol Renan
imagines that the advance of Chemistry and

the arts of war may one day place in the
hands of a superior order means, hitherto un-
imagined, of mastering the many. Plato also
had dreamed of the Tyrant - Sage, the man
who should unite political with philosophic
authority.

" Unless those who govern States be serious
philosophers the perfect State will never see the
light," runs the theme of the Republic. " Authority must be confided to those who think little of
authority, to men of science and philosophers
pursuing a more than mortal aim." And the
Athenian had already propounded a system of
social selection by which the most gifted, most
temperate, strongest and wisest of a nation should
be raised from the body of the people into a
superior caste, entrusted with supreme power.
. . . The outburst of anarchy, of simple instincts,
which defaced the end of the Franco-Prussian
war, revealed how little power over a people
has the small class of free, enlightened spirits.
Renan looked on in a melancholy too deep for
tears ; and he too murmured—" Instinct would
play the tyrant ; we must find a stronger tyrant
to put Instinct in chains." So he came to dream
of his caste of Tyrant-Sages, having at their
disposal an authentic Hell, " not without the
limits of biology," the product of, as yet, un-

dreamed-of discoveries in Chemistry and Balistic Science. The philosopher then would not refute the barbarian, but annihilate him on the first threat of insurrection. Against such authority, after one or two unfortunate attempts, there could be no possibility of rebellion. An élite of intelligent beings would govern the world for good ; and the whole force of Humanity, concentrated in a syndicate of demi-gods, would hasten the advent of perfect Reason. Sombre imaginings, unworthy of that liberal spirit ! How should the world be saved by a false principle ? Perish even the tyranny of the best ! But the Reign of Terror of the Commune had jangled out of tune the sweet bells of Renan's harmony. For one moment of discord, he sought to meet injustice with its own arms and to attain a noble end by infamous means. The conception, harsh, false, profound, was worthy of the echo it found in the most singular brain of our time. The Prussian, Nietzsche, read of M. Renan's *Dævas* and dreamed of the *Uebermensch*, of the super-human master whose motto, worthy of ↙ Prussia, reads :—Might is Right.

As for us, we will hold rather (with Emerson) that the demi-gods must go ere God shall appear. Let us diffuse our light rather than concentre its life-giving rays. . . . Reflect, M. Renan, in what peril you place the great age-long structures of Truth, Beauty, Wisdom, Civilization, by giving them too narrow a base. . . . Once I was talking to an eminent anarchist, a being kind and wise as M. Renan's *Dævas :*—

"We object to moderate fortunes," said he : " We admit millionaires. Our ideal would be the concentration of the wealth of the nation in a dozen pockets. . . . There would be only a dozen heads to fall." . . .

And ere now the Titans have fallen. The Tyrant-Sage might fall ! Suppose that by some deep-plotted combination the mass should arise and murder the demi-gods in their sleep ! Suppose that—owing, perhaps, to an imperfect sterilization of their instruments of torture— an epidemic should prevail among the *Dævas ?* Science, Truth, Power, Civilization would disappear at one fell swoop ! No, dream for dream, play for play, give us the pretty chimæra of '48 : Let us ennoble the barbarians !

Meanwhile, dreaming not only of Hell but of Heaven, the sad philosopher tried to invent a less redoubtable conpensation for Virtue and Wisdom. They do not meet their reward on earth. Lo, their homes are burned and pillaged, a cruel enemy slays their sons, and a brother arises to stab them from behind ! Yet *in sinu meo est haec spes reposita:* the just shall not perish! The Elect shall see God! Those who have contributed to the fund of the Universe their atom of disinterested thought or feeling shall receive, in exchange for the imperishable spark which they emit, a part in the eternity of the World-Soul. Eye hath not seen, tongue may not tell, how that due return shall be rendered unto them. But they shall be a part of the consciousness of the Over-Soul. And when the Divine shall become at last all-perfect and all-powerful, every particle of that unimaginable Being shall thrill, irradiate with life at once separate and blended, at once individual and general, at once a Soul and God.

PART IV

CHAPTER I

THE ANTICHRIST

IN this crisis of his life, Renan returned to his work with new ardour, disgusted with politics. The professional Discourager's is a melancholy business, and it is sad to be in the right against the illusions of one's country. Renan had tried to point out the reasons for the superiority of Prussia ; he had tried to make his country accept a discipline and an ideal. He had worn, as it were, on his shoulders the yoke of Jeremiah ;[1] he had sat on the temple-steps and cried to the people ; but they had not listened. The task of his own life, after all, was the quest of Truth. Let Martha be busied with appearances: one thing alone is needful ; and they who choose the better part sit in long contemplation at the feet of the Eternal Realities.

---

[1] See a remarkable conversation recorded in *Goncourt's Journal* under the date 18 April 1871. Renan says, in substance—" I am disgusted with the lack of courage of the Deputies of Paris. They should parade the streets and harangue the people group by group. If I had been elected I would have done so—had I worn on my shoulders the yoke of Jeremiah."

The German invasion, with its terrible sequels, had proved to our sage that brute force is still, alas, the mistress of the material world, leading it whither she listeth; that, in the conduct of events, the enlightened portion of humanity— the disciples of reason — have little influence, scant importance, and no true cohesion among themselves. A Mommsen, and a Strauss, and a Wagner, had each in turn revealed the soul of a Prussian corporal, and a view of practical politics quite unmodified by their proficiency in History, Philosophy, or Art. Europe was not yet in the hands of an international Elite. Renan sighed at the narrowness of broad minds, went into his study, and turned to the Past, since the Present would none of him.

His own mind was the broadest of his age, and therefore the least passionate. He was incapable of taking a side, accepting a limit to the laws of reason. If Truth spoke from the mouth of an opponent, he was eager with his unqualified assent. In his rare affirmations he never forgot that things have always their unseen side, which may possibly contradict all that we should predicate from those surfaces within our range of vision. For the human eye—and the mind's eye also—is so constructed that it cannot see every face of an object at the same time. Renan, however, saw them so immediately one after the other, as in a series of rapid dissolving views, that his vision of things was never simple, but blended, as it were, from a set of contraries. No aspect of Truth engrossed him so entirely as to exclude an instinctive divination of its opposite. A sort of *contranitency*, — if we may use the word — an elastic reaction against pressure, which became the main quality of his mind, assured him that the truth of one thing does not necessarily establish the falsehood of its apparent negation. The air through which we all see the world is in fact a sort of vivid prism, iridescent, opalescent, only habit has dulled our sense of it. But Renan kept in his mind's eye unimpaired that intellectual iridescence which illuminates the inner vision. The truth of his most considered assertions is qualified with subtle reservations. And the unity of his mind, exceptionally sincere and veracious, is made of a thousand diversities in fusion, as a painter mixes his white from a medley of many colours.

Hence inherent contradictions : a love of giving himself the lie. Hence many a disconcerting strange *predella* painted underneath his sacred pictures. In no book is this so marked as in the book of these years : *The Antichrist.* He cannot contrast the terrible hieratic Christ of

the Apocalypse with the tender Elder Brother
of the Gospel stories, but he exclaims : " Who
knows ?   The image of the Gospel may be false.
Jesus may have been the centre of a group more
pedantic, more scholastic, nearer to the Scribes
and Pharisees than the Evangelists would have
us think." He cannot consider the obscurity
which envelops the end of St Paul without re-
flecting that the convert may be converted more
than once : the disenchanted saint may have
passed over to the creed of Ecclesiastes and the
Sceptics.   Convinced that he had given his life
for a dream, Paul may have wandered despair-
ing, resigned, on some Iberian shore, aware of
the nothingness of life. . . . . Then, in a
twinkling, the ironic little transformation scene
flashes out of sight, and leaves us face to face
with a soberer vision of the Past.

None of these brief glimpses into the interior
of a thinker's mind are so cruel as the sacrilegious
page wherein Renan ascribes to Nero, tearing
their last veils from the Virgin Martyrs in the
arena, the invention of a new order of beauty :
the supreme grace of Christian modesty.   Such
pages bear too clear the disfiguring hall-mark
of the dilettante.   In fact Renan, after 1871,
retraversed more seriously the crisis which had
menaced his moral health after the disasters of

1848. A second journey to Italy in 1875 led him again to the feet of his old enchantress, visible beauty—again he heard her whisper—

> " *Flecte ramos, arbor alta,*
> *Tensa laxa viscera,*
> *Et lentescat rigor ille*
> *Quem dedit nativitas.*"

The fourth volume of the *Origins of Christianity* is in some sense the masterpiece of the series. It is the record of the most memorable struggle between the hostile ideals of moral and material perfection, written at a time when that same struggle was a constant preoccupation of the author's spirit. In his profound disappointment with Life there were moments when Art, and Art only, seemed precious and imperishable in Renan's eyes ; when the spiritual enthusiasm of arid Palestine appeared, after all, a poor thing to him compared with the divine and innocent grace of Attic beauty. He had given his life to the Holy Land, to the worship of holiness ; there were hours when he half regretted that he had not offered it to Hellas. There are hours in most lives, perhaps, when that which creates and represents appears more satisfying, more positive, than that which suggests and inspires ; when the frieze of the Parthenon

strikes us as more real than the shadow of the
Cross on Calvary.   And yet the Galilean conquers.

In the first century of Christianity, its history
shifts gradually from Asia Minor to imperial
Rome.   Two Romes were soon in presence.   St
Paul in prison was weaving, no longer the coarse
Cilician tissue of his loom, but the spiritual
fabric of the future, while Nero, the circus rider,
the æsthetic athlete, worshipped the art and the
splendour of the decadent Greeks.   How Renan
makes us see them both : the prophet, illuminated by suffering ; and Nero, "the poor young
man," whose deplorable taste in Art had so
unfortunate an effect on his morals ; a mere
Tenorino devoured by vanity, not wholly bad
but wholly artificial, debased, of irritable nerves—
and entrusted with the government of a world.
No less vivid are the portraits of Titus and
Vespasian : serious military men, a little provincial in tone and therefore all the more en-
slaved by the elderly graces of the aristocratic
Berenice.

For life, brilliance, irony, force, this volume is
unmatched.   But we miss the moral charm, the
rare deep fraternal kindness of St Paul and
the Apostles.

"Perhaps our race alone[1] is capable of re-

[1] *The Antichrist*, p. 102.

alising virtue without faith, of blending hope and
doubt inextricably together.   An hour strikes
in the life of European men of genius when
they agree with Epicurus. . . . Whilst continuing their task with ardour, they feel a chill dis-
relish for life creep over them.   Victorious, they
wonder whether the cause for which they fought
were worth so many sacrifices, and, whilst continuing to push the battle, many of them admit
that wisdom begins on the day when they are
content to contemplate Nature and enjoy her.
There is, perhaps, scarce one self-sacrificing
person, priest or nun, who, at fifty, has not
deplored a vow which they continue to observe.
A spice of scepticism appears to us integral in good
breeding.   We like to hear the just man say :
'Virtue, thou art but a name !'   The essential
quality of distinction is this faculty of soaring
up and dominating our own beliefs, of rising
superior to the cause for which we are content to
give our lives, of smiling at our own most stringent
effort.   And we love our heroes the better when
we watch them sink a moment by the road-
side, aware of the vanity of absolute convictions."

What a disenchantment rings in these accents
of crystal and silver !   It is well, indeed, that
advancing years should take from us something of

the substance of our personality—that we should grow wider, fainter, and, as it were, diaphanous : mere cobwebs to catch the grace of Heaven. But such a diminution of fibre as Renan shows us at this moment is nothing less than a moral malady. Let us not hold victory too cheap ! Our heroes do well to be victorious, for they continue to live in their triumph ; their dead hands mould and modify us from the other side the grave ; their effort has shaped our future. And influence is a sort of immortality.

CHAPTER II

THE incapacity to affirm does not imply the incapacity to choose and resolve. The least consistent in theory, in practice Renan was the most persistent of men. He followed his meandering paths to the very goal. He was willing to admit that all is vanity; but he acted as though nothing were so important as the finishing of the task he had found to his hand. His scepticism never paralyzed the continuity of his effort: a hermetic compartment separated his intelligence and his moral self.

Nil expedit . . . Laboremus ! Our task is of no importance, yet give us, O Lord, our daily task! Vanity of Vanities! But let us finish the fifth and sixth volumes of the *Origins of Christianity !* . . . Without a lapse, without a pause, this solid and inveterate worker brought the considerable sequence to a close. As we have said, this great piece of history is also, in some sort, an autobiography. *The Anti-*

christ reflects Renan's discouragement, his dilet-
tantism. The *Christian Church* and *Marcus
Aurelius* show us a Renan reconciled with
democracy, confident in the gradual ascent of
man, aware that the greatest cataclysms do not
really interrupt the imperceptible progress of the
world.

Truths had a knack of flashing their contraries
into the eyes of our philosopher. In the *Philosophic
Dialogues* he had elaborated his doctrine of the
élite, of a world saved by the tyranny of a privileged
circle of adepts. And so, in the last volumes
of the *Origins* he shows us the peril of an aristocracy of science, all the danger and the sterility of
the oligarchic theory. For, at one moment, a
chimerical, intellectual syndicate attempted to
govern Christianity: the Church was only saved
by breaking the yoke of the Gnostics. Rome and
the world were entrusted, at one moment, to the
rule of a philosopher and a saint: and Renan shows
us the intimate miseries of the reign of a Marcus
Aurelius. That wise emperor only succeeded
in giving a veneer of hypocrisy to the evil forces
which raged around him, and which he refused to
recognise. May it not be that Stoicism and Gnos-
ticism perished for lack of a public? That antiquity
was misguided on seeking to specialise Truth
and Virtue, in neglecting the education of the

lower classes! "I speak for one in a thousand," said Basilides; "the rest are dogs and swine." . . . "Suffer the little children to come unto me," said He who spake through the mouths of babes and sucklings. May it not be that the brain can not work without the pulse of the heart, that Wisdom cannot be nourished without the warm current of a live fraternity?

With the doctrine of the Gnostics, as mere doctrine, Renan had little fault to find. The metaphysics of Basilides forecast the main ideas of Hegel. His polytheistic cosmogony covers, but does not conceal, a philosophic system. . . . Life is the gradual development of a series of seeds or germs contained in the original matter of the Universe. Filiation is the great secret: each organism, abstract or concrete, produces its successor and dies. The sum of the aspiration of Humanity makes for righteousness. The recompense of the individual is Rest: complete absorption into the substance of Deity, a divine unconsciousness, a μεγάλη ἄγνοια. Man passes, but the Universe remains, and progresses. The Residue of Perfection is secured by the Frontier-Spirit. The Frontier-Spirit is a mystic interplanetary influence which carries the current of Being from the domain of pure spirit into the domain of pure matter, thus mingles either and

thus strengthens each. This free, starry secret
of a life continually renewed, this Breath from
Over-the-Border, this μεθόριον πνεῦμα, answers, in
Renan's own philosophy, to the Spirit of Love.
Renan could have no intellectual quarrel with
the Gnostics.

What he feared and loathed in them was their
sterile pride. Woe to the Truth which crystal-
lises too soon ! These thinkers, who imagined
themselves to form a close syndicate of Truth
for the sole use of the initiate, begat a vanity
fatal to progress. Their wisdom was a system
for solitaries. Had it endured it must have
caused at last the establishment of a society not
unlike the castes of India. The Gnostic Saint
was already a Buddhist *in posse*.

The Church fought tooth and nail against this
hermetic aristocracy. For the Catholic ideal was
the good of the masses ; her holiest instinct to im-
prove the average man whilst diminishing the sum
of his sufferings. Her means were Faith and Works.
She preached Hope in the Man of Sorrows,
Trust in the Beyond. She needed no metaphysical system : the Primitive Church had little
or no theology. It is certain that Jesus, and his
immediate disciples, neglected that part of the
human mind which desires to know.

In their house Science had no mansion. They

spoke to the heart, to the imagination, not to the mind. Christianity came not to satisfy our curiosity, but to console the unhappy, to stimulate the moral sense, to teach men to say "Our Father," to bind them together in a brotherly bond. In more things than one, the Church and Marcus Aurelius pursued the same ideal. But Christianity counted on the masses, the Stoic Philosophers upon the Few. As we know, the Galilean vanquished. And yet, after her victory, the Church was compelled to assimilate something of the principles she had conquered. You cannot say to the world at large, Be ye perfect! Christianity, in her turn, felt the necessity of an *élite*— of a Chosen Few set apart to practice a superior morality. Without diminishing the broad, general movement of her main current, Catholicism began to reserve, as in some peaceful backwater, the clearer, holier space of the conventual life. To the Monk and the Nun, it was said : Be ye perfect! And the average churchman, soiled with the dust of the world, struggled content, knowing that somewhere, out of sight, the Gospel was not preached in vain.

In demonstrating the secret of Christian influence Renan fell again, to some extent, under the charm which had ruled his early years. Not that ever again he was to say *Credo !* Faith remained to him a fountain sealed, a garden enclosed—a garden at which one slants regretful glances from the sun-beaten steep highway. . . . It was the beauty of Catholicism which fascinated Ernest Renan, which appealed to his æsthetic faculty, which revived the souvenir of his pious youth. His mind still accepted a modified Pantheism as the most reasonable solution of the problem of the Infinite. But, more and more, his fancy harked back to the conception of a Providence exterior to the universe, of a sympathetic intimate spectator of the struggles of the soul. " Man is always more anthropomorphic than he thinks," said Goethe. As old age steals on, leaving our brain intact, nay, enriched by the experience and thought of our maturity, threatening the springs of life only, the craving for a continuation of our activity beyond the grave is natural to man. More than once the ex-pupil of St Sulpice will demand of the Unknown God some survival of the holier instincts of our nature, some possibility of progress after death. " Thou art too resigned, dear Master ! " he cries to Marcus Aurelius[1]; "if it be true that even those among us who have lived in communion with Deity be extinguished for ever, then of a truth we have the right to complain. If this world have not

[1] *Marcus Aurelius*, p. 268.

its counterpart Beyond, how shall he who has sacrificed himself to Right and Truth die contented?
No, such an one has the right to blaspheme!
Heaven has taken advantage of his good faith.
Why has Heaven implanted in his heart instincts
of rectitude to which he falls a victim? Why
should the ungodly triumph? Is it *he* after all
who sees clear? If there be no Beyond, accurséd
be the gods who place so ill their favours! . . .
I am content that the Future remain an enigma.
But if there be *no* Future, then this world of ours
is a hideous trap for Virtue. Mind ye, I crave
not the desire of the vulgar. What I ask is
neither to witness the downfall of the ungodly,
nor to enjoy the interest of my good behaviour.
No selfish reward! Only to be, only to exist
in relation to the light, only to continue the
thought begun on earth. . . . To know more
and more, to enjoy the truth at last, to behold
the Triumph of the Good which I have loved!"

More than once at the close of his history
of the *Origins of Christianity*, Renan asked himself, What should be the future of the Catholic
Church? He saw one portion doomed to corruption, for the letter killeth. The Church will
resist the gradual growth of Truth, will heap
dogma on dogma, invent miracle after miracle.
Lourdes and Tilly-sur-Seules will not save the

Church.   No Papal Bull will make the sun stand still in heaven—*E pur si muove!*   But there shall be a remnant.   Abandoning the excesses of supernaturalism, Christianity once more shall worship the Father in spirit and in truth.   The freer thought of Catholicism will find a new force in its combination with the Liberal forms of Protestantism, with enlightened Judaism, and Idealist Philosophy.   From these shall spring a new Church which, in its turn, for its time, shall serve the progress of the Soul, no less abundantly, no less vitally, than those elder altars which it shall inevitably supersede.

CHAPTER III

SOUVENIRS

THERE comes an hour to all objective minds —too occupied with the world and its great problems to keep a constant register of their own sensations—an hour when they recognise that they are growing old. This revelation came to Ernest Renan in 1875, one twentieth of September, towards the evening, as he watched the dews thicken on the vineyards of Ischia, and the white sea deepen in tone as the light grew less intense. He was but two-and-fifty years of age. Rheumatism, not the weight of years, stiffened and impeded his gait, affected his heart, took the elasticity from his veins and muscles. He had grown old ten years too soon. With his habitual mild serenity, he recognised the fact without impatience—with a movement of thankfulness, rather, towards all the benign influences which had shaped his life. Even so, long ago, on the banks of the Grau, Marcus Aurelius had let his mind turn piously towards the tutors of his early years. Renan, likewise, passed a happy hour in casting up his debt to each of these. That September evening he wrote but a few pages. The idea of writing some record of his childhood was born, however, into his reflective mind.

Five years later, M. Quellien asked our sage to preside at the annual banquet of the Bretons in Paris: the *Diner Celtique.* Renan agreed to be the permanent president of this humble festivity: a reunion of Celtic men of letters held in the purlieus of the Western Railway Station. And this accident helped to revive in his heart the love of his native place. "Quellien prolonged my life by a good ten years," cried Renan. "I felt fifty years slip from my shoulders as I refound myself in contact with my earliest memories." . . . The historian's peculiar curiosity, which was ever so responsive a fibre in him, began to vibrate in answer to this image of the Past. "I had seen the primitive world!" It was a world of immense moral solidity, but filigreed all over on the surface with poetic Pagan superstitions,—it was, we may say, a *menhir*, thick with harebells. Now the great block had fallen out of place, and the flowers with it. With every year Brittany becomes more and more a mere agglomeration of western departments—an integral part of France.

But Renan could remember the royal and Catholic Brittany of Charles the Tenth.

Renan's special gift as a historian was his art of divining the origin of things. There was something singularly primitive and archaic at the root of his supple, and apparently decadent, imagination. This vision of Celtic Brittany interested him, even as the wanderings of the Beni-Israel in Chaldea, or the small Christian communities on the shores of Nero's Asia Minor. His mother's tales, his own first memories, put him in touch with a society, pious, primitive, simple, such as he loved to delineate. In his own childhood, he had contemplated a page of the Origins of Contemporary France. This page he wrote one day, and treated it as Taine, for all his genius, could never have done.

A meditative moralist, a student of history, Renan was no less a man of feeling. Save Rousseau or Samuel Johnson, no writer's peculiar temperament has been destined so greatly to influence modern times. He had his own magic by which he knew how to revive all the tender, confused, rudimentary forces which blend in a heart of fifteen : love of home, unconscious love, awakening thought, the first pursuit of Truth, the first elusive escape of Faith. All these rule and inspire the *Souvenirs d'Enfance et de Jeunesse.*

P

On the threshold of old age, the philosopher
turned and cast a last long lingering glance
at the days of his childhood, before the Angel
of Knowledge had troubled the waters of his
heart. He heard the drowned church bells of
the town of Ys peal again through all the waves
that have gone over them—obstinate carillons,
still convoking his renegade thoughts to a divine
service long since silent. The priests of Tréguier
rose again on his inner eye. He saw the haggard
silhouette of the Bonhomme Système, and the
dazed melancholy figure of the flax-crusher's
daughter. He saw, in a more delicate aureole,
the little girls he had played with before his first
communion, and whose smile had haunted him
ever since. Most men begin with the heart and
end with the mind. Renan began with the mind,
and never thought so much of Love as after fifty.
The women and the priests, to whom he owed
his breeding, had bequeathed him the sentimental
turn of their imagination ; and, as he grew old,
this trait showed clearer—as our likeness to our
forbears comes out with our grey hairs—in the
oddest contrast to the sceptical attitude of his
mind. As we climb down the slope of later life, the
world of our fifteenth year, long since cast aside
as the thing of a child, revisits us, and revives,
singularly fresh and dear. And in the best-filled

life, there are hours in which we are glad to amuse ourselves again with the old vain toys which we broke a life-time ago.

Thus, nearing sixty, Renan sought to compress into an hour the aroma of all his early life ; to evoke, in the twinkling of an eye, all he had once loved so much, so long ago. The *Souvenirs* are neither an autobiography nor a confession : they are, in Goethe's phrase, " Truth and Poetry " —a long conversation with remembrance, born of our instinctive pity for all that dies with us when we perish, of our instinctive wish that something, at least, of the heart of us survive. . . .

No man writing of himself was ever more natural, more simple. Renan's egotism is so devoid of display, so mere an outpouring, that it seldom irritates and never wearies. He takes us into his confidence. He sits down beside us, as it were, and beguiles us with his Past ; as we show our children a picture book, to pass the time and cultivate their imagination.

The *Souvenirs* took the world by storm. They possess that lyric note of personal utterance which the public prizes in a man already famous And what shall we say of their success in Renan's old home ? Disraeli's novels are not more elo-quent of the " Semitic secret " than these souvenirs of the prerogative of the Celt. The writer himself is regarded as a mere epitome of his race. He is eloquent with the treasured silence of generations, rich with their economies of thought and imagination—but not other than they. The clear green springs; the misty skies; the moors dotted with *menhirs*, and sprinkled with the silver gleam of trembling lady birches; the Atlantic breakers rolling on the coast against the great granite promontories; the pious, stolid, fisher folk; the women of Ar-Mor, demure in their black gowns and coifs of white; the priests of Tréguier; the skyward sweep of the cathedral steeple—all these animate and inspire their faithful spokesman. These are responsible for the genius of Ernest Renan, and his glory reflects on them. . . . Such, at least, is the refrain of the *Souvenirs*.

In the middle of August 1884, Renan returned to Tréguier. He had scarcely seen the place since he left it forty years before. He had doubtless dreaded the return. But he came back as the local prophet. Despite some natural opposition on the part of the ultra-Catholics, the author of the *Souvenirs* was received so warmly that he determined to spend a part of every year in his native clime. Near Lannion, and nearer Perros Guirec, he discovered a comfortable manor-house—Rosmapamon—which his children continue to inhabit. It is a pleasant, long, low old house, standing among woods close to the sea. Thence the name and fame of Ernest Renan spread through the country side. The peasants and fisher folk, who treated him with a rustic familiarity never repulsed, were aware of the fame of the sage of Rosmapamon, though they knew not what had earned it. The women inclined to suppose him a Saint — " C'est un bien grand Saint, Monsieur ! " said one old dame, I believe, to M. Spronck. The men, seated in the tavern, swore that he was a great Republican. Quite lately there was a public fête at Tréguier to inaugurate an inscription on M. Renan's natal house, at present the property of his children. On this occasion our philosopher was greatly extolled for his Republican principles. . . . Were they so much out of count, these simple people, in their definition of the greatest Religious Critic, the truest Liberal, after all, of Modern France ?

CHAPTER IV

ECCLESIASTES IN A DEMOCRACY

THE *Souvenirs d'Enfance et de Jeunesse* had appeared in 1883. They reflect the picturesque and emotional side of Renan— Celtic, Catholic in spite of all, and curious of the Past. Another view of his complex temperament is given in a volume which came out a few months earlier : a translation of *Ecclesiastes* with an introduction. Here we see his disenchanted self,—modern, agnostic, dilettante. ·

"The author of *Ecclesiastes*," says the translator, "is the author of the Book of Job grown seven centuries older. His objurgations against God, his eloquent and terrible blasphemies, have sunk into the trick of a hopeless trifling. The patriarch has suffered a change into the man of letters about town. He has no longer the strength to be angry with the Eternal : Where is the use of it?"

After a great experience of human things, Ecclesiastes has lost his faith in progress.—

The world offers a succession of phenomena which repeat themselves without essential change. What has been, will be. The wheel of things revolves, and must revolve, ever in the same circle. Our attempts at reform and progress are mere chimæras. Nothing worth knowing is knowable. ✔ Man is hopelessly limited by his faculties as by his destiny. All is vanity ! The only wisdom is not to be unnecessarily miserable about that which it is certain we were never meant to alter.

Such is the melancholy philosophy of Cohelet. " No man," says Renan, " was ever less of a pedant. The clearest view of a truth never prevents him from seeing, a second later, the contrary aspect of that truth in just as sharp relief. His disenchantment does not make him in the least out of temper with the conventions of society. In him, the motives for living are all slackened and relaxed ; but his lively taste for life and its pleasures remains unimpaired. He no longer seeks to explain the scheme of things, nor to invent symbols in which to incarnate a precise religion. He amuses himself rather with delightful philosophic vagaries. ' There is another evil under the sun ' (he might have said) —and haply is it the greatest of them all. And this is the presumption of spirit which seeks to explain the universe in a sentence four words long.   Woe unto him who shall not contradict himself at least once a day."

The soul of Ernest Renan animates this Ecclesiastes of 1882.   The portrait is a living likeness.   Only, save in quite his darkest hours, Renan would scarcely have agreed that the world revolves eternally in an unalterable circle.   However pessimistic, he was still a Liberal.   Almost always he saw the course of the universe slowly spinning down the grooves of Time, *in a spiral*, imperceptibly advancing even when it appears to recede.   If nothing be wholly good, nothing also is wholly harmful.   " My philosophy," he wrote in the *Souvenirs*, " inclines me to believe that good and evil, pain and pleasure, the beautiful and the ugly, slide into one another as imperceptibly as the tints which blend on the neck of a dove."   There is no Absolute—All is relative.   Or if an absolute exist in the region of the infinite, we, by the constitution of our natures, are condemned to perceive only the relative. The Order of things is no Finality, " knowing what and why it worketh in a most exact order or law," but a sort of happy accident without purpose or precision.   And yet—who knows? From this fortuitous combination there may proceed the Conscient Soul, whose presentiment is deep implanted in our heart.   The progress of

the Universe is, perchance, the long and painful
Advent of the unborn God. "Nothing proves`
that there exists a Soul of the Universe ; nothing
proves the contrary. Let us deny nothing, affirm
nothing. We may hope."

In reading Mr Tollemache's "Recollections
of Mark Pattison" I have been much struck by
many similarities between his melancholy "Pis-
gah-sights" (as Browning would have said) and
Ernest Renan's. Both indeed were disenchanted
men, both still under the emotional sway of a
creed in which their reason had ceased to ac-
quiesce. Pattison observed that the idea of Deity
has now been "defecated to a pure transparency,"
and Renan might have used the phrase : yet each
was haunted by a more personal religious Ideal,
while for ever baffled by philosophical per-
plexities. Only, in this baffling, Renan took, on
the whole, a certain pleasure, such as robust constitutions find in walking against a wind, while
Pattison's slighter nature shivered and dwindled
in the blast. Both inclined to imagine a conceivable survival of the soul, contingent on its progress
in this mortal sphere ; and either would have
defined this hoped-for after life—so dimly adum-
brated, so faintly apprehended, — rather as a
possible posthumous influence for good than as
a renewal of our human personality ; and yet,

each in softer hours, dreamed, half playfully, of
his childhood's Paradise.   "Shall I have my
library in Heaven?" queried the scholarly Rector of Lincoln, and Renan, the dreamer, laid up
stores of pleasant visions for the eternal night,
as though he were half persuaded that, after
death, he might still need an amusement.

An optimist at heart, Renan did not despair.
"This life of four days produces some enduring
fruits. . . . I can not suffer to hear our Humanity
insulted — poor thing of grief, thrown like an
orphan upon the earth, scarce sure of the morrow,
which finds means, between the birth-throe and
the death-agony, to invent art, science, virtue."
Renan had, as he confessed, despite experience
of the Dead Sea fruit, "a lively taste for the
universe."   He looked forward, though with but
a moderate cheerfulness.   He thought with Pattison that, when Reform has finished her perfect
work, the world, destitute of originality and
variety, will become a sort of universal China.
He foresaw that everything tended towards
Democracy, towards Socialism even, towards an
Americanising of our frame of life, a prosperous
vulgarity, repugnant to a man of taste.   But
after all, who knows?   A sort of modified
Chicago may be a less insupportable condition
of existence than we imagine.   Pattison was

too innately the Don, the College Man, to contemplate such a change without a shudder. But
Renan, who was a human being and a dreamer
first and a scholar afterwards—mingled some
indulgence and much curiosity with his personal
distaste. "Who knows, the general commonness
may guarantee the happiness of the Chosen
Few! American vulgarity would not have
buried Giordano Bruno, nor persecuted Galileo "
(Preface to *Souvenirs*).

On this subject Renan has embodied his reflections in a series of philosophical comedies,
which he composed, during his autumn holidays
in the Isle of Ischia in 1877 and in 1879, and
which he completed later at Rosmapamon. The
book appeared as a whole in 1888 under the
title of *Philosophical Dramas*. Three of these
tragi-comedies, *Caliban*, *The Fountain of Youth*,
The Priest of Nemi, are priceless documents for
the critic of Renan's character and opinions,
which the fourth, *The Abbess of Jouarre*, on the
whole a regrettable performance, obscures from
the height of its bad eminence.

The dramas we have mentioned are chiefly
concerned with the problems of Democracy.
They show the attitude towards uncultured
socialism of a Liberal Philosopher. Aristocratic
by temperament and education, for no aristocracy

is so close as the sacerdotal, Renan was by principle a sort of Socialist, or at least Republican, *malgré lui*. After the Commune, through fear of the tyranny of the mob, he had warmly advocated the restoration of the legitimate Bourbon.[1] After the stifling experience of the *Ordre Moral*, he had seen what a restoration of the Throne and Altar would really mean : the dominion of ortho- doxy, that is to say, tyranny *plus* hypocrisy, the most monstrous regimen of all.

"I love Prospero (he writes in *Caliban*), but I do not love the men who would re-establish him upon the throne. Caliban, improved by power, is more to my liking. Caliban, after all, is more useful to us scholars than Prospero would be with the Jesuits for his wire-pullers. In the present circumstances, the Government of Prospero would be, not a renaissance, but a crushing-flat of all free intelligence. Let us keep Caliban!"—that is to say, Democracy. Under all his airs of ironic aristocracy, Renan kept the staunchest sense of the rights of the people. He was indeed at heart more Radical, more anti-clerical, than he cared to appear. When Jules Ferry launched his famous Article VII., almost all cultured France deplored the system of petty religious persecution which it inaugurated : clerical colleges closed, monks and

---

[1] *Réforme intellectuelle et morale.*

nuns expelled from their pious homes, convents in-
ordinately taxed. "A most illiberal persecution !"
assented Renan, "and, what is more . . . insufficient!
I would not close a single clerical college : I would
only debar the pupils of the Regular Orders from
every public career." At heart, in his old age,
Renan returned to the democratic point of view
exhibited in his first social study, the "Future
of Science." The vision is less brilliant, but
it is not hopeless. Caliban (Democracy), the
unformed, mindless brute, educated by his own
responsibility, makes an adequate ruler after all,
no worse, if not wiser, than those who went before.
Prospero (the Aristocratic Principle, or, if we will,
the Mind) accepts, not unwillingly, his own de-
thronement from practical affairs for the sake of
greater liberty in the intellectual life : for Caliban
proves an effective policeman, and leaves his
superiors the freest of hands in the laboratory. Ariel
(the Religious Principle[1]) learns at last not to give up
the ghost at the faintest hint of change. Robuster,
if less ethereal, he, too, flourishes in the service of
Prospero under the external government of the
many-headed Brute. The future of Ariel is in
fact secured by the unconscious co-operation of
Prospero and Caliban. Every great religion is

[1] Compare with *The Tempest* Isaiah xxix., where Jerusalem is
figured under the symbolic name of Ariel.

the result of some such fecund misunderstanding. Nor is the future of Science less secure. " In the Ledger of Knowledge every truth is added up, every error omitted. Error is sterile, essentially perishable." [1] Truth alone knows how to capitalise her vast, her continually multiplying resources, which, as it were at compound interest, increase from year to year. In spite of all, the only needful things are *not* destined to succumb : Religion and Knowledge are as imperishable as the world which they dignify.

Thus, out of the depths, rises unvanquished the essential idealism of Ernest Renan.

Faith and Science had ever occupied his mind. On the threshold of old age, his philosophy became aware of another great entity, of Love, which, up to the age of five-and-fifty or thereabouts, had appeared to him a personal accident, of keen interest doubtless to the individuals it concerned, but scarcely a problem, hardly an immense universal force such as Beauty, Virtue, Truth, or Faith. When we are old, we secretly prize that which we disregarded most in its due season. Love and the charm of woman took a great importance in the eyes of our philosopher, grown prematurely aged, the unwieldiest of mortals, the wittier Dr Johnson of Parisian society. There

---

[1] Preface to *Feuilles Détachées.*

is something, we must own, a little grotesque in this tardy Cupid perched on the rim of Socrates' basket. Love as the interplanetary essence, the running music of the spheres binding all existence in one harmony, Love the μιθόριον πνεῦμα may occupy the sage at any decade. And we are moved and pleased by the ageing scholar's recollection of the girlish faces which had brightened existence for him some forty years ago. But that were enough; we did not desire the *Abbesse de Jouarre* !

"At Christmas we no more desire a rose"—

And the rose, of an odd blue unhealthy-looking sort, takes to blooming in Renan's frostiest season.

His life, as all who knew him can aver, was ever the life of a saint, and would appear of the purest, judged by the canons of any doctrine. Quaintly enough, he considered that this white apex of his gave him a singularly favourable point of view for scrutinising the nice enigmas of the heart. In the *Abbesse of Jouarre* he writes the apology of instinct. Chastity, says he, is often only another name for the merest social prudence : were the world to end to-morrow we should all abandon ourselves without remorse to our most passionate desires. His excuse must be that, in his peculiar mind, the most frivolous fantasies slide into philosophic symbols. . . . In the course of the universe Renan descried two impelling forces — the gradual process which develops, and the rare divine capricious impulse of spontaneity, which, as with a leap and a bound, hurries on the slow progress of cosmic elaboration ; steps in, at difficult moments, like a god out of a machine ; suggests Speech to the bleating and calling Bushmen ; makes the perplexed savage, as he notches his tally, dream of writing and arithmetic ; which, in fact, is continually intervening with the happiest effect, in the interminable evolution of the god from the sea-anemone. Love, in the eyes of Renan, was the constant manifestation of this force of spontaneity without which no great thing had fully achieved its being. Woman is the pure depositary of instinct; and, as such, she is precious above all things in the eyes of the philosopher.

" The more man develops his brain, the more he dreams of the opposite pole, of the Irrational, of a repose in complete ignorance—of the woman who is only a woman, of the instinctive being whose acts are guided by the impulse of an obscurer consciousness. . . . When our meditations have led us to the last term of doubt—then the spontaneous affirmation of the Good and the Beautiful in a woman's soul enchants us, and may yet give the casting vote. . . . Through her we are still in union with that eternal source of things, wherein God is reflected."[1]

It was this difference in woman which attracted Renan. Here was something at his hand whose movements he could not predicate, whose organs and whose instincts obeyed apparently different laws to those which regulated his own being. The curiosity of the philosopher was invincibly attracted. We all know how, in the Indian drama, the men speak in Sanscrit, the heroines in Pracrit. Renan knew his Sanscrit grammar by heart ; it was stale to him. In his old age he longed to learn this Pracrit poetry of woman. " If born again," he said in one of his last prefaces, " I would be born a woman."

Woman, divinised in Renan's later philosophy, repaid a hundredfold the adulation of the sage. Uncouth in frame and gait, as some gnome-like Breton saint, unworldly as the village *curé* he always looked like, Renan became the arbiter of the more intellectual elegancies of Paris. Fair ladies slept happy when they had exhibited him in their salons ; bonnets from Virot drooped a trifle disconcerted at the uncompromising scholarship of his lectures at the College of France ; latter-day Magdalenes consulted him as to the

[1] *Préface au Souvenirs d'Enfance et de Jeunesse.*

Q

state of their conscience, and music-hall singers asked his opinion on their songs. We have spoken of Samuel Johnson. The great Doctor himself did not yield a more undisputed or a less-to-be-expected social sway over last-century London than Ernest Renan over the Paris of the Eighties. Victor Hugo, perhaps, was more of a popular enthusiasm, but Renan was both Society's and Caliban's special prophet. Perhaps the good opinion they entertained of him may have influenced our philosopher's estimate of Society, and of Caliban. For to both of these, in his latter days, he became extraordinarily indulgent.

In 1879 Renan had been elected to the French Academy. The Academy accepted him with reluctance; but we may say that he reigned there, even as he reigned—a placid, benevolent, ambiguous divinity—over most of the learned societies of Paris. President of the Asiatic Society in 1882, he was, in the summer of 1884, appointed Administrator of the College of France —Principal, or Rector, as we should say at Oxford. He came into residence on his return from Rosmapamon. The local divinity was poorly housed in the old building of the Rue des Ecoles; a meagre study looking north did not spare his rheumatism; the narrow bedrooms were

worthy of a convent, but there was a fair-sized
salon to frame Scheffer's pictures, and endless
garrets for the innumerable books. It is doubtful
if Renan was ever happier than in this inconvenient
apartment. After his death his devoted wife, in
setting his papers in order, found in a drawer
a collection of old half-sheets, backs of envelopes,
and such like, on which, from time to time, her
husband had scrawled his reflections. On one
of these she read: "I have known the grip of
poverty, but never have I been so badly housed
as at the College of France." Since then the
residence has been twice enlarged to suit two
successive Administrators, and at present it is
all that health and commodity require. As
much, and more, would have been done for
Renan had it occurred to him to ask for repairs.
But it is charmingly characteristic of the man
that he never thought of it. In some moment
of irritation he confided to a private *Bocca di
Leone*, and perhaps to the ear of the Eternal, his
just dissatisfaction . . . and then forgot it. I
doubt if he would have suffered an improvement.
It is certain that he would not have exchanged
his beloved college for the palace of the Elysée.

The least practical of men, Renan proved an
admirable Administrator. Whatever he set his
hand to do, he did it with all his might. One

of his colleagues has set on record the unsuspected
firmness that underlay his charming genius :—

"Very indulgent to others, and convinced that
few of the things for which men torment themselves are really worth the trouble, there was *one*
thing as to which he was ever inflexible ; for if
we seek the continual motive of his life, in the
sphere of action, we shall find it to have been
the most abstract sense of duty.   This man, who
seemed to prize especially the grace of courtesy,
among all the virtues of St Sulpice, who always
seemed to seek for the phrase most pleasant to
the ear of his interlocutor, be he whom he might,
and who often carried the caress of his amiability
to the verge of an apparent irony—this man,
so indifferent and so pliant in appearance, became
a bar of iron so soon as one sought to wrest from
him an act or a word contrary to the intimate
sense of his conscience." [1]

No man had a stronger sense of a professional
engagement.   Tortured with rheumatism, faint
with the oppressed action of his heart, he never
let his ill-health interfere with his lectures.   I
have seen him carried down the steep staircase
of the College by hired porters—his bulk made
it no easy thing to do—in order to attend an

[1] James Darmesteter, *Ernest Renan.   See Critique et Politique,*
p. 64.

election of the Academy. The least personal, the least glorious of his labours occupied him most. The last months of his life were given to the volume on the Rabbis of France in the fourteenth century, which he was compiling from the notes of Dr Neubauer, and which, I suppose, scarce one of my readers will have read, or even heard of. The most arid, the most ungrateful of tasks, Renan was delighted to subject himself to this labour, which he deemed useful, and which no one certainly would undertake if he left it undone. At the same moment all Paris, nay, all the *élite* of Europe, was smiling over the exquisite *Feuilles Détachées*. I have little doubt that in his heart of hearts, Renan preferred the Rabbis.

Traversed by ill-health, disciplined by hard work, these years of apotheosis, these years of the eighties, were very happy years, full of family love, full of a just fame, to which Renan was never indifferent; full of the flattery of popular applause. Surrounded by those he loved—his delightful wife ("She must have been specially made for me," he used to say); his gifted, sensitive son; his exquisite daughter, in whom his dreams of Celtic grace had come to a perfect flower; with his grandchildren about his knees, Paris at his feet, Renan spent happy winters_in

his high-perched study of the College, and happy
summers in his Breton manor.   With Ecclesiastes,
he exclaimed, more than once, that this, at least,
is not vanity : to grow old with the wife of our
youth, and to enjoy the modest fortune amassed
by one's honest labours.   That fortune was very
modest, it is true ; but no shadow of money cares,
no thought for the morrow, ever touched the
serene self-detachment of this inveterate disciple
of Mary.   His children still smile when they recall how, one afternoon, in their private, domestic
Commission of the Budget, Madame Renan exposed the narrow extent of the family resources.
" 'Tis true, 'tis true," said Renan, with sagacious
impersonal calm, as he swayed himself from side
to side.   " Money shows no signs of rolling our
way ! "   But the fact appeared less important to
him, it was evident, than the date of the last discovered Himyarite inscription.   Care and trouble
came not nigh him.

It was at this moment that I made the acquaintance of M. and Madame Renan and their
children.   Well do I remember the day, the year,
the season !   It was in September 1880.   I was
travelling in Italy with my parents.   At Venice
we fell in with a friend of my father's—Signor
Castellani, the archæologist.   He invited us to
spend a day at Torcello with the Renans, Sir

Henry Layard, and his wife. I was a young girl then, more familiar with the Nineveh Courts of the British Museum (for which I worshipped Sir Henry Layard) and with Signor Castellani's exquisite Bronze Mask in the same collection, than with any writing of M. Renan's. In fact, save for a lecture on Marcus Aurelius, which I had heard him deliver a few months before, I knew him only by repute, as a heretic (that was attractive), and a philologist (which seemed less interesting). But after the first half-hour in his company I saw that here, here was the Man of Genius! I thought him like the enchanter Merlin—not Burne-Jones' graceful wizard, but some rough-hewn, gnome-like, Saint-Magician of Armor. What a leonine head, with its silvery mane of soft, grey hair, surmounted that massive girth! What an elfin, delicate light shone in the clear eyes, and lurked in the sinuous lines of the smile! How lucid, how natural, how benign the intelligence which mildly radiated from him! M. Renan was at his best on that occasion. We all felt ourselves in the glad society of an Immortal. . . . I still see the little Italian gunboat cutting through the bright lagoon towards the desolate shores of Torcello, fringed with scarlet-dotted pomegranate hedges and wastes of lilac-tipped sea-lavender! How bril-

liant the mother-island looked in her abandonment. The brown old church inspired M. Renan.
At that moment, with a heart divided between
the glory of Hellas and the spiritual grace of
Christianity, few things, indeed, could have
touched him nearer than that ancient Mosaic,
where the Apocalyptic Angels pour the Wrath
of God from vials shaped like the purest classic
cornucopiæ. He stood long in front of it. He
discoursed to the eminent archæologists who
accompanied him ; we all listened, we girls no
less earnestly than they, if with less understanding.
At first I had thought him ugly, I confess. But, as
he spoke, he grew almost handsome. The great
head, held on one side, half in criticism, half in
propitiation, was so puissant in its mass ; the
blue eyes beamed with wit and playful kindness.
How he savoured, and made us savour, that
image of the anger of the Eternal elegantly
treasured in the horns of plenty. How he revived for us the soul of the mother-church of
Venice—the handful of poor refugees: primitive
people, shipwrecked, as it were, upon that lonely
island ; yet, in their way, refined thinkers, with a
command of art and image, as became the heirs
of more than one immeasurable ideal.

Seven years later I went to see the Renans at
the College of France, and thenceforward they

both are blended with the happy memories of my married life. Madame Renan bestowed her kind protecting friendship on the foreign bride. Her husband, as Head of the College, as President of the Asiatic Society where M. Darmesteter was Secretary, was my husband's "chief"—and in more ways than these, for was he not first among the students of old faiths, and the leader of Oriental philologists in France? Though much firmness and an unalterable decision were masked by that benignant affability of his, he was the most genial of chiefs. I remember one afternoon, when we were in mourning and my husband ill, how he walked quickly into our little salon, embraced James on either cheek, tapped him on the shoulder, and pinned the Cross of the Legion of Honour in his coat.

If we went to see him in his study at the College, how wise were his counsels, never volunteered! No man made less of a fetish of his work. Those golden phrases of his were often interrupted, for his time was at the disposal of those who needed it. When a visitor arrived, he would lay down his pen, give his mind to his guest until the door shut upon him, and then he would resume, without a pause, the unfinished sentence. So he threw off the first jet, generally copied by Madame Renan, recorrected, set up by

the printer, and polished slowly and lovingly on
proof after proof of his interminable revise.

He was somewhat disquieted by the drones
and butterflies drawn to the College by the honey
of his hive.   One cannot imagine his serenity
ruffled.   But a summer lightning of irony would
play in his eyes when too many tall English
tourists, too many marvellous Parisian toilettes, occupied the narrow benches of the little " Salle des
Langues."   I am told that on one such occasion,
seeing his own students ousted, he bowed to the
motley company as amiably as ever—" I am enchanted," he began, " to observe the vogue for
abstruse Hebrew studies which obtains to-day.
In the presence of so choice an audience (another
bow) there can be no need of an introduction to
our subject.   We will therefore read our text,
phrase after phrase, in turn—in the original
Hebrew "—a quick dispersion left the scholars to
their book.

M. Renan talked marvellously well, and he
loved talking.   He had little of the ready give-
and-take which is the most usual form of wit,
yet he had a colloquial magic of his own.   His
conversation was an attentive silence, interrupted
by long pauses of solitary meditation, and by
outbursts of radiant monologue.   He liked dining
out.   Some of my most agreeable recollections

are of the subtle and singular reflections with which, as with the wave of a fairy wand, our enchanter would turn a Paris dinner-party into an elect symposium. He could be grave—he could be gay. That night, for instance, when he told us—with what charm! with what elegant lightness!—the story of the Babylonian Tobias. Rash and young, this Chaldæan brother of our Tobit, discouraged by the difficult approaches of prosperity, had entered into partnership with a demi-god or Demon, who made all his schemes succeed and pocketed fifty per cent. upon the profits. The remaining fifty sufficed to make Tobias as rich as Oriental fancy can imagine. The young man fell in love, married his bride and brought her home. . . . On the threshold stood the Demon : " How about my fifty per cent.? " The Vénus d'Ille, you see, was not born yesterday. From the dimmest dawn of time, sages have taught us not to trust the gods too far !

Μυριάνους ἀνήρ—M. Renan had far other moods. I remember a more serious banquet. It was at the house of the dear philosopher of the Rue Cassette. The Renans were there, some others, the Lyttons, I believe, and ourselves. That morning M. Taine had received a bundle of the papers of the Psychical Research Society. The psychologist—much interested at that time in

the problems of dual personality and so forth—
let the conversation wander into the dubious
sphere of the phantoms of the living. M. Renan
appeared sunk in a dream of his own. From
time to time he shook his mane, like a slumber-
ing lion. Suddenly he looked up and spoke,
with a flash in his blue eyes—θεὸς ὢν τις ἐλεγχτικός.
Briefly indeed, and with a rare scorn in his irony,
did the cross-examining God dispose of those
vague approximations, those imprecise reminiscences of another's experience, which suffice to
found a fact in the annals of unscientific ob-
servers. Truth, Science, were eloquently bid to
the rescue, enjoined to engulph and swallow up
the miracle-mongery, the wonder-worship, still
so dear to the fashionable uneducated. And
suddenly the prophet relented, cast up his hands
in kindly deprecation—"O les gens du monde!
la science des gens du monde!" In spite of
all, he knew he had a weakness for these well-
bred culprits.

Such outbursts were rare. The affable Arch-
angel concealed them, as it were, under a cassock of non-committal ecclesiastical courtesy. He
generally acquiesced. I used to wonder what
assertion would be too wild to provoke his
amiable "Mais certainement, Madame!" He
would let any young lady explain to him the

nicest points in Semitic archæology without a protest. Sometimes I tried, I admit, how far one could go. Perhaps there was a twinkle in the kindly indifferent eye. Never anything so pedantic as a contradiction.

M. Renan and I were born on the same day — at an interval of some five - and - thirty years—or rather we thought we were so born. For it is characteristic of the idealist that all his life he thought himself a day older than he was. On the 27th of February, notes and flowers went gaily between us. For M. Renan was gay : M. Lemaître has reproached him with the fact, and it is true. Despite old age, and constant pain, lack of breath, and sometimes lack of means— despite the prospect of the end at hand, M. Renan was gay, unfailingly patient, cheerful, and serene. One 27th of February there were no more good wishes, and yet, as we talked with Madame Renan, the kind sage seemed almost one among us. "A widow," said Michelet, "should be her husband's soul delayed among us." Such was she. The thoughts, the wishes, the counsels, the memories of M. Renan lingered with us eighteen months after we had bidden him fare-well. The past abided with her. She would spend hours contentedly reviving the episodes of their journey in Asia Minor, living over again the first years of her marriage. Happy years full of youth and love and poverty, when, at the end of his long day's work, she used to carry off her young husband on some inexpensive adventure. "We used to call on the cats of the Quarter! M. Renan had names for them all. You may put that in your book!" she would say with a smile. This book was a favourite project of her's. We made plans for writing it together; and, indeed, I could never have written it without her. But she missed too sorely, she mourned too faithfully, the hero of our biography, and, before a line of it was set down, I learned one day, at her door, that she would never read it.

But remembrance carries me too fast. Those days have not yet dawned. A brief spell of life and noble labour remains to Ernest Renan.

CHAPTER V

THE HISTORY OF ISRAEL

IN that writing-table drawer to which our philosopher confided so many private ejaculations, Madame Renan found a slip of paper on which was written : "Of all that I have done, I prefer the *Corpus.*" Of average, well-read persons, taking an interest in European literature, I suppose some fifty per cent. may have read the *Souvenirs* of Ernest Renan, and perhaps twenty per cent. the *Life of Jesus*, and ten, at most, let us say, some other work of the master's — usually the *Feuilles Détachées*, or the recently published *Letters*, but occasionally *St Paul*, or the *Apostles*, or perhaps one of the two lovely volumes of *Religious Studies*, or the *Essays on Moral Science and Criticism.* But for every hundred cultured readers, scarce the fraction of a unit can be placed to the account of the *Corpus.* The *Corpus Semiticarum Inscriptionum* is not in any sense a book. It is a tool for scholars. It is a collection of all

the Semitic inscriptions as yet discovered on
Jewish, Aramean, Phœnician, Himyarite, Cartha-
ginian, Cypriote, Greek, Egyptian, Sicilian, Mal-
tese, Sardinian, Arabian, Assyrian, and Chaldæan
monuments. The comparison of these inscriptions — the unsuspected details, the singular
rapprochements, which result from such a comparison—is, perhaps, the most important factor in the
exegesis and the historical discoveries of the
future. In the study of the Past no detail is
insignificant; the most patient analysis of the
greatest possible quantity of authentic material
is the first condition of historic insight. A poet,
a prophet may touch the dry bones and make
them live. But without these dry bones, apparently so mouldered and remote, even an Ezekiel
were of no avail. Renan never forgot this
essential truth. His soaring genius was constantly refreshed from the humble springs of
fact and certainty.

It was in 1867 that M. Renan proposed to the
Academy of Science and Belle Lettres the formation of a *Corpus* for Semitic inscriptions on the
model of Bœkh's Greek Corpus; but it was only
in 1881 that the first number was given to the
world. Semitic epigraphy is a recent science,
and every year adds to its scanty store, and
patiently reanimates the past of Israel, and of the

neighbours of Israel, too long transfigured by an
exclusively sacred tradition into something out of
the likeness of human days and works.   The
materials are slowly accumulating for a definite
history of the Semitic kingdoms.   M. Renan,
nourished on the Bible, familiar with the sites and
races of the Holy Land, was almost the first to
perceive the extent of the fresh resources offered
by recent epigraphy.

Renan commenced his " History of the People
of Israel " at sixty years of age—the first volume
appeared in 1887—having spent his whole life
in studying the materials which critics, scholars,
archæologists, and explorers have gathered concerning the Semitic peoples.   Forty years before
he had planned his great work on the " Origins
of Christianity."   " I ought to have begun with
the Prophets," he said later ; but the figure of
Jesus attracted him with an incessant magnetism,
and besides, a delicate lad of twenty, he had
not dared to count upon so long a future.   Now
he determined to fill up the weak places in his
foundations, and to found Christianity, as in
truth it is founded, on the teachings of Amos,
of Isaiah, of Ezekiel, and especially of the great
nameless prophet, who wrote the latter chapters
of the book we call Isaiah's.

The originality of Renan's "History of Israel "

R

lies in this fact, that he places the Prophets at
the very core and centre of Jewish thought—
the Prophets, not Moses or Elias. The first
volume of his history is perhaps disappointing;
it is less a history than a vague poetic rhapsody
—such as we expect from a Michelet rather
than a Renan — a piece of cosmic folk-lore,
too merely grandiose and picturesque. Yet
it contains a page on the civilisation of Babylonia
which no reader can forget; and the idyll of
Father Orcham, the ideal king of the Chaldæan
golden age, whom the pastors of Israel adopted
for their ancestor, has the true ring of a primitive
fable.   But surely M. Renan exaggerates the
monotheism of these tribal wanderers?   He
is never so happy as when divining in its ultimate
recesses, calling up from its deepest hiding-places,
the different forms of religious feeling.   And
yet we think he antedates the religious tendency
of these primitive tribesmen.   Surely in their
attitude towards the Unknown there was little
but dread and mere propitiation.

Something of the same fatigue, the same in-
adequacy, is shown in the history of David and
Solomon, however picturesque, however full of
recondite and charming detail.   Yet David, the
brigand chief, ruling Israel by means of his Cretan
mercenaries; Solomon, the intelligent, unpreju-

diced, wise man of the East, much like many a
Jew of our days—shrewd, epicurean, materialist,
blind to the true vocation of his race : these are
figures which impress us by their reality despite
the defects of the volume which contains them.
Of these defects the greatest is an excessive use
of Renan's peculiar irony. The immensity of his
mental horizon is such as to include, and as it
were to associate, objects which appear to belong
to different spheres of thought. What can be
more disconcerting than his serene and candid
fashion of assuring us how much the Book
of Jonah resembles *La Belle Hélène ?* — that
Jeremiah was a journalist of the type of Félix
Pyat, and Ezekiel a sort of Victor Hugo at
Hauteville House, unless, indeed, we consider him
more like Fourier ? These unexpected compari-
sons startle and shock the attention of readers less
familiar with the antipodes of history ; and, while
acquitting our placid sage of any childish desire
to merely dazzle or astonish. I own that I consider these " actualities " misplaced. They may
occasionally illuminate, as by a searchlight, some
obscure and dusty purlieu of the Past. But more
often they merely serve to irritate the student ;
and, after a short lapse of years, they will seem
even more incomprehensible : two Pasts, neither
familiar, will then confuse each other. This con-

tinual blemish mars the third volume of the
History of Israel no less, and perhaps even more,
than the two earlier ones.   But, at this point, it
is caught up and, as it were, whirled out of sight
in the noble and living current of the work.   For
M. Renan touches his true subject at last in dealing with the Prophets of Israel.   The notion of
justice, of righteousness unto God and Man, the
divine necessity of self-amelioration, was born into
the world with Amos and Hosea, and their religion
is big with our future.

[Renan's *History of Israel* is, in fact, a history of
the religious Idea ; a chronicle of the divine thirst
after justice done, not to ourselves, but to all men,
for the greater glory of God.   The prehistoric
cosmogony of Israel is, in this sense, not religious
at all : neither the Elohim, the multiple sprites of
the air, nor Yahveh, the storm-god of Sinai, have
any clear idea of right and wrong.   They have
not plucked as yet the fruit of the Tree of Knowledge.   Their will is capricious, inexplicable,
absurd ; the Elohim wrestle all night with the
sons of earth, and are wounded by a man at
cock-crow ; they enter into a chief's garden, and
sit at meat with him.   Yahveh is of a revolting
partiality ; he protects his favourites, he takes
care of his own, however little exemplary their
conduct, so that it is wise indeed to be the servant

of Yahveh. The world which these deities govern is quite small; a ladder connects it with the heaven which they inhabit. One may say that up to the death of Solomon true religion was unknown. The deity was still the tribal god : his prophet was still a sorcerer, a medicine-man, a sort of mythic wonder-worker. But let us not despair of that divine instinct in humanity which knows how to turn dross into gold, how to evolve, from the primitive terror of soothsay, the idea of justice, the search for truth, the thirst after righteousness. " Behold the days come (saith the Lord) that I will send a famine in the land, not a famine of bread nor a thirst after water, but of hearing the words of the Lord " (Amos, viii. 11). And behold, the Word of the Lord has grown in its significance. Yahveh no longer says " worship me and prosper " ; he says " eschew evil and do good." He commands no more "take thy brother's birthright," but "love thy neighbour as thyself."

It is this moral evolution which is the secret of the undying importance of the *History of Israel.* Full of ruse and guile, destitute of the sense of Beauty which ennobled Greece, or of the political and military grandeur which made the force of Rome, this small Syrian tribe is no less immortal than Greece or Rome, for it first interpreted the

secret oracle within the heart of humanity.   All
the great fibres of spiritual being vibrate in the
soul of Israel.   Wonder of wonders, the instinct
of religion reveals to the prophet even how
the day shall dawn when religion shall be
other than he may conceive it—freer, ampler,
tied to no ritual, bound upon the horns of no
altar.

" And it shall come to pass (saith the Lord)
that ye shall say no more : ' The Ark of the
Covenant of the Lord' : neither shall it come to
mind : neither shall ye remember it ; neither
shall ye visit it ; neither shall these things be
done any more — neither shall ye walk any
more after the imagination of an evil heart "
(Jeremiah iii. 16).

Every great gift is developed and nourished
at the expense of the exhausted organism which
produces it.   The soul, that perfect flower of
Israel, ruined the material prosperity of Israel.
The doctrines of the Prophets are not compatible
with any strong military or civic organisation.
Preoccupied with individual justice,—individual
well-doing and well-being—Amos and Jeremiah
conceived as iniquity the nation which deliber-
ately devotes thousands of its offspring to the
brutal and stupid life of tent and camp.   The
Assyrian hoplite appeared to them even lower

in the scale than the captive of the Assyrians
—for him, at least, there should be no return
from exile, no promised restoration. And in
a primitive civilisation, the country which means
to conquer, which means to dominate, can
only do so at the cost of the enforced service
of the mass : a colossal unconsented slavery in
the interests of a fatherland which absorbs and
does not reward the factors of its grandeur.
There is its fine side, too, in the military glory
of an Assyria or an Egypt. But Israel only sees
the innocent blood, the endless tears of the just
man offended, with which the stones of their
pyramids are welded together. And she will
none of the magnificence of Assur.

More than once, in writing the *History of*
Israel, Renan's thoughts reverted to his own
times. In Amos and Hosea, in Jeremiah and
Isaiah, he saw the forerunners of the socialists
of our age. In Nineveh and Babylon he saw
the ancestors of feudal Germany. Which is
the wiser ? Almost invariably, the nation which
labours for Humanity and the Future works its
own destruction in the process. The Kingdom of
God is not of this world. In the administration
of a great power, in the maintenance of a national
army, there are abuses which are almost necessary. A society which is always just is disarmed

before the strength of the unscrupulous. A people whose teachers are concerned only with the eternal verities will be far behind Babylon, not simply in practical affairs, but also in natural science. It was Babylon, after all, which first attempted to explain the Universe; Israel borrowed the ten opening chapters of Genesis from the *savants* of Chaldæa. An exclusive preoccupation with piety and morals is apt to produce a very mediocre standard of culture. The ideal of Israel is the ideal of a saint, a prophet, a monk, a Savonarola. But which did the most for Florence, Savonarola or the Medici?

The happiness and the sanctity of the individual, or the splendour and force of the organism of which he is an atom: whether of these is desirable? More than once Renan has asked himself the question, to which there are only too many answers. Whichever response we accept may be an error, for, when all is said, which of us can be sure of what is in fact the real object of Humanity?

" He, at least, is not wholly mistaken who fears lest he be in the wrong and treats no one as blind; who, ignoring the goal of Man, loves him as he strives, he and his work; who seeks the Truth in doubting of heart, and who says to his opponent : ' Perchance seest thou clearer than I.'

He, in fine, who accords his fellows the wide liberty he takes for himself;—he surely may sleep in peace and await the judgment of all things, if such a judgment there shall be." [1]

[1] *Hist. du peuple d'Israel*, III., p. 279.

CHAPTER VI

LAST DAYS

" IN the Name of Life, the vast, the mysterious, the excellent! " So begins the Bible of the Mendaïtes, and under this invocation would I place the last philosophy of Ernest Renan. The final reaction of his mind was, after all, optimistic. Man is full of errors, but error is essentially transitory, and the eternal result of his passage through the universe is Truth. God is absent from the scheme of things in the sense of Action ; in all the ages of human history no trustworthy evidence attests a divine intervention to protect the innocent or to relieve the sufferer. But the law and condition of so much of the Universe as we may understand is ever a perpetual *Fieri*, a divine Becoming, an eternal development towards an unknown end, which may become at last a manifestation of the Hidden Divinity. Nor, because His ways are not as our ways, His thoughts as our thoughts, let us too hastily conclude the eternal absence of that Heavenly Father which the heart of man claims, and to which he calls

incessantly without response. Out of our tears
and our prayers He may yet be born. Moreover, rightly considered, is not that call of ours
its own answer ? Disinterested prayer is not
a petition but an act of praise, an act of
Hope, an inner communing with the principle
of things, an affirmation of the spiritual Reality
which governs appearances. "And our day-
dreams themselves are another fashion of adoring—a poor inferior prayer, full of long re-
mainders of the ardour of our youth, warm as
covered embers are, instinct with the secret
assurance that the Absolute Night itself is, perchance, not devoid of this same lingering warmth
and life!"[1] The unselfish man—the only one
who counts—prays in secret a hundred times a
day. For an acquiescence in the laws of that
Universe, in which alone we may see God,—"as
in a glass, darkly,"—is not this also Prayer and
an act of Faith ?

We must fain believe in Something independent of the Finite and the Knowable, when
in our own hearts, in our own lives, in the
lives of all around us we observe the persistence
and the universality of certain great guiding
principles which are folly, according to the wisdom of this world : self-sacrifice, love, disin-

---

[1] Preface to the *Nouvelles Etudes Religieuses.*

terestedness, the instinct of Duty. These are the voice of the Universe, " a language which hails from the Infinite, perfectly clear in its commands, obscure in its promises "[1]—a language, which in some fashion and degree, we all obey. No man is absolutely and consistently a monster ; in every life there is *some* effort towards Love, Truth, or Beauty ; the worst man drops one of these priceless gold coins into the world's coffer against the millions of mere brass counters which he squanders out of window. And in the scheme of things, Good is a coin of great price, Evil is poor trash of no value. Thus there is scarce any existence which, rightly summed up, does not show an imperceptible balance to the good.

Like Francis of Assisi, whom he understood so well ("St Francis will save him !" once cried a Capuchin friar), Renan had arrived at the supreme indulgence—he no longer believed in the existence of sin. Evil appeared to him a void, a vacuum, a gap to be filled up in the gradual process of Creation ; but not a substance to be vanquished and destroyed. Of him also might it be said : "He would not admit the reality of evil. It is not that he was indifferent, but, in probing the heart of man, he found no irre-

[1] *Feuilles Détachées* : Examen de Conscience Philosophique.

missible guilt in it: the one sin is baseness; weakness, error, seemed to him scarcely sin."[1] He would have said with Plato, that when the Soul is alienate from Truth, it is always momentarily so constrained against its will : the natural growth of our spirits being towards the light. An involuntary opinion can not be a crime. Let us believe that the sin of our neighbour is no affair of ours, and probably infinitely less important than we deem it. In time, the Truth will certainly prevail, and convince even them that sit in outer darkness.

The two fundamental doctrines of religion remain undemonstrable : no man can prove the existence of a personal God, nor the immortality of the Soul. The task of the modern thinker is the task of Kant—the task of the Prophets of Israel. *They* justified the ways of God to man with little more than the minimum of faith ; from the rebellious stuff of humanity they extracted righteousness and resignation, and patient depths of long self-sacrifice, with no sure promise of a future life. They loved God for God, and the right for the sake of righteousness. Happy those who can so inspire their fellows without alleging anything unproven, anything with which their conscience may reproach them

[1] *Nouvelles Études Religieuses:* St François d'Assise, p. 333.

as a lure. Piety may exist independent of all dogma, and may prove the inner strength and consolation of the Soul. We may still "seek God," like the wise men of Israel, and find much sweetness in that seeking. We may weep to Him alone in our trouble, nor our tears be shed in vain. For in the end, in the infinite end of ages, Humanity creates the thing which it desires. And at last, at last, all the dreams of Man come true.

Thus "the most logical attitude of the thinker towards Religion is: to behave as though Religion were true. We must act as though God and the Soul were proven. Religion is one of the numerous hypotheses, such as the waves of ether, or the electric, luminous, caloric and nervous fluids, nay, the atom itself, which we know to be mere symbols and manners of speech, convenient for the explaining of certain phenomena, but which, none the less, we maintain."[1] The more we reflect, the more we see the impossibility of proving, but also the *moral necessity* of believing in, these great premisses : God and the Soul. Let us keep the category of the Unknowable ! Parallels meet at the Infinite : Science and Religion doubtless meet there. And

[1] Examen de Conscience.— *Feuilles Détachées*, p. 432.

if not ?—Why, then, Renan would have said with
Goethe :

"Wen Gott betrügt ist wohl betrogen."

The most intelligent course of Man, as well
as the most virtuous, is to act in the general
sense of Universal Law. *Domine, si error est, a
te decepti sunt!*

In philosophy the consolatory hypothesis is,
after all, as good an hypothesis as any other. It
is the only one which could abidingly content a
man like Renan, who,—dilettante and scholar as
he remained, no doubt,—was none the less, by
the inner constitution of his being, a profoundly
religious man. The needs of his nature were
triple : his heart desired Beauty and his mind
Truth ; but the earnest problem of Man's virtue
in Nature's ruthlessness was the fundamental preoccupation of his soul.

"I often reproach myself (he said, in almost
the last pages that fell from his hand) because
at my age, I am sometimes occupied with other
things than these Eternal Verities. My excuse
is that my chief duty here below is accomplished.
. . . That last arch of the bridge which I had
still to throw between Christianity and Judaism,
is now established. . . . I have still much to do
in the way of proof-correcting ; but, if I died

to-morrow, with the aid of a good corrector, my *History of Israel* could appear in its completeness." [1]

The third and finest volume of this last and great work appeared in 1891. Renan did not live to see the publication of the two concluding tomes, which he left almost finished, lacking, indeed, those fine last touches, those delicate elaborations and reservations, which he was wont to add—patiently, interminably—on page after page of his proofs. The pearl has less gloss, and a dimmer orient, it may be; but its orb is perfect, and its structure sound. The chapters on Philo and the Essenians, which adorn the fifth volume, are among the most vivid and the purest which we owe to Renan's singular genius. Age could not stale nor custom wither that infinite variety. The extraordinary freshness, the divine youth of his spirit remained almost unimpaired by suffering, to his last hour. It is a freshness as of thyme and dew on a spring morning; something natural, and sweet, and pure; and it was never more conspicuous, as mere style, than in those *Feuilles Détachées*, which he collected and published in the very year of his death.

For long enough his health had been failing. He took all the little miseries of age and a broken

---

[1] Preface to *Feuilles Détachées*.

constitution in that spirit of mingled irony and
sweetness which never left him. Before mere
physical suffering, he was ever serene as an
image of Buddha. Enforced idleness was a
sorer burden, and sometimes he would half complain that in his childhood he had never learned
to play. His little grandchildren began his
instruction in that wise art. But the sage was
too tired to prove an apt pupil. He liked best to
look on and listen, thinking of many things, and
enjoying that last pleasure of watching life's
morning windows brighten when the sun forsakes
us in the west.

Few people suffer more than he in his last
illness. Protracted neuralgia tortured him month
by month. He admitted the fact, but never
murmured, and would certainly not have owned
himself unhappy. For he loved Life, and saw that
it was good. Self-pity was a weakness which he
knew not. Nor did his own pain ever blind him
to the immense sum of virtue, love, beauty,
knowledge, and innocent happiness, which, all
round him, at that instant, the universe was
yielding undiminished. That tiny but eternal
residue of good, that drop of immortal aroma,
which the scheme of things secretes from day
to day, appeared to impregnate every moment
of his life, and to embalm even the pangs of his

S

agony. I think there was no day, even of that cruel last year, from which he would not have offered from a sincere heart, his *Te Deum Laudamus*. If there were hours in it racked with intercostal neuralgia, stupefied with oppressive weakness, there were also moments — divine moments whose superior value outweighed those hours—in which he was able to complete the great task of his life ; or which he gave to the management of that beloved College whose good genius he was ; or he spent them in discussing with a few chosen spirits—M. Berthelot, M. Taine, M. Gaston Paris, and some others ever welcome— the questions which occupied his unfailing mind in sickness as in health ; or, simply, he let himself rest in the tender love of his dear wife and children.

He knew that he was dying. The physicians continued to speak of gout, of rheumatism, of neuralgia—but it is, I think, impossible to have a mortal disease and not to know it : for years he had told his wife that his heart was affected. But he was dying at the end of his chosen task, having completed the immense circle which he had dared to trace. He had married his daughter, and had embraced her children. The sensitive artistic spirit of his son, the painter, showed itself calmed and fortified by the first draught of success.

His wife, the trusted confidante and secretary of more than thirty years, would execute his last wishes, and would see his History through the press. One of his favourite pupils would succeed him in his chair at the College of France, and in the direction of the Corpus. He could repeat with the ancient Simeon : *Nunc dimittis servum tuum, Domine, secundum verbum tuum, in pace.* . . .

The future, in fine, was a spectacle which he could regard with a great satisfaction. He had given his life to Truth, and he had certainly furthered her progress. He had chosen the better part, and it had not been taken away from him. The things in which he had put the truest part of his life would survive him, and would be fruitful in his absence. Untimely death may be terrible, for it may mean a waste of immense possibilities. But death when our task is achieved? Why rebel against the law of nature? Did we ever believe ourselves exempt from mortality?

At the New Year of 1892 the Renans went to Cap Martin for a few weeks of sun and sea. The blue Mediterranean shore enveloped the dying sage with its enchantment. He felt better, well, saw the future brighten and lengthen before him. But the south in winter is a cup of which a sick man should drink deep, or not at all.

Despite his wasted health, Renan could not make up his mind to desert the College even for a season. Before the month was out he returned to resume his course of Hebrew. On the return journey, at Dijon, he took a chill. And after that, again, he was less well all winter.

Those who knew him as well as I did will never forget his quiet heroism, his unassuming devotion, all through the first *semestre* of 1892. With my eyes shut, I can still see the heavy quaint figure painfully descending the steep stairs of the College, and serenely accosting, with oppressed breath, but without complaint, the colleagues he directed, with a smile. He delivered his lectures with exactitude. He presided over the Asiatic Society. He completed his studies on the Mediæval Rabbis for the Academy of Inscriptions ;—and this was a great joy. On Friday evenings, in his wife's *salon*, his friends found him willing to converse with them on any subject. His unimpaired curiosity continued to interrogate the universe. He was dying, but he had not abdicated.

At midsummer he moved with his family to the Breton coast. And for a while things went well with him. He loved his calm manor of Rosmapamon, the fresh quiet country, with its green fields and spinnies, its commons golden with gorse, its great granite rocks, its sombre and splendid sea. It was there, perhaps, that he spent his happiest days. "My ideal"—(he says in the *Eau de Jouvence*, speaking as usual through the lips of Prospero).—"My ideal would be an old patriarchal country house, full of children singing, full of lads and lasses light of heart, where everyone would eat, drink, and be merry at my expense." Rosmapamon supplied his kind old age with that hospitable holiday. There were long quiet mornings for work : evenings in which the tired enchanter saw, as he wished, the young people unchecked by his presence in their merry-making. In the afternoons, in the long, lazy, summer afternoons, almost every day he went a little walk, leaning on his wife's arm. He would sit on a bank by the side of a field, and look placidly over the Celtic landscape which he had loved in childhood—of which he felt himself an animate part. But there was one thing he loved more than Nature, and that was knowledge; the service of Truth. When, at the end of September, he had an attack of the heart, he said to Madame Renan : "Take me back to the College." And there on the 12th of October 1892, he died at his post.

He died happy. His mind kept to the end its

serene lucidity, his temper its kind sweetness, unalloyed by personal repining. All he asked was that his illness should put nothing out of its due order, that his death should cost no excessive grief—the only thing in which his wife ever disobeyed him. " I have done my work," he said to Madame Renan, " I die happy." And again he said, " It is the most natural thing in the world to die: let us accept the Laws of the Universe "—and he added : " the heavens and the earth remain."

So he passed away, and his death struck France with a sort of stupor. He was the greatest man of genius our generation had known : in style, sentiment, poetry of feeling no less a Master than Victor Hugo ; in history and philosophy the compeer of Taine ; in philology the heir of Burnouf. There was scarce one branch of thought in France but it was impoverished by his disappearance.

He was buried with great honours. The grey old College was decked as for a national festivity. The best and wisest men in France bade a public farewell to his sacred ashes. There had been a question of laying him to rest under the dome of the Panthéon. At the last moment the Government feared the protest of the Right at the opening of the Chambers. And the great Idealist had not where to lay his head. . . . His wife buried him with her people in the vault of the Sheffers at Mont-Martre. But where he should have lain, where he would have wished to lie, is in the small, green space which the cloister of Tréguier encloses. "It is there I would sleep," he said once, " under a stone engraved with these words—

Veritatem Dilexi."

Who knows? the day may dawn when the Church of his youth may yet accept the guardianship of the grave of Ernest Renan.

" All religions are vain (he said), but religion is not vain." . . . " Let us not abjure our Heavenly Father. Let us not deny the possibility of a final justice. Perchance we have never known one of those tragic situations where God is the sole Confidant, the necessary Consoler. . . . Where else shall we seek the true witness, if not on high ? How often have we felt the need of an appeal to Absolute Truth ; how often we would cry to it : ' Speak ! Speak !' Who knows ? At that instant we were, perhaps, on the threshold of Truth. But the strange thing is that nothing

shows if our protestations have found a hearing.
When Nimrod shot his arrows into Heaven, they
came back to him tipped with blood. We have
never received any response at all. O God,
whom we adore in spite of all, Thou art in truth
a Hidden God!"[1]

These were almost the last written words of
Ernest Renan. They are characteristic. They
might be taken from his earliest pages. Instinct
and Reason speak to us in different voices, equally
imperious, equally insistent; only we are most of
us a little deaf with one ear! But Renan lost no
word of either of these eternal monitors. There
is his secret, there his charm, there the peculiar
value of his genius. But therein also the something unconvinced—or only momentarily convinced
—which leaves his purest harmonies for ever un-
resolved. We know that, in one other moment,
he will hear the other Voice, he will deliver a
different message: *le cœur a ses raisons que la
raison ne connait pas*. One lobe of his brain is
continually engaged in supplementing the thoughts
produced by the other: we can imagine them as
two mirrors so placed as to show the opposing
faces of the object they reflect. Fortunately this
variety is saved from chaos by certain dominating

[1] Preface to *Feuilles Détachées*.

principles which remain unaltered in the midst of mutability.

Religion may or may not be true ; it is not vain ; even though it answer to no supernatural reality. Our conscience is a moral fact as important as our reason, and the man who says " I ought " as superior to the savage as the man who says " I reflect."

The Good exists ; and indeed we may say that it alone exists. Evil is transitory. In its different forms of Truth, Virtue, Knowledge, Beauty, the Good endures and accumulates, and, by the impulse of its own force, must develop more and more. " The world's our oyster " : slowly, surely, it secretes the inevitable pearl which may survive it. Meanwhile Evil is with us certainly. We suffer, we are oppressed by material circumstances, we may even die before our time in anguish and never bring forth the fruit which we were destined to produce. Yet the construction of the universe allows for infinite waste. Other germs will bear ; all will not be blasted. Evil is a sort of moral carbonic acid gas, mortal when isolated and a real danger to our existence ; and yet, when combined with other forces, not only innocuous, but even necessary to our vital powers, in the present state of their development. The important thing in life is not our misery, our despair,

T

however crushing, but the one good moment which outweighs it all. Man is born to suffer, but he is born to hope. And the message of the universe still runs, as of old : αἰλίνον, αλλίνον, εἶπε, τὸ δ'εὐ νικάτω.

PRINTED BY
TURNBULL AND SPEARS
EDINBURGH

A CATALOGUE OF BOOKS
AND ANNOUNCEMENTS OF
METHUEN AND COMPANY
PUBLISHERS : LONDON
36 ESSEX STREET
W.C.

CONTENTS

NOVEMBER 1897

MESSRS. METHUEN'S
ANNOUNCEMENTS

Poetry

SHAKESPEARE'S POEMS. Edited, with an Introduction and Notes, by GEORGE WYNDHAM, M.P. *Crown 8vo. Buckram.* 6s.

This is a volume of the sonnets and lesser poems of Shakespeare, and is prefaced with an elaborate Introduction by Mr. Wyndham.

ENGLISH LYRICS. Selected and Edited by W. E. HENLEY, *Crown 8vo. Buckram.* 6s.
Also 15 copies on Japanese paper. *Demy 8vo. £2, 2s. net.*

Few announcements will be more welcome to lovers of English verse than the one that Mr. Henley is bringing together into one book the finest lyrics in our language.

NURSERY RHYMES. With many Coloured Pictures. By F. D. BEDFORD. *Small 4to.* 5s.

This book has many beautiful designs in colour to illustrate the old rhymes.

THE ODYSSEY OF HOMER. A Translation by J. G. CORDERY. *Crown 8vo.* 7s. 6d.

Travel and Adventure

BRITISH CENTRAL AFRICA. By Sir H. H. JOHNSTON, K.C.B. With nearly Two Hundred Illustrations, and Six Maps. *Crown 4to.* 30s. net.

CONTENTS.—(1) The History of Nyasaland and British Central Africa generally. (2) A detailed description of the races and languages of British Central Africa. (3) Chapters on the European settlers and missionaries; the Fauna, the Flora, minerals, and scenery. (4) A chapter on the prospects of the country.

WITH THE GREEKS IN THESSALY. By W. KINNAIRD ROSE, Reuter's Correspondent. With Plans and 23 Illustrations. *Crown 8vo.* 6s.

A history of the operations in Thessaly by one whose brilliant despatches from the seat of war attracted universal attention.

THE BENIN MASSACRE. By CAPTAIN BOISRAGON. With Portrait and Map. *Crown 8vo.* 3s. 6d.

This volume is written by one of the two survivors who escaped the terrible massacre in Benin at the beginning of this year. The author relates in detail his adventures and his extraordinary escape, and adds a description of the country and of the events which led up to the outbreak.

FROM TONKIN TO INDIA. By PRINCE HENRI OF
ORLEANS. Translated by HAMLEY BENT, M.A. With 80 Illustrations and a Map. *Crown 4to.* 25*s.*

The travels of Prince Henri in 1895 from China to the valley of the Bramaputra
covered a distance of 2100 miles, of whith 1600 was through absolutely unexplored
country. No fewer than seventeen ranges of mountains were crossed at altitudes
of from 11,000 to 13,000 feet. The journey was made memorable by the discovery
of the sources of the Irrawaddy. To the physical difficulties of the journey were
added dangers from the attacks of savage tribes. The book deals with many of
the burning political problems of the East, and it will be found a most important
contribution to the literature of adventure and discovery.

THREE YEARS IN SAVAGE AFRICA. By LIONEL DECLE.
With an Introduction by H. M. STANLEY, M.P. With 100 Illustrations and 5 Maps. *Demy 8vo.* 21*s.*

Few Europeans have had the same opportunity of studying the barbarous parts of
Africa as Mr. Decle. Starting from the Cape, he visited in succession Bechuana-
land, the Zambesi, Matabeleland and Mashonaland, the Portuguese settlement on
the Zambesi, Nyasaland, Ujiji, the headquarters of the Arabs, German East
Africa, Uganda (where he saw fighting in company with the late Major 'Roddy'
Owen), and British East Africa. In his book he relates his experiences, his
minute observations of native habits and customs, and his views as to the work
done in Africa by the various European Governments, whose operations he was
able to study. The whole journey extended over 7000 miles, and occupied
exactly three years.

WITH THE MOUNTED INFANTRY IN MASHONA-
LAND. By Lieut.-Colonel ALDERSON. With numerous Illustrations and Plans. *Demy 8vo.* 12*s.* 6*d.*

This is an account of the military operations in Mashonaland by the officer who
commanded the troops in that district during the late rebellion. Besides its
interest as a story of warfare, it will have a peculiar value as an account of the
services of mounted infantry by one of the chief authorities on the subject.

THE HILL OF THE GRACES: OR, THE GREAT STONE
TEMPLES OF TRIPOLI. By H. S. COWPER, F.S.A. With Maps,
Plans, and 75 Illustrations. *Demy 8vo.* 10*s.* 6*d.*

A record of two journeys through Tripoli in 1895 and 1896. The book treats of a
remarkable series of megalithic temples which have hitherto been uninvestigated,
and contains a large amount of new geographical and archæological matter.

ADVENTURE AND EXPLORATION IN AFRICA. By
Captain A. ST. H. GIBBONS, F.R.G.S. With Illustrations by
C. WHYMPER, and Maps. *Demy 8vo.* 21*s.*

This is an account of travel and adventure among the Marotse and contiguous tribes,
with a description of their customs, characteristics, and history, together with the
author's experiences in hunting big game. The illustrations are by Mr. Charles
Whymper, and from photographs. There is a map by the author of the hitherto
unexplored regions lying between the Zambesi and Kafukwi rivers and from 18°
to 15° S. lat.

History and Biography

A HISTORY OF EGYPT, FROM THE EARLIEST TIMES TO
THE PRESENT DAY. Edited by W. M. FLINDERS PETRIE, D.C.L.,
LL.D., Professor of Egyptology at University College. *Fully Illustrated. In Six Volumes. Crown 8vo. 6s. each.*
VOL. V. ROMAN EGYPT. By J. G. MILNE.

THE DECLINE AND FALL OF THE ROMAN EMPIRE.
By EDWARD GIBBON. A New Edition, edited with Notes,
Appendices, and Maps by J. B. BURY, M.A., Fellow of Trinity
College, Dublin. *In Seven Volumes. Demy 8vo, gilt top. 8s. 6d.
each. Crown 8vo. 6s. each. Vol. IV.*

THE LETTERS OF VICTOR HUGO. Translated from the
French by F. CLARKE, M.A. *In Two Volumes. Demy 8vo.
10s. 6d. each. Vol. II.* 1835-72.
This is the second volume of one of the most interesting and important collection of
letters ever published in France. The correspondence dates from Victor Hugo's
boyhood to his death, and none of the letters have been published before.

A HISTORY OF THE GREAT NORTHERN RAILWAY,
1845-95. By C. H. GRINLING. With Maps and Illustrations.
Demy 8vo. 10s. 6d.
A record of Railway enterprise and development in Northern England, containing
much matter hitherto unpublished. It appeals both to the general reader and to
those specially interested in railway construction and management.

A HISTORY OF BRITISH COLONIAL POLICY. By
H. E. EGERTON, M.A. *Demy 8vo. 12s. 6d.*
This book deals with British Colonial policy historically from the beginnings of
English colonisation down to the present day. The subject has been treated by
itself, and it has thus been possible within a reasonable compass to deal with a
mass of authority which must otherwise be sought in the State papers. The
volume is divided into five parts:—(1) The Period of Beginnings, 1497-1650;
(2) Trade Ascendancy, 1651-1830; (3) The Granting of Responsible Government,
1831-1860; (4) *Laissez Aller*, 1861-1885; (5) Greater Britain.

A HISTORY OF ANARCHISM. By E. V. ZENKER.
Translated from the German. *Demy 8vo. 7s. 6d.*
A critical study and history, as well as a powerful and trenchant criticism, of the
Anarchist movement in Europe. The book has aroused considerable attention
on the Continent.

THE LIFE OF ERNEST RENAN By MADAME DARMES-
TETER. With Portrait. *Crown 8vo. 6s.*
A biography of Renan by one of his most intimate friends.

A LIFE OF DONNE. By AUGUSTUS JESSOPP, D.D. With
Portrait. *Crown 8vo. 3s. 6d.*
This is a new volume of the 'Leaders of Religion' series, from the learned and witty
pen of the Rector of Scarning, who has been able to embody the results of much
research.

OLD HARROW DAYS. By J. G. COTTON MINCHIN. *Crown 8vo. 5s.*
A volume of reminiscences which will be interesting to old Harrovians and to many of the general public.

Theology

A PRIMER OF THE BIBLE. By Prof. W. H. BENNETT. *Crown 8vo. 2s. 6d.*
This Primer sketches the history of the books which make up the Bible, in the light of recent criticism. It gives an account of their character, origin, and composition, as far as possible in chronological order, with special reference to their relations to one another, and to the history of Israel and the Church. The formation of the Canon is illustrated by chapters on the Apocrypha (Old and New Testament); and there is a brief notice of the history of the Bible since the close of the Canon.

LIGHT AND LEAVEN : HISTORICAL AND SOCIAL SERMONS. By the Rev. H. HENSLEY HENSON, M.A., Fellow of All Souls', Incumbent of St. Mary's Hospital, Ilford. *Crown 8vo. 6s.*

𝔇𝔢𝔳𝔬𝔱𝔦𝔬𝔫𝔞𝔩 𝔖𝔢𝔯𝔦𝔢𝔰

THE CONFESSIONS OF ST. AUGUSTINE. Newly Translated, with an Introduction, by C. BIGG, D.D., late Student of Christ Church. With a Frontispiece. *18mo. 1s. 6d.*
This little book is the first volume of a new Devotional Series, printed in clear type, and published at a very low price.
This volume contains the nine books of the 'Confessions' which are suitable for devotional purposes. The name of the Editor is a sufficient guarantee of the excellence of the edition.

THE HOLY SACRIFICE. By F. WESTON, M.A., Curate of St. Matthew's, Westminster. *18mo. 1s.*
A small volume of devotions at the Holy Communion.

Naval and Military

A HISTORY OF THE ART OF WAR. By C. W. OMAN, M.A., Fellow of All Souls', Oxford. *Demy 8vo. Illustrated. 21s.*

Vol. II. MEDIÆVAL WARFARE.

Mr. Oman is engaged on a History of the Art of War, of which the above, though covering the middle period from the fall of the Roman Empire to the general use of gunpowder in Western Europe, is the first instalment. The first battle dealt with will be Adrianople (378) and the last Navarette (1367). There will appear later a volume dealing with the Art of War among the Ancients, and another covering the 15th, 16th, and 17th centuries.
The book will deal mainly with tactics and strategy, fortifications and siegecraft, but subsidiary chapters will give some account of the development of arms and armour, and of the various forms of military organization known to the Middle Ages.

A SHORT HISTORY OF THE ROYAL NAVY, FROM
EARLY TIMES TO THE PRESENT DAY. By DAVID HANNAY.
Illustrated. 2 *Vols. Demy 8vo.* 7*s.* 6*d. each.* Vol. I.

This book aims at giving an account not only of the fighting we have done at sea,
but of the growth of the service, of the part the Navy has played in the development of the Empire, and of its inner life.

THE STORY OF THE BRITISH ARMY. By Lieut.-Colonel
COOPER KING, of the Staff College, Camberley. Illustrated. *Demy*
8vo. 7*s.* 6*d.*

This volume aims at describing the nature of the different armies that have been
formed in Great Britain, and how from the early and feudal levies the present
standing army came to be. The changes in tactics, uniform, and armament are
briefly touched upon, and the campaigns in which the army has shared have
been so far followed as to explain the part played by British regiments in them.

General Literature

THE OLD ENGLISH HOME. By S. BARING-GOULD.
With numerous Plans and Illustrations. *Crown 8vo.* 7*s.* 6*d.*

This book, like Mr. Baring-Gould's well-known 'Old Country Life,' describes the
life and environment of an old English family.

OXFORD AND ITS COLLEGES. By J. WELLS, M.A.,
Fellow and Tutor of Wadham College. Illustrated by E. H. NEW.
Fcap. 8vo. 3*s.* *Leather.* 4*s.*

This is a guide—chiefly historical—to the Colleges of Oxford. It contains numerous
illustrations.

VOCES ACADEMICÆ. By C. GRANT ROBERTSON, M.A.,
Fellow of All Souls', Oxford. *With a Frontispiece.* *Fcap. 8vo.*
3*s.* 6*d.*

This is a volume of light satirical dialogues and should be read by all who are interested in the life of Oxford.

A PRIMER OF WORDSWORTH. By LAURIE MAGNUS.
Crown 8vo. 2*s.* 6*d.*

This volume is uniform with the Primers of Tennyson and Burns, and contains a
concise biography of the poet, a critical appreciation of his work in detail, and a
bibliography.

NEO-MALTHUSIANISM. By R. USSHER, M.A. *Cr. 8vo.* 6*s.*

This book deals with a very delicate but most important matter, namely, the voluntary limitation of the family, and how such action affects morality, the individual,
and the nation.

PRIMÆVAL SCENES. By H. N. HUTCHINSON, B.A., F.G.S.,
Author of 'Extinct Monsters,' 'Creatures of Other Days,' 'Pre-
historic Man and Beast,' etc. With numerous Illustrations drawn
by JOHN HASSALL and FRED. V. BURRIDGE. 4*to.* 6*s.*

A set of twenty drawings, with short text to each, to illustrate the humorous aspects
of pre-historic times. They are carefully planned by the author so as to be
scientifically and archæologically correct and at the same time amusing.

THE WALLYPUG IN LONDON. By G. E. FARROW,
Author of 'The Wallypug of Why.' With numerous Illustrations.
Crown 8vo. 3s. 6d.
An extravaganza for children, written with great charm and vivacity.

RAILWAY NATIONALIZATION. By CLEMENT EDWARDS.
Crown 8vo. 2s. 6d.   [*Social Questions Series.*

Sport

SPORTING AND ATHLETIC RECORDS. By H. MORGAN
BROWNE. *Crown 8vo.* 1s. *paper;* 2s. *cloth.*
This book gives, in a clear and complete form, accurate records of the best perform-
ances in all important branches of Sport. It is an attempt, never yet made, to
present all-important sporting records in a systematic way.

THE GOLFING PILGRIM. By HORACE G HUTCHINSON.
Crown 8vo. 6s.
This book, by a famous golfer, contains the following sketches lightly and humorously
written :—The Prologue—The Pilgrim at the Shrine—Mecca out of Season—The
Pilgrim at Home—The Pilgrim Abroad—The Life of the Links—A Tragedy by
the Way—Scraps from the Scrip—The Golfer in Art—Early Pilgrims in the West
—An Interesting Relic.

Educational

EVAGRIUS. Edited by PROFESSOR LÉON PARMENTIER of
Liége and M. BIDEZ of Gand. *Demy 8vo.* 7s. 6d.
        [*Byzantine Texts.*

THE ODES AND EPODES OF HORACE. Translated by
A. D. GODLEY, M.A., Fellow of Magdalen College, Oxford.
Crown 8vo. buckram. 2s.

ORNAMENTAL DESIGN FOR WOVEN FABRICS. By
C. STEPHENSON, of The Technical College, Bradford, and
F. SUDDARDS, of The Yorkshire College, Leeds. With 65 full-page
plates, and numerous designs and diagrams in the text. *Demy 8vo.*
7s. 6d.
The aim of this book is to supply, in a systematic and practical form, information on
the subject of Decorative Design as applied to Woven Fabrics, and is primarily
intended to meet the requirements of students in Textile and Art Schools, or of
designers actively engaged in the weaving industry. Its wealth of illustration is
a marked feature of the book.

ESSENTIALS OF COMMERCIAL EDUCATION. By
E. E. WHITFIELD, M.A. *Crown 8vo.* 1s. 6d.
A guide to Commercial Education and Examinations.

PASSAGES FOR UNSEEN TRANSLATION. By E. C. MARCHANT, M.A., Fellow of Peterhouse, Cambridge; and A. M. COOK, M.A., late Scholar of Wadham College, Oxford: Assistant Masters at St. Paul's School. *Crown 8vo.* 3s. 6d.

This book contains Two Hundred Latin and Two Hundred Greek Passages, and has been very carefully compiled to meet the wants of V. and VI. Form Boys at Public Schools. It is also well adapted for the use of Honour men at the Universities.

EXERCISES IN LATIN ACCIDENCE. By S. E. WINBOLT, Assistant Master in Christ's Hospital. *Crown 8vo.* 1s. 6d.

An elementary book adapted for Lower Forms to accompany the shorter Latin primer

NOTES ON GREEK AND LATIN SYNTAX. By G. BUCKLAND GREEN, M.A., Assistant Master at the Edinburgh Academy, late Fellow of St. John's College, Oxon. *Cr. 8vo.* 3s. 6d.

Notes and explanations on the chief difficulties of Greek and Latin Syntax, with numerous passages for exercise.

A DIGEST OF DEDUCTIVE LOGIC. By JOHNSON BARKER, B.A. *Crown 8vo.* 2s. 6d.

A short introduction to logic for students preparing for examinations.

TEST CARDS IN EUCLID AND ALGEBRA. By D. S. CALDERWOOD, Headmaster of the Normal School, Edinburgh. In a Packet of 40, with Answers. 1s.

A set of cards for advanced pupils in elementary schools.

HOW TO MAKE A DRESS. By J. A. E. WOOD. Illustrated. *Crown 8vo.* 1s. 6d.

A text-book for students preparing for the City and Guilds examination, based on the syllabus. The diagrams are numerous.

Fiction

LOCHINVAR. By S. R. CROCKETT, Author of 'The Raiders,' etc. Illustrated by FRANK RICHARDS. *Crown 8vo.* 6s.

BYEWAYS. By ROBERT HICHENS. Author of 'Flames,' etc. *Crown 8vo.* 6s.

THE MUTABLE MANY. By ROBERT BARR, Author of 'In the Midst of Alarms,' 'A Woman Intervenes,' etc. *Crown 8vo.* 6s.

THE LADY'S WALK. By Mrs. OLIPHANT. *Crown 8vo.* 6s.

A new book by this lamented author, somewhat in the style of her 'Beleagured City.'

TRAITS AND CONFIDENCES. By The Hon. EMILY LAW-
LESS, Author of ' Hurrish,' ' Maelcho,' etc.   *Crown 8vo.*   6s.

BLADYS.   By S. BARING GOULD, Author of 'The Broom
Squire,' etc.   Illustrated by F. H. TOWNSEND.   *Crown 8vo.*   6s.
A Romance of the last century.

THE POMP OF THE LAVILETTES. By GILBERT PARKER,
Author of ' The Seats of the Mighty,' etc.   *Crown 8vo.*   3s. 6d.

A DAUGHTER OF STRIFE. By JANE HELEN FINDLATER,
Author of ' The Green Graves of Balgowrie.'   *Crown 8vo.*   6s.
A story of 1710.

OVER THE HILLS. By MARY FINDLATER. *Crown 8vo.* 6s.
A novel by a sister of J. H. Findlater, the author of ' The Green Graves of Balgowrie.'

A CREEL OF IRISH STORIES. By JANE BARLOW, Author
of ' Irish Idylls.'   *Crown 8vo.*   6s.

THE CLASH OF ARMS. By J. BLOUNDELLE BURTON,
Author of ' In the Day of Adversity.'   *Crown 8vo.*   6s.

A PASSIONATE PILGRIM. By PERCY WHITE, Author of
' Mr. Bailey-Martin.'   *Crown 8vo.*   6s.

SECRETARY TO BAYNE, M.P.   By W. PETT RIDGE.
Crown 8vo.   6s.

THE BUILDERS. By J. S. FLETCHER, Author of ' When
Charles I. was King.'   *Crown 8vo.*   6s.

JOSIAH'S WIFE. By NORMA LORIMER. *Crown 8vo.* 6s.

BY STROKE OF SWORD.   By ANDREW BALFOUR.   Illustrated by W. CUBITT COOKE.   *Crown 8vo.*   6s.
A romance of the time of Elizabeth

THE SINGER OF MARLY. By I. HOOPER.   Illustrated
by W. CUBITT COOKE.   *Crown 8vo.*   6s.
A romance of adventure.

KIRKHAM'S FIND.   By MARY GAUNT, Author of 'The
Moving Finger.'   *Crown 8vo.*   6s.

THE FALL OF THE SPARROW. By M. C. BALFOUR.
Crown 8vo.   6s.

SCOTTISH BORDER LIFE.   By JAMES C. DIBDIN.   *Crown
8vo.*   3s. 6d.

MESSRS. METHUEN'S
PUBLICATIONS

———◆———

Poetry

RUDYARD KIPLING'S NEW POEMS

Rudyard Kipling. THE SEVEN SEAS. By RUDYARD
KIPLING. *Third Edition. Crown 8vo. Buckram, gilt top. 6s.*
'The new poems of Mr. Rudyard Kipling have all the spirit and swing of their pre-
    decessors. Patriotism is the solid concrete foundation on which Mr. Kipling has
    built the whole of his work.'—*Times.*
'Full of passionate patriotism and the Imperial spirit.'—*Yorkshire Post.*
'The Empire has found a singer; it is no depreciation of the songs to say that states-
    men may have, one way or other, to take account of them.'—*Manchester
    Guardian.*
'Animated through and through with indubitable genius.'—*Daily Telegraph.*
'Packed with inspiration, with humour, with pathos.'—*Daily Chronicle.*
'All the pride of empire, all the intoxication of power, all the ardour, the energy,
    the masterful strength and the wonderful endurance and death-scorning pluck
    which are the very bone and fibre and marrow of the British character are here.'
    —*Daily Mail.*

Rudyard Kipling. BARRACK-ROOM BALLADS; And
Other Verses. By RUDYARD KIPLING. *Twelfth Edition. Crown
8vo. 6s.*
'Mr. Kipling's verse is strong, vivid, full of character. . . . Unmistakable genius
    rings in every line.'—*Times.*
The ballads teem with imagination, they palpitate with emotion. We read them
    with laughter and tears; the metres throb in our pulses, the cunningly ordered
    words tingle with life; and if this be not poetry, what is?'—*Pall Mall Gazette.*

'Q." POEMS AND BALLADS. By "Q.," Author of 'Green
Bays,' etc. *Crown 8vo. Buckram. 3s. 6d.*
'This work has just the faint, ineffable touch and glow that make poetry 'Q.' has
    the true romantic spirit.'—*Speaker.*

"Q." GREEN BAYS: Verses and Parodies. By "Q.," Author
of 'Dead Man's Rock,' etc. *Second Edition. Crown 8vo. 3s. 6d.*
'The verses display a rare and versatile gift of parody, great command of metre, and
    a very pretty turn of humour.'—*Times.*

E. Mackay. A SONG OF THE SEA. By ERIC MACKAY,
Author of 'The Love Letters of a Violinist.' *Second Edition.
Fcap. 8vo. 5s.*
'Everywhere Mr. Mackay displays himself the master of a style marked by all the
    characteristics of the best rhetoric. He has a keen sense of rhythm and of general
    balance; his verse is excellently sonorous.'—*Globe.*

Ibsen. BRAND. A Drama by HENRIK IBSEN. Translated by WILLIAM WILSON. *Second Edition. Crown 8vo.* 3s. 6d.

'The greatest world-poem of the nineteenth century next to "Faust." It is in the same set with "Agamemnon," with "Lear," with the literature that we now instinctively regard as high and holy.'—*Daily Chronicle.*

"A. G." VERSES TO ORDER. By "A. G." *Cr. 8vo.* 2s. 6d. *net.*

A small volume of verse by a writer whose initials are well known to Oxford men.
'A capital specimen of light academic poetry. These verses are very bright and engaging, easy and sufficiently witty.'—*St. James's Gazette.*

Belles Lettres, Anthologies, etc.

R. L. Stevenson. VAILIMA LETTERS. By ROBERT LOUIS STEVENSON. With an Etched Portrait by WILLIAM STRANG, and other Illustrations. *Second Edition. Crown 8vo. Buckram.* 7s. 6d.

'Few publications have in our time been more eagerly awaited than these "Vailima Letters," giving the first fruits of the correspondence of Robert Louis Stevenson. But, high as the tide of expectation has run, no reader can possibly be disappointed in the result.'—*St. James's Gazette.*

Henley and Whibley. A BOOK OF ENGLISH PROSE. Collected by W. E. HENLEY and CHARLES WHIBLEY. *Crown 8vo.* 6s.

'A unique volume of extracts—an art gallery of early prose.'—*Birmingham Post.*
'An admirable companion to Mr. Henley's "Lyra Heroica."'—*Saturday Review.*
'Quite delightful. A greater treat for those not well acquainted with pre-Restoration prose could not be imagined.'—*Athenæum.*

H. C. Beeching. LYRA SACRA : An Anthology of Sacred Verse. Edited by H. C. BEECHING, M.A. *Crown 8vo. Buckram.* 6s.

'A charming selection, which maintains a lofty standard of excellence.'—*Times.*

"Q." THE GOLDEN POMP : A Procession of English Lyrics from Surrey to Shirley, arranged by A. T. QUILLER COUCH. *Crown 8vo. Buckram.* 6s.

'A delightful volume : a really golden "Pomp."'—*Spectator.*

W. B. Yeats. AN ANTHOLOGY OF IRISH VERSE. Edited by W. B. YEATS. *Crown 8vo.* 3s. 6d.

'An attractive and catholic selection.'—*Times.*

G. W. Steevens. MONOLOGUES OF THE DEAD. By G. W. STEEVENS. *Foolscap 8vo.* 3s. 6d.

A series of Soliloquies in which famous men of antiquity—Julius Cæsar, Nero, Alcibiades, etc., attempt to express themselves in the modes of thought and language of to-day.
The effect is sometimes splendid, sometimes bizarre, but always amazingly clever —*Pall Mall Gazette.*

Victor Hugo. THE LETTERS OF VICTOR HUGO. Translated from the French by F..CLARKE, M.A. *In Two Volumes. Demy 8vo.* 10*s.* 6*d. each. Vol. I.* 1815-35.

This is the first volume of one of the most interesting and important collection of letters ever published in France. The correspondence dates from Victor Hugo's boyhood to his death, and none of the letters have been published before. The arrangement is chiefly chronological, but where there is an interesting set of letters to one person these are arranged together. The first volume contains, among others, (1) Letters to his father; (2) to his young wife; (3) to his confessor, Lamennais; a very important set of about fifty letters to Sainte-Beauve; (5) letters about his early books and plays.

'A charming and vivid picture of a man whose egotism never marred his natural kindness, and whose vanity did not impair his greatness.'—*Standard.*

C. H. Pearson. ESSAYS AND CRITICAL REVIEWS. By C. H. PEARSON, M.A., Author of 'National Life and Character.' Edited, with a Biographical Sketch, by H. A. STRONG, M.A., LL.D. With a Portrait. *Demy 8vo.* 10*s.* 6*d.*

'Remarkable for careful handling, breadth of view, and knowledge.'—*Scotsman.*
'Charming essays.'—*Spectator.*

W. M. Dixon. A PRIMER OF TENNYSON. By W. M. DIXON, M.A., Professor of English Literature at Mason College. *Crown 8vo.* 2*s.* 6*d.*

'Much sound and well-expressed criticism and acute literary judgments. The bibliography is a boon.'—*Speaker.*

W. A. Craigie. A PRIMER OF BURNS. By W. A. CRAIGIE. *Crown 8vo.* 2*s.* 6*d.*

This book is planned on a method similar to the 'Primer of Tennyson.' It has also a glossary.
'A valuable addition to the literature of the poet.'—*Times.*
'An excellent short account.'—*Pall Mall Gazette.*
'An admirable introduction.'—*Globe.*

Sterne. THE LIFE AND OPINIONS OF TRISTRAM SHANDY. By LAWRENCE STERNE. With an Introduction by CHARLES WHIBLEY, and a Portrait. 2 *vols.* 7*s.*

'Very dainty volumes are these; the paper, type, and light-green binding are all very agreeable to the eye. *Simplex munditiis* is the phrase that might be applied to them.'—*Globe.*

Congreve. THE COMEDIES OF WILLIAM CONGREVE. With an Introduction by G. S. STREET, and a Portrait. 2 *vols.* 7*s.*

'The volumes are strongly bound in green buckram, are of a convenient size, and pleasant to look upon, so that whether on the shelf, or on the table, or in the hand the possessor is thoroughly content with them.'—*Guardian.*

Morier. THE ADVENTURES OF HAJJI BABA OF ISPAHAN. By JAMES MORIER. With an Introduction by E. G. BROWNE, M.A., and a Portrait. 2 *vols.* 7*s.*

Walton. THE LIVES OF DONNE, WOTTON, HOOKER, HERBERT, AND SANDERSON. By IZAAK WALTON. With an Introduction by VERNON BLACKBURN, and a Portrait. 3*s.* 6*d.*

Johnson. THE LIVES OF THE ENGLISH POETS. By SAMUEL JOHNSON, LL.D. With an Introduction by J. H. MILLAR, and a Portrait. 3 *vols.* 10*s.* 6*d.*

Burns. THE POEMS OF ROBERT BURNS. Edited by ANDREW LANG and W. A. CRAIGIE. With Portrait. *Demy 8vo,* *gilt top.* 6*s.*

This edition contains a carefully collated Text, numerous Notes, critical and textual, a critical and biographical Introduction, and a Glossary.
'Among the editions in one volume, Mr. Andrew Lang's will take the place of authority.'—*Times.*

F. Langbridge. BALLADS OF THE BRAVE : Poems of Chivalry, Enterprise, Courage, and Constancy. Edited, with Notes, by Rev. F. LANGBRIDGE. *Crown 8vo. Buckram.* 3*s.* 6*d.* *School Edition.* 2*s.* 6*d.*

'A very happy conception happily carried out. These "Ballads of the Brave" are intended to suit the real tastes of boys, and will suit the taste of the great majority.' —*Spectator.* 'The book is full of splendid things.'—*World.*

Illustrated Books

Jane Barlow. THE BATTLE OF THE FROGS AND MICE, translated by JANE BARLOW, Author of 'Irish Idylls,' and pictured by F. D. BEDFORD. *Small 4to.* 6*s. net.*

S. Baring Gould. A BOOK OF FAIRY TALES retold by S. BARING GOULD. With numerous illustrations and initial letters by ARTHUR J. GASKIN. *Second Edition. Crown 8vo. Buckram.* 6*s.*

'Mr. Baring Gould is deserving of gratitude, in re-writing in honest, simple style the old stories that delighted the childhood of "our fathers and grandfathers." As to the form of the book, and the printing, which is by Messrs. Constable, it were difficult to commend overmuch. —*Saturday Review.*

S. Baring Gould. OLD ENGLISH FAIRY TALES. Collected and edited by S. BARING GOULD. With Numerous Illustrations by F. D. BEDFORD. *Second Edition. Crown 8vo. Buckram.* 6*s.*

'A charming volume, which children will be sure to appreciate. The stories have been selected with great ingenuity from various old ballads and folk-tales, and, having been somewhat altered and readjusted, now stand forth, clothed in Mr. Baring Gould's delightful English, to enchant youthful readers.'—*Guardian.*

S. Baring Gould. A BOOK OF NURSERY SONGS AND RHYMES. Edited by S. BARING GOULD, and Illustrated by the Birmingham Art School. *Buckram, gilt top. Crown 8vo.* 6*s.*

'The volume is very complete in its way, as it contains nursery songs to the number of 77, game-rhymes, and jingles. To the student we commend the sensible introduction, and the explanatory notes. The volume is superbly printed on soft, thick paper, which it is a pleasure to touch ; and the borders and pictures are among the very best specimens we have seen of the Gaskin school.'—*Birmingham Gazette.*

H. C. Beeching. A BOOK OF CHRISTMAS VERSE. Edited by H. C. BEECHING, M.A., and Illustrated by WALTER CRANE. *Crown 8vo, gilt top.* 5s.

A collection of the best verse inspired by the birth of Christ from the Middle Ages to the present day. A distinction of the book is the large number of poems it contains by modern authors, a few of which are here printed for the first time.

'An anthology which, from its unity of aim and high poetic excellence, has a better right to exist than most of its fellows.'—*Guardian.*

History

Gibbon. THE DECLINE AND FALL OF THE ROMAN EMPIRE. By EDWARD GIBBON. A New Edition, Edited with Notes, Appendices, and Maps, by J. B. BURY, M.A., Fellow of Trinity College, Dublin. *In Seven Volumes. Demy 8vo. Gilt top.* 8s. 6d. each. *Also crown 8vo.* 6s. each. *Vols. I., II., and III.*

'The time has certainly arrived for a new edition of Gibbon's great work. . . . Professor Bury is the right man to undertake this task. His learning is amazing, both in extent and accuracy. The book is issued in a handy form, and at a moderate price, and it is admirably printed.'—*Times.*

'The edition is edited as a classic should be edited, removing nothing, yet indicating the value of the text, and bringing it up to date. It promises to be of the utmost value, and will be a welcome addition to many libraries.'—*Scotsman.*

'This edition, so far as one may judge from the first instalment, is a marvel of erudition and critical skill, and it is the very minimum of praise to predict that the seven volumes of it will supersede Dean Milman's as the standard edition of our great historical classic.'—*Glasgow Herald.*

'The beau-ideal Gibbon has arrived at last.'—*Sketch.*

'At last there is an adequate modern edition of Gibbon. . . . The best edition the nineteenth century could produce.'—*Manchester Guardian.*

Flinders Petrie. A HISTORY OF EGYPT, FROM THE EARLIEST TIMES TO THE PRESENT DAY. Edited by W. M. FLINDERS PETRIE, D.C.L., LL.D., Professor of Egyptology at University College. *Fully Illustrated. In Six Volumes. Crown 8vo.* 6s. each.

    Vol. I. PREHISTORIC TIMES TO XVI. DYNASTY. W. M. F. Petrie. *Third Edition.*

    Vol. II. THE XVIITH AND XVIIITH DYNASTIES. W. M. F. Petrie. *Second Edition.*

'A history written in the spirit of scientific precision so worthily represented by Dr. Petrie and his school cannot but promote sound and accurate study, and supply a vacant place in the English literature of Egyptology.'—*Times.*

Flinders Petrie. EGYPTIAN TALES. Edited by W. M. FLINDERS PETRIE. Illustrated by TRISTRAM ELLIS. *In Two Volumes. Crown 8vo.* 3s. 6d. each.

'A valuable addition to the literature of comparative folk-lore. The drawings are really illustrations in the literal sense of the word.'—*Globe.*

'It has a scientific value to the student of history and archæology.'—*Scotsman.*

'Invaluable as a picture of life in Palestine and Egypt.'—*Daily News.*

Flinders Petrie. EGYPTIAN DECORATIVE ART. By W. M. FLINDERS PETRIE, D.C.L. With 120 Illustrations. *Crown 8vo. 3s. 6d.*

'Professor Flinders Petrie is not only a profound Egyptologist, but an accomplished student of comparative archæology. In these lectures, delivered at the Royal Institution, he displays both qualifications with rare skill in elucidating the development of decorative art in Egypt, and in tracing its influence on the art of other countries.'—*Times.*

S. Baring Gould. THE TRAGEDY OF THE CÆSARS. The Emperors of the Julian and Claudian Lines. With numerous Illustrations from Busts, Gems, Cameos, etc. By S. BARING GOULD, Author of 'Mehalah,' etc. *Fourth Edition. Royal 8vo.* 15s.

'A most splendid and fascinating book on a subject of undying interest. The great feature of the book is the use the author has made of the existing portraits of the Caesars, and the admirable critical subtlety he has exhibited in dealing with this line of research. It is brilliantly written, and the illustrations are supplied on a scale of profuse magnificence.'—*Daily Chronicle.*
'The volumes will in no sense disappoint the general reader. Indeed, in their way, there is nothing in any sense so good in English. . . . Mr. Baring Gould has presented his narrative in such a way as not to make one dull page.'—*Athenæum.*

H. de B. Gibbins. INDUSTRY IN ENGLAND : HISTORI-CAL OUTLINES. By H. DE B. GIBBINS, M.A., D.Litt. With 5 Maps. *Second Edition. Demy 8vo.* 10s. 6d.

This book is written with the view of affording a clear view of the main facts of English Social and Industrial History placed in due perspective. Beginning with prehistoric times, it passes in review the growth and advance of industry up to the nineteenth century, showing its gradual development and progress. The book is illustrated by Maps, Diagrams, and Tables.

A. Clark. THE COLLEGES OF OXFORD : Their History and their Traditions. By Members of the University. Edited by A. CLARK, M.A., Fellow and Tutor of Lincoln College. *8vo.* 12s. 6d.

'A work which will certainly be appealed to for many years as the standard book on the Colleges of Oxford.'—*Athenæum.*

Perrens. THE HISTORY OF FLORENCE FROM 1434 TO 1492. By F. T. PERRENS. Translated by HANNAH LYNCH. *8vo.* 12s. 6d.

A history of Florence under the domination of Cosimo, Piero, and Lorenzo de Medicis.
'This is a standard book by an honest and intelligent historian, who has deserved well of all who are interested in Italian history.'—*Manchester Guardian.*

J. Wells. A SHORT HISTORY OF ROME. By J. WELLS, M.A., Fellow and Tutor of Wadham Coll., Oxford. With 4 Maps. *Crown 8vo. 3s. 6d.*

This book is intended for the Middle and Upper Forms of Public Schools and for Pass Students at the Universities. It contains copious Tables, etc.
'An original work written on an original plan, and with uncommon freshness and vigour.'—*Speaker.*

E. L. S. Horsburgh. THE CAMPAIGN OF WATERLOO.
By E. L. S. HORSBURGH, B.A. *With Plans. Crown 8vo. 5s.*

'A brilliant essay—simple, sound, and thorough.'—*Daily Chronicle.*
'A study, the most concise, the most lucid, the most critical that has been produced.
—*Birmingham Mercury.*

H. B. George. BATTLES OF ENGLISH HISTORY. By H. B.
GEORGE, M.A., Fellow of New College, Oxford. *With numerous
Plans. Third Edition. Crown 8vo. 6s.*

'Mr. George has undertaken a very useful task—that of making military affairs intelligible and instructive to non-military readers—and has executed it with laudable intelligence and industry, and with a large measure of success.'—*Times.*

O. Browning. A SHORT HISTORY OF MEDIÆVAL ITALY,
A.D. 1250-1530. By OSCAR BROWNING, Fellow and Tutor of King's
College, Cambridge. *Second Edition. In Two Volumes. Crown
8vo. 5s. each.*

> VOL. I. 1250-1409.—Guelphs and Ghibellines.
> VOL. II. 1409-1530.—The Age of the Condottieri.

'A vivid picture of mediæval Italy.'—*Standard.*
'Mr. Browning is to be congratulated on the production of a work of immense labour and learning.'—*Westminster Gazette.*

O'Grady. THE STORY OF IRELAND. By STANDISH
O'GRADY, Author of 'Finn and his Companions.' *Cr. 8vo. 2s. 6d.*

'Most delightful, most stimulating. Its racy humour, its original imaginings, make it one of the freshest, breeziest volumes.'—*Methodist Times.*

Biography

S. Baring Gould. THE LIFE OF NAPOLEON BONA-
PARTE. By S. BARING GOULD. With over 450 Illustrations in
the Text and 12 Photogravure Plates. *Large quarto. Gilt top. 36s.*

'The best biography of Napoleon in our tongue, nor have the French as good a biographer of their hero. A book very nearly as good as Southey's "Life of Nelson."'—*Manchester Guardian.*
'The main feature of this gorgeous volume is its great wealth of beautiful photogravures and finely-executed wood engravings, constituting a complete pictorial chronicle of Napoleon I.'s personal history from the days of his early childhood at Ajaccio to the date of his second interment under the dome of the Invalides in Paris.'—*Daily Telegraph.*
'The most elaborate account of Napoleon ever produced by an English writer.'—*Daily Chronicle.*
'A brilliant and attractive volume. Never before have so many pictures relating to Napoleon been brought within the limits of an English book.'—*Globe.*
'Particular notice is due to the vast collection of contemporary illustrations.'—*Guardian.*
'Nearly all the illustrations are real contributions to history.'—*Westminster Gazette.*
'The illustrations are of supreme interest.'—*Standard.*

Morris Fuller. THE LIFE AND WRITINGS OF JOHN
DAVENANT, D.D. (1571-1641), President of Queen's College,
Lady Margaret Professor of Divinity, Bishop of Salisbury. By
MORRIS FULLER, B.D. *Demy 8vo.* 10s. 6d.

'A valuable contribution to ecclesiastical history.'—*Birmingham Gazette.*

J. M. Rigg. ST. ANSELM OF CANTERBURY: A CHAPTER
IN THE HISTORY OF RELIGION. By J. M. RIGG. *Demy 8vo.* 7s. 6d.

'Mr. Rigg has told the story of the great Primate's life with scholarly ability, and
has thereby contributed an interesting chapter to the history of the Norman period.'
—*Daily Chronicle.*

F. W. Joyce. THE LIFE OF SIR FREDERICK GORE
OUSELEY. By F. W. JOYCE, M.A. With Portraits and Illustrations. *Crown 8vo.* 7s. 6d.

'This book has been undertaken in quite the right spirit, and written with sympathy
insight, and considerable literary skill.'—*Times.*

W. G. Collingwood. THE LIFE OF JOHN RUSKIN. By
W. G. COLLINGWOOD, M.A., Editor of Mr. Ruskin's Poems. With
numerous Portraits, and 13 Drawings by Mr. Ruskin. *Second
Edition.* 2 vols. 8vo. 32s.

'No more magnificent volumes have been published for a long time.'—*Times.*
'It is long since we had a biography with such delights of substance and of form.
Such a book is a pleasure for the day, and a joy for ever.'—*Daily Chronicle.*

C. Waldstein. JOHN RUSKIN: a Study. By CHARLES
WALDSTEIN, M.A., Fellow of King's College, Cambridge. With a
Photogravure Portrait after Professor HERKOMER. *Post 8vo.* 5s.

'A thoughtful, impartial, well-written criticism of Ruskin's teaching, intended to
separate what the author regards as valuable and permanent from what is transient
and erroneous in the great master's writing.'—*Daily Chronicle.*

W. H. Hutton. THE LIFE OF SIR THOMAS MORE. By
W. H. HUTTON, M.A., Author of 'William Laud.' *With Portraits.*
Crown 8vo. 5s.

'The book lays good claim to high rank among our biographies. It is excellently,
even lovingly, written.'—*Scotsman.*   'An excellent monograph.'—*Times.*

Clark Russell. THE LIFE OF ADMIRAL LORD COL-
LINGWOOD. By W. CLARK RUSSELL, Author of 'The Wreck
of the Grosvenor.' With Illustrations by F. BRANGWYN. *Third
Edition. Crown 8vo.* 6s.

'A book which we should like to see in the hands of every boy in the country.'—
St. James's Gazette.   'A really good book.'—*Saturday Review.*

A 3

Southey. ENGLISH SEAMEN (Howard, Clifford, Hawkins, Drake, Cavendish). By ROBERT SOUTHEY. Edited, with an Introduction, by DAVID HANNAY. *Second Edition. Crown 8vo.* 6s.

'Admirable and well-told stories of our naval history.'—*Army and Navy Gazette.*
'A brave, inspiriting book.'—*Black and White.*

Travel, Adventure and Topography

R. S. S. Baden-Powell. THE DOWNFALL OF PREMPEH. A Diary of Life with the Native Levy in Ashanti, 1895. By Colonel BADEN-POWELL. With 21 Illustrations and a Map. *Demy 8vo.* 10s. 6d.

'A compact, faithful, most readable record of the campaign.'—*Daily News.*
'A bluff and vigorous narrative.'—*Glasgow Herald.*

R. S. S. Baden-Powell. THE MATEBELE CAMPAIGN 1896. By Colonel R. S. S. BADEN-POWELL. With nearly 100 Illustrations. *Second Edition. Demy 8vo.* 15s.

'Written in an unaffectedly light and humorous style.'—*The World.*
'A very racy and eminently readable book.'—*St. James's Gazette.*
'As a straightforward account of a great deal of plucky work unpretentiously done, this book is well worth reading. The simplicity of the narrative is all in its favour, and accords in a peculiarly English fashion with the nature of the subject.' *Times.*

Captain Hinde. THE FALL OF THE CONGO ARABS. By SIDNEY L. HINDE. With Portraits and Plans. *Demy 8vo.* 12s. 6d.

'The book is full of good things, and of sustained interest.'—*St. James's Gazette.*
A graphic sketch of one of the most exciting and important episodes in the struggle for supremacy in Central Africa between the Arabs and their Europeon rival. Apart from the story of the campaign, Captain Hinde's book is mainly remarkable for the fulness with which he discusses the question of cannibalism. It is, indeed, the only connected narrative—in English, at any rate—which has been published of this particular episode in African history.'—*Times.*
'Captain Hinde's book is one of the most interesting and valuable contributions yet made to the literature of modern Africa.'—*Daily News.*

W. Crooke. THE NORTH-WESTERN PROVINCES OF INDIA: THEIR ETHNOLOGY AND ADMINISTRATION. By W. CROOKE. With Maps and Illustrations. *Demy 8vo.* 10s. 6d.

'A carefully and well-written account of one of the most important provinces of the Empire. In seven chapters Mr. Crooke deals successively with the land in its physical aspect, the province under Hindoo and Mussulman rule, the province under British rule, the ethnology and sociology of the province, the religious and social life of the people, the land and its settlement, and the native peasant in his relation to the land. The illustrations are good and well selected, and the map is excellent.'—*Manchester Guardian.*

W. B. Worsfold. SOUTH AFRICA : Its History and its Future. By W. BASIL WORSFOLD, M.A. *With a Map. Second Edition. Crown 8vo. 6s.*

'An intensely interesting book.'—*Daily Chronicle.*

'A monumental work compressed into a very moderate compass.'—*World.*

General Literature

S. Baring Gould. OLD COUNTRY LIFE. By S. BARING GOULD, Author of ' Mehalah,' etc. With Sixty-seven Illustrations by W. PARKINSON, F. D. BEDFORD, and F. MASEY. *Large Crown 8vo.* 10s. 6d. *Fifth and Cheaper Edition.* 6s.

' "Old Country Life," as healthy wholesome reading, full of breezy life and move-ment, full of quaint stories vigorously told, will not be excelled by any book to be published throughout the year. Sound, hearty, and English to the core.'—*World.*

S. Baring Gould. HISTORIC ODDITIES AND STRANGE EVENTS. By S. BARING GOULD. *Third Edition. Crown 8vo.* 6s.

'A collection of exciting and entertaining chapters. The whole volume is delightful reading.'—*Times.*

S. Baring Gould. FREAKS OF FANATICISM. By S. BARING GOULD. *Third Edition. Crown 8vo.* 6s.

'Mr. Baring Gould has a keen eye for colour and effect, and the subjects he has chosen give ample scope to his descriptive and analytic faculties. A perfectly fascinating book.'—*Scottish Leader.*

S. Baring Gould. A GARLAND OF COUNTRY SONG : English Folk Songs with their Traditional Melodies. Collected and arranged by S. BARING GOULD and H. FLEETWOOD SHEPPARD. *Demy 4to.* 6s.

S. Baring Gould. SONGS OF THE WEST : Traditional Ballads and Songs of the West of England, with their Traditional Melodies. Collected by S. BARING GOULD, M.A., and H. FLEET-WOOD SHEPPARD, M.A. Arranged for Voice and Piano. In 4 Parts (containing 25 Songs each), *Parts I., II., III., 3s. each. Part IV., 5s. In one Vol., French morocco, 15s.*

'A rich collection of humour, pathos, grace, and poetic fancy.'—*Saturday Review.*

S. Baring Gould. YORKSHIRE ODDITIES AND STRANGE EVENTS. *Fourth Edition. Crown 8vo. 6s.*

S. Baring Gould. STRANGE SURVIVALS AND SUPER-STITIONS. With Illustrations. By S. BARING GOULD. *Crown 8vo. Second Edition. 6s.*

'We have read Mr. Baring Gould's book from beginning to end. It is full of quaint and various information, and there is not a dull page in it.'—*Notes and Queries.*

S. Baring Gould. THE DESERTS OF SOUTHERN FRANCE. By S. BARING·GOULD. With numerous Illustrations by F. D. BEDFORD, S. HUTTON, etc. *2 vols. Demy 8vo. 32s.*

'His two richly-illustrated volumes are full of matter of interest to the geologist, the archæologist, and the student of history and manners.'--*Scotsman.*

G. W. Steevens. NAVAL POLICY: WITH A DESCRIP-TION OF ENGLISH AND FOREIGN NAVIES. By G. W. STEEVENS. *Demy 8vo. 6s.*

This book is a description of the British and other more important navies of the world, with a sketch of the lines on which our naval policy might possibly be developed. It describes our recent naval policy, and shows what our naval force really is. A detailed but non-technical account is given of the instruments of modern warfare—guns, armour, engines, and the like—with a view to determine how far we are abreast of modern invention and modern requirements. An ideal policy is then sketched for the building and manning of our fleet; and the last chapter is devoted to docks, coaling-stations, and especially colonial defence.

'An extremely able and interesting work.'—*Daily Chronicle.*

W. E. Gladstone. THE SPEECHES AND PUBLIC AD-DRESSES OF THE RT. HON. W. E. GLADSTONE, M.P. Edited by A. W. HUTTON, M.A., and H. J. COHEN, M.A. With Portraits. *8vo. Vols. IX. and X. 12s. 6d. each.*

J. Wells. OXFORD AND OXFORD LIFE. By Members of the University. Edited by J. WELLS, M.A., Fellow and Tutor of Wadham College. *Crown 8vo. 3s. 6d.*

'We congratulate Mr. Wells on the production of a readable and intelligent account of Oxford as it is at the present time, written by persons who are possessed of a close acquaintance with the system and life of the University.'—*Athenæum.*

L. Whibley. GREEK OLIGARCHIES: THEIR ORGANISA-TION AND CHARACTER. By L. WHIBLEY, M.A., Fellow of Pembroke College, Cambridge. *Crown 8vo. 6s.*

'An exceedingly useful handbook: a careful and well-arranged study of an obscure subject.'—*Times.*

'Mr. Whibley is never tedious or pedantic.'—*Pall Mall Gazette.*

L. L. Price. ECONOMIC SCIENCE AND PRACTICE. By L. L. PRICE, M.A., Fellow of Oriel College, Oxford. *Crown 8vo.* 6s.

'The book is well written, giving evidence of considerable literary ability, and clear mental grasp of the subject under consideration.'—*Western Morning News.*

C. F. Andrews. CHRISTIANITY AND THE LABOUR QUESTION. By C. F. ANDREWS, B.A. *Crown 8vo.* 2s. 6d.

'A bold and scholarly survey.'—*Speaker.*

J. S. Shedlock. THE PIANOFORTE SONATA : Its Origin and Development. By J. S. SHEDLOCK. *Crown 8vo.* 5s.

'This work should be in the possession of every musician and amateur, for it not only embodies a concise and lucid history of the origin of one of the most important forms of musical composition, but, by reason of the painstaking research and accuracy of the author's statements, it is a very valuable work for reference.' —*Athenæum.*

E. M. Bowden. THE EXAMPLE OF BUDDHA : Being Quotations from Buddhist Literature for each Day in the Year. Compiled by E. M. BOWDEN. With Preface by Sir EDWIN ARNOLD. *Third Edition.* 16mo. 2s. 6d.

Science

Freudenreich. DAIRY BACTERIOLOGY. A Short Manual for the Use of Students. By Dr. ED. VON FREUDENREICH. Translated from the German by J. R. AINSWORTH DAVIS, B.A., F.C.P. *Crown 8vo.* 2s. 6d.

Chalmers Mitchell. OUTLINES OF BIOLOGY. By P. CHALMERS MITCHELL, M.A., F.Z.S. *Fully Illustrated. Crown 8vo.* 6s.

A text-book designed to cover the new Schedule issued by the Royal College of Physicians and Surgeons.

G. Massee. A MONOGRAPH OF THE MYXOGASTRES. By GEORGE MASSEE. With 12 Coloured Plates. *Royal 8vo.* 18s. net.

'A work much in advance of any book in the language treating of this group of organisms. It is indispensable to every student of the Myxogastres. The coloured plates deserve high praise for their accuracy and execution.'—*Nature.*

Philosophy

L. T. Hobhouse. THE THEORY OF KNOWLEDGE. By L. T. HOBHOUSE, Fellow and Tutor of Corpus College, Oxford. *Demy 8vo.* 21*s.*

'The most important contribution to English philosophy since the publication of Mr. Bradley's "Appearance and Reality." Full of brilliant criticism and of positive theories which are models of lucid statement.'—*Glasgow Herald.*

'An elaborate and often brilliantly written volume. The treatment is one of great freshness, and the illustrations are particularly numerous and apt.'—*Times.*

W. H. Fairbrother. THE PHILOSOPHY OF T. H. GREEN. By W. H. FAIRBROTHER, M.A., Lecturer at Lincoln College, Oxford. *Crown 8vo.* 3*s.* 6*d.*

This volume is expository, not critical, and is intended for senior students at the Universities and others, as a statement of Green's teaching, and an introduction to the study of Idealist Philosophy.

'In every way an admirable book. As an introduction to the writings of perhaps the most remarkable speculative thinker whom England has produced in the present century, nothing could be better.'—*Glasgow Herald.*

F. W. Bussell. THE SCHOOL OF PLATO: its Origin and its Revival under the Roman Empire. By F. W. BUSSELL, M.A., Fellow and Tutor of Brasenose College, Oxford. *Demy 8vo.* 10*s.* 6*d.*

'A highly valuable contribution to the history of ancient thought.'—*Glasgow Herald.*

'A clever and stimulating book, provocative of thought and deserving careful reading.'
—*Manchester Guardian.*

F. S. Granger. THE WORSHIP OF THE ROMANS. By F. S. GRANGER, M.A., Litt.D., Professor of Philosophy at University College, Nottingham. *Crown 8vo.* 6*s.*

'A scholarly analysis of the religious ceremonies, beliefs, and superstitions of ancient Rome, conducted in the new instructive light of comparative anthropology.'—*Times.*

Theology

E. C. S. Gibson. THE XXXIX. ARTICLES OF THE CHURCH OF ENGLAND. Edited with an Introduction by E. C. S. GIBSON, D.D., Vicar of Leeds, late Principal of Wells Theological College. *In Two Volumes. Demy 8vo.* 15*s.*

'The tone maintained throughout is not that of the partial advocate, but the faithful exponent.'—*Scotsman.*

'There are ample proofs of clearness of expression, sobriety of judgment, and breadth of view. . . . The book will be welcome to all students of the subject, and its sound, definite, and loyal theology ought to be of great service.'—*National Observer.*

'So far from repelling the general reader, its orderly arrangement, lucid treatment, and felicity of diction invite and encourage his attention.'—*Yorkshire Post.*

R. L. Ottley. THE DOCTRINE OF THE INCARNATION. By R. L. OTTLEY, M.A., late fellow of Magdalen College, Oxon., Principal of Pusey House. *In Two Volumes. Demy 8vo.* 15s.

'Learned and reverent : lucid and well arranged.'—*Record.*
'Accurate, well ordered, and judicious.'—*National Observer.*
'A clear and remarkably full account of the main currents of speculation. Scholarly precision . . . genuine tolerance . . . intense interest in his subject—are Mr. Ottley's merits.'—*Guardian.*

F. B. Jevons. AN INTRODUCTION TO THE HISTORY OF RELIGION. By F. B. JEVONS, M.A., Litt.D., Principal of Bishop Hatfield's Hall. *Demy 8vo.* 10s. 6d.

Mr. F. B. Jevons' 'Introduction to the History of Religion' treats of early religion, from the point of view of Anthropology and Folk-lore ; and is the first attempt that has been made in any language to weave together the results of recent investigations into such topics as Sympathetic Magic, Taboo, Totemism, Fetishism, etc., so as to present a systematic account of the growth of primitive religion and the development of early religious institutions.
' Dr. Jevons has written a notable work, and we can strongly recommend it to the serious attention of theologians, anthropologists, and classical scholars.'—*Manchester Guardian.*
' The merit of this book lies in the penetration, the singular acuteness and force of the author's judgment. He is at once critical and luminous, at once just and suggestive. It is but rarely that one meets with a book so comprehensive and so thorough as this, and it is more than an ordinary pleasure for the reviewer to welcome and recommend it. Dr. Jevons is something more than an historian of primitive belief—he is a philosophic thinker, who sees his subject clearly and sees it whole, whose mastery of detail is no less complete than his view of the broader aspects and issues of his subject is convincing.'—*Birmingham Post.*

S. R. Driver. SERMONS ON SUBJECTS CONNECTED WITH THE OLD TESTAMENT. By S. R. DRIVER, D.D., Canon of Christ Church, Regius Professor of Hebrew in the University of Oxford. *Crown 8vo.* 6s.

' A welcome companion to the author's famous ' Introduction.' No man can read these discourses without feeling that Dr. Driver is fully alive to the deeper teaching of the Old Testament.'—*Guardian.*

T. K. Cheyne. FOUNDERS OF OLD TESTAMENT CRITICISM : Biographical, Descriptive, and Critical Studies. By T. K. CHEYNE, D.D., Oriel Professor of the Interpretation of Holy Scripture at Oxford. *Large crown 8vo.* 7s. 6d.

This book is a historical sketch of O. T. Criticism in the form of biographical studies from the days of Eichhorn to those of Driver and Robertson Smith.
' A very learned and instructive work.'—*Times.*

C. H. Prior. CAMBRIDGE SERMONS. Edited by C. H. PRIOR, M.A., Fellow and Tutor of Pembroke College. *Crown 8vo.* 6s.

A volume of sermons preached before the University of Cambridge by various preachers, including the Archbishop of Canterbury and Bishop Westcott.
A representative collection. Bishop Westcott's is a noble sermon.'—*Guardian.*

E. B. Layard. RELIGION IN BOYHOOD. Notes on the Religious Training of Boys. With a Preface by J. R. ILLINGWORTH. By E. B. LAYARD, M.A. 18mo. 1s.

W. Yorke Faussett. THE *DE CATECHIZANDIS RUDIBUS* OF ST. AUGUSTINE. Edited, with Introduction, Notes, etc., by W. YORKE FAUSSETT, M.A., late Scholar of Balliol Coll. *Crown 8vo.* 3*s.* 6*d.*

An edition of a Treatise on the Essentials of Christian Doctrine, and the best methods of impressing them on candidates for baptism.

'Ably and judiciously edited on the same principle as the ordinary Greek and Latin texts.'—*Glasgow Herald.*

Devotional Books.

With Full-page Illustrations. Fcap. 8vo. Buckram. 3*s.* 6*d.*
Padded morocco, 5*s.*

THE IMITATION OF CHRIST. By THOMAS À KEMPIS. With an Introduction by DEAN FARRAR. Illustrated by C. M. GERE, and printed in black and red. *Second Edition.*

'Amongst all the innumerable English editions of the "Imitation," there can have been few which were prettier than this one, printed in strong and handsome type, with all the glory of red initials.'—*Glasgow Herald.*

THE CHRISTIAN YEAR. By JOHN KEBLE. With an Introduction and Notes by W. LOCK, D.D., Warden of Keble College, Ireland, Professor at Oxford. Illustrated by R. ANNING BELL.

'The present edition is annotated with all the care and insight to be expected from Mr. Lock. The progress and circumstances of its composition are detailed in the Introduction. There is an interesting Appendix on the MSS. of the "Christian Year," and another giving the order in which the poems were written. A "Short Analysis of the Thought" is prefixed to each, and any difficulty in the text is explained in a note.'—*Guardian.*

'The most acceptable edition of this ever-popular work.'—*Globe.*

Leaders of Religion

Edited by H. C. BEECHING, M.A. *With Portraits, crown 8vo.*

A series of short biographies of the most prominent leaders of religious life and thought of all ages and countries.

3/6

The following are ready—

CARDINAL NEWMAN. By R. H. HUTTON.
JOHN WESLEY. By J. H. OVERTON, M.A.
BISHOP WILBERFORCE. By G. W. DANIEL, M.A.
CARDINAL MANNING. By A. W. HUTTON, M.A.
CHARLES SIMEON. By H. C. G. MOULE, M.A.
JOHN KEBLE. By WALTER LOCK, D.D.
THOMAS CHALMERS. By Mrs. OLIPHANT.
LANCELOT ANDREWES. By R. L. OTTLEY, M.A.
AUGUSTINE OF CANTERBURY. By E. L. CUTTS, D.D.
WILLIAM LAUD. By W. H. HUTTON, B.D.

JOHN KNOX. By F. M'CUNN.
JOHN HOWE. By R. F. HORTON, D.D.
BISHOP KEN. By F. A. CLARKE, M.A.
GEORGE FOX, THE QUAKER. By T. HODGKIN, D.C.L.
Other volumes will be announced in due course.

Fiction

SIX SHILLING NOVELS

Marie Corelli's Novels

Crown 8vo. 6s. each.

A ROMANCE OF TWO WORLDS. *Sixteenth Edition.*
VENDETTA. *Thirteenth Edition.*
THELMA. *Seventeenth Edition.*
ARDATH. *Eleventh Edition.*
THE SOUL OF LILITH *Ninth Edition.*
WORMWOOD. *Eighth Edition.*
BARABBAS : A DREAM OF THE WORLD'S TRAGEDY.
Thirty-first Edition.

' The tender reverence of the treatment and the imaginative beauty of the writing
have reconciled us to the daring of the conception, and the conviction is forced on
us that even so exalted a subject cannot be made too familiar to us, provided it be
presented in the true spirit of Christian faith. The amplifications of the Scripture
narrative are often conceived with high poetic insight, and this "Dream of the
World's Tragedy" is, despite some trifling incongruities, a lofty and not inade-
quate paraphrase of the supreme climax of the inspired narrative.'—*Dublin
Review.*

THE SORROWS OF SATAN. *Thirty-sixth Edition.*

' A very powerful piece of work. . . . The conception is magnificent, and is likely
to win an abiding place within the memory of man. . . . The author has immense
command of language, and a limitless audacity. . . . This interesting and remarkable romance will live long after much of the ephemeral literature of the day
is forgotten. . . . A literary phenomenon . . . novel, and even sublime,'—W. T.
STRAD in the *Review of Reviews.*

Anthony Hope's Novels

Crown 8vo. 6s. each.

THE GOD IN THE CAR. *Seventh Edition.*

' A very remarkable book, deserving of critical analysis impossible within our limit ;
brilliant, but not superficial ; well considered, but not elaborated ; constructed
with the proverbial art that conceals, but yet allows itself to be enjoyed by readers
to whom fine literary method is a keen pleasure.'—*The World.*

A CHANGE OF AIR. *Fourth Edition.*

'A graceful, vivacious comedy, true to human nature. The characters are traced
with a masterly hand.'—*Times.*

A MAN OF MARK. *Fourth Edition.*

' Of all Mr. Hope's books, "A Man of Mark" is the one which best compares with
"The Prisoner of Zenda." '—*National Observer.*

THE CHRONICLES OF COUNT ANTONIO. *Third Edition.*

'It is a perfectly enchanting story of love and chivalry, and pure romance. The outlawed Count is the most constant, desperate, and withal modest and tender of lovers, a peerless gentleman, an intrepid fighter, a very faithful friend, and a most magnanimous foe.'—*Guardian.*

PHROSO. Illustrated by H. R. MILLAR. *Third Edition.*

'The tale is thoroughly fresh, quick with vitality, stirring the blood, and humorously, dashingly told.'—*St. James's Gazette.*

'A story of adventure, every page of which is palpitating with action and excitement.' —*Speaker.*

'From cover to cover " Phroso " not only engages the attention, but carries the reader in little whirls of delight from adventure to adventure.'—*Academy.*

S. Baring Gould's Novels

Crown 8vo. 6s. each.

'To say that a book is by the author of "Mehalah" is to imply that it contains a story cast on strong lines, containing dramatic possibilities, vivid and sympathetic descriptions of Nature, and a wealth of ingenious imagery.'—*Speaker.*

'That whatever Mr. Baring Gould writes is well worth reading, is a conclusion that may be very generally accepted. His views of life are fresh and vigorous, his language pointed and characteristic, the incidents of which he makes use are striking and original, his characters are life-like, and though somewhat exceptional people, are drawn and coloured with artistic force. Add to this that his descriptions of scenes and scenery are painted with the loving eyes and skilled hands of a master of his art, that he is always fresh and never dull, and under such conditions it is no wonder that readers have gained confidence both in his power of amusing and satisfying them, and that year by year his popularity widens.'—*Court Circular.*

ARMINELL : A Social Romance. *Fourth Edition.*

URITH : A Story of Dartmoor. *Fifth Edition.*

'The author is at his best.'—*Times.*

IN THE ROAR OF THE SEA. *Sixth Edition.*

'One of the best imagined and most enthralling stories the author has produced. —*Saturday Review.*

MRS. CURGENVEN OF CURGENVEN. *Fourth Edition.*

'The swing of the narrative is splendid.'—*Sussex Daily News.*

CHEAP JACK ZITA. *Fourth Edition.*

'A powerful drama of human passion.'—*Westminster Gazette.*

'A story worthy the author.'—*National Observer.*

THE QUEEN OF LOVE. *Fourth Edition.*

'You cannot put it down until you have finished it.'—*Punch.*

'Can be heartily recommended to all who care for cleanly, energetic, and interesting fiction.'—*Sussex Daily News.*

KITTY ALONE. *Fourth Edition.*

'A strong and original story, teeming with graphic description, stirring incident, and, above all, with vivid and enthralling human interest.'—*Daily Telegraph.*

NOÉMI : A Romance of the Cave-Dwellers. Illustrated by R. CATON WOODVILLE. *Third Edition.*

'"Noémi" is as excellent a tale of fighting and adventure as one may wish to meet. The narrative also runs clear and sharp as the Loire itself.'—*Pall Mall Gazette.*

'Mr. Baring Gould's powerful story is full of the strong lights and shadows and vivid colouring to which he has accustomed us.'—*Standard.*

THE BROOM-SQUIRE. Illustrated by FRANK DADD.
Fourth Edition.

'A strain of tenderness is woven through the web of his tragic tale, and its atmosphere is sweetened by the nobility and sweetness of the heroine's character.'—*Daily News.*

'A story of exceptional interest that seems to us to be better than anything he has written of late.'—*Speaker.*

THE PENNYCOMEQUICKS. *Third Edition.*

DARTMOOR IDYLLS.

'A book to read, and keep and read again; for the genuine fun and pathos of it it will not early lose their effect.'—*Vanity Fair.*

GUAVAS THE TINNER. Illustrated by Frank Dadd. *Second Edition.*

'Mr. Baring Gould is a wizard who transports us into a region of visions, often lurid and disquieting, but always full of interest and enchantment.'—*Spectator.*

'In the weirdness of the story, in the faithfulness with which the characters are depicted, and in force of style, it closely resembles "Mehalah."'—*Daily Telegraph.*

'There is a kind of flavour about this book which alone elevates it above the ordinary novel. The story itself has a grandeur in harmony with the wild and rugged scenery which is its setting.'—*Athenæum.*

Gilbert Parker's Novels

Crown 8vo. 6s. each.

PIERRE AND HIS PEOPLE. *Fourth Edition.*

'Stories happily conceived and finely executed. There is strength and genius in Mr. Parker's style.'—*Daily Telegraph.*

MRS. FALCHION. *Fourth Edition.*

'A splendid study of character.'—*Athenæum.*

'But little behind anything that has been done by any writer of our time.'—*Pall Mall Gazette.* 'A very striking and admirable novel.'—*St. James's Gazette.*

THE TRANSLATION OF A SAVAGE.

'The plot is original and one difficult to work out; but Mr. Parker has done it with great skill and delicacy. The reader who is not interested in this original, fresh, and well-told tale must be a dull person indeed.'—*Daily Chronicle.*

THE TRAIL OF THE SWORD. *Fifth Edition.*

'Everybody with a soul for romance will thoroughly enjoy "The Trail of the Sword."'—*St. James's Gazette.*

'A rousing and dramatic tale. A book like this, in which swords flash, great surprises are undertaken, and daring deeds done, in which men and women live and love in the old straightforward passionate way, is a joy inexpressible to the reviewer.'—*Daily Chronicle.*

WHEN VALMOND CAME TO PONTIAC: The Story of a Lost Napoleon. *Fourth Edition.*

'Here we find romance—real, breathing, living romance, but it runs flush with our own times, level with our own feelings. The character of Valmond is drawn unerringly; his career, brief as it is, is placed before us as convincingly as history itself. The book must be read, we may say re-read, for any one thoroughly to appreciate Mr. Parker's delicate touch and innate sympathy with humanity.'—*Pall Mall Gazette.*

'The one work of genius which 1895 has as yet produced.'—*New Age.*

AN ADVENTURER OF THE NORTH: The Last Adventures of 'Pretty Pierre.' *Second Edition.*

'The present book is full of fine and moving stories of the great North, and it will add to Mr. Parker's already high reputation.'—*Glasgow Herald.*

THE SEATS OF THE MIGHTY. *Illustrated. Eighth Edition.*

'The best thing he has done; one of the best things that any one has done lately.'—
St. James's Gazette.

'Mr. Parker seems to become stronger and easier with every serious novel that he
attempts. . . . In "The Seats of the Mighty" he shows the matured power which
his former novels have led us to expect, and has produced a really fine historical
novel. . . . Most sincerely is Mr. Parker to be congratulated on the finest
novel he has yet written.'—*Athenæum.*

'Mr. Parker's latest book places him in the front rank of living novelists. "The
Seats of the Mighty" is a great book.'—*Black and White.*

'One of the strongest stories of historical interest and adventure that we have read
for many a day. . . . A notable and successful book.'—*Speaker.*

Conan Doyle. ROUND THE RED LAMP. By A. CONAN
DOYLE, Author of 'The White Company,' 'The Adventures of
Sherlock Holmes,' etc. *Fifth Edition. Crown 8vo. 6s.*

'The book is, indeed, composed of leaves from life, and is far and away the best view
that has been vouchsafed us behind the scenes of the consulting-room. It is very
superior to "The Diary of a late Physician."'—*Illustrated London News.*

Stanley Weyman. UNDER THE RED ROBE. By STANLEY
WEYMAN, Author of 'A Gentleman of France.' With Twelve Illustrations by R. Caton Woodville. *Twelfth Edition. Crown 8vo. 6s.*

'A book of which we have read every word for the sheer pleasure of reading, and
which we put down with a pang that we cannot forget it all and start again.'—
Westminster Gazette.

'Every one who reads books at all must read this thrilling romance, from the first
page of which to the last the breathless reader is haled along. An inspiration of
"manliness and courage."'—*Daily Chronicle.*

Lucas Malet. THE WAGES OF SIN. By LUCAS
MALET. *Thirteenth Edition. Crown 8vo. 6s.*

Lucas Malet. THE CARISSIMA. By LUCAS MALET,
Author of 'The Wages of Sin,' etc. *Third Edition. Crown 8vo. 6s.*

Arthur Morrison. TALES OF MEAN STREETS. By ARTHUR
MORRISON. *Fourth Edition. Crown 8vo. 6s.*

'Told with consummate art and extraordinary detail. He tells a plain, unvarnished
tale, and the very truth of it makes for beauty. In the true humanity of the book
lies its justification, the permanence of its interest, and its indubitable triumph.'—
Athenæum.

'A great book. The author's method is amazingly effective, and produces a thrilling
sense of reality. The writer lays upon us a master hand. The book is simply
appalling and irresistible in its interest. It is humorous also; without humour
it would not make the mark it is certain to make.'—*World.*

Arthur Morrison. A CHILD OF THE JAGO. By ARTHUR
MORRISON. *Third Edition. Crown 8vo. 6s.*

This, the first long story which Mr. Morrison has written, is like his remarkable
'Tales of Mean Streets,' a realistic study of East End life.

'The book is a masterpiece.'—*Pall Mall Gazette.*

'Told with great vigour and powerful simplicity.'—*Athenæum.*

Mrs. Clifford. A FLASH OF SUMMER. By Mrs. W. K. CLIF-
FORD, Author of 'Aunt Anne,' etc. *Second Edition. Crown 8vo. 6s.*

'The story is a very sad and a very beautiful one, exquisitely told, and enriched with
many subtle touches of wise and tender insight. It will, undoubtedly, add to its
author's reputation—already high—in the ranks of novelists.'—*Speaker.*

Emily Lawless. HURRISH. By the Honble. EMILY LAW-
LESS, Author of 'Maelcho,' etc. *Fifth Edition. Crown 8vo.* 6s.
A reissue of Miss Lawless' most popular novel, uniform with 'Maelcho.'

Emily Lawless. MAELCHO : a Sixteenth Century Romance.
By the Honble. EMILY LAWLESS. *Second Edition. Crown 8vo.* 6s.
'A really great book.'—*Spectator.*
'There is no keener pleasure in life than the recognition of genius. Good work is
commoner than it used to be, but the best is as rare as ever. All the more
gladly, therefore, do we welcome in "Maelcho" a piece of work of the first order,
which we do not hesitate to describe as one of the most remarkable literary
achievements of this generation. Miss Lawless is possessed of the very essence
of historical genius.'—*Manchester Guardian.*

J. H. Findlater. THE GREEN GRAVES OF BALGOWRIE.
By JANE H. FINDLATER. *Fourth Edition. Crown 8vo,* 6s.
'A powerful and vivid story.'—*Standard.*
'A beautiful story, sad and strange as truth itself.'—*Vanity Fair.*
'A work of remarkable interest and originality.'—*National Observer.*
'A very charming and pathetic tale.'—*Pall Mall Gazette.*
'A singularly original, clever, and beautiful story.'—*Guardian.*
'"The Green Graves of Balgowrie" reveals to us a new Scotch writer of undoubted
faculty and reserve force.'—*Spectator.*
'An exquisite idyll, delicate, affecting, and beautiful.'—*Black and White.*

H. G. Wells. THE STOLEN BACILLUS, and other Stories.
By H. G. WELLS, Author of 'The Time Machine.' *Second Edition.
Crown 8vo.* 6s.
'The ordinary reader of fiction may be glad to know that these stories are eminently
readable from one cover to the other, but they are more than that ; they are the
impressions of a very striking imagination, which, it would seem, has a great deal
within its reach.'—*Saturday Review.*

H. G. Wells. THE PLATTNER STORY AND OTHERS. By H.
G. WELLS. *Second Edition. Crown 8vo.* 6s.
'Weird and mysterious, they seem to hold the reader as by a magic spell.'—*Scotsman.*
'Such is the fascination of this writer's skill that you unhesitatingly prophesy that
none of the many readers, however his flesh do creep, will relinquish the volume
ere he has read from first word to last.'—*Black and White.*
'No volume has appeared for a long time so likely to give equal pleasure to the
simplest reader and to the most fastidious critic.'—*Academy.*
'Mr. Wells is a magician skilled in wielding that most potent of all spells—the fear
of the unknown.'—*Daily Telegraph.*

E. F. Benson. DODO : A DETAIL OF THE DAY. By E. F.
BENSON. *Sixteenth Edition. Crown 8vo.* 6s.
'A delightfully witty sketch of society.'—*Spectator.*
'A perpetual feast of epigram and paradox.'—*Speaker.*

E. F. Benson. THE RUBICON. By E. F. BENSON, Author of
'Dodo.' *Fifth Edition. Crown 8vo.* 6s.
'An exceptional achievement ; a notable advance on his previous work.'—*National
Observer.*

Mrs. Oliphant. SIR ROBERT'S FORTUNE. By MRS.
OLIPHANT. *Crown 8vo.* 6s.
'Full of her own peculiar charm of style and simple, subtle character-painting comes
her new gift, the delightful story before us. The scene mostly lies in the moors,
and at the touch of the authoress a Scotch moor becomes a living thing, strong,
tender, beautiful, and changeful.'—*Pall Mall Gazette.*

Mrs. Oliphant. THE TWO MARYS. By MRS. OLIPHANT. *Second Edition. Crown 8vo. 6s.*

W. E. Norris. MATTHEW AUSTIN. By W. E. NORRIS, Author of 'Mademoiselle de Mersac,' etc. *Fourth Edition. Crown 8vo. 6s.*

"Matthew Austin" may safely be pronounced one of the most intellectually satisfactory and morally bracing novels of the current year.'—*Daily Telegraph.*

W. E. Norris. HIS GRACE. By W. E. NORRIS. *Third Edition. Crown 8vo. 6s.*

' Mr. Norris has drawn a really fine character in the Duke of Hurstbourne, at once unconventional and very true to the conventionalities of life.'—*Athenæum.*

W. E. Norris. THE DESPOTIC LADY AND OTHERS. By W. E. NORRIS. *Crown 8vo. 6s.*

' A budget of good fiction of which no one will tire.'—*Scotsman.*

W. E. Norris. CLARISSA FURIOSA. By W. E. NORRIS, Author of 'The Rogue,' etc. *Crown 8vo. 6s.*

' One of Mr. Norris's very best novels. As a story it is admirable, as a *jeu d'esprit* it is capital, as a lay sermon studded with gems of wit and wisdom it is a model which will not, we imagine, find an efficient imitator.'—*The World.*
' The best novel he has written for some time : a story which is full of admirable character-drawing.'—*The Standard.*

Robert Barr. IN THE MIDST OF ALARMS. By ROBERT BARR. *Third Edition. Crown 8vo. 6s.*

' A book which has abundantly satisfied us by its capital humour.'—*Daily Chronicle.*
' Mr. Barr has achieved a triumph whereof he has every reason to be proud.'—*Pall Mall Gazette.*

J. Maclaren Cobban. THE KING OF ANDAMAN : A Saviour of Society. By J. MACLAREN COBBAN. *Crown 8vo. 6s.*

' An unquestionably interesting book. It would not surprise us if it turns out to be the most interesting novel of the season, for it contains one character, at least, who has in him the root of immortality, and the book itself is ever exhaling the sweet savour of the unexpected. . . . Plot is forgotten and incident fades, and only the really human endures, and throughout this book there stands out in bold and beautiful relief its high-souled and chivalric protagonist, James the Master of Hutcheon, the King of Andaman himself.'—*Pall Mall Gazette.*

J. Maclaren Cobban. WILT THOU HAVE THIS WOMAN ? By J. M. COBBAN, Author of 'The King of Andaman.' *Crown 8vo. 6s.*

' Mr. Cobban has the true story-teller's art. He arrests attention at the outset, and he retains it to the end.'—*Birmingham Post.*

H. Morrah. A SERIOUS COMEDY. By HERBERT MORRAH. *Crown 8vo. 6s.*

' This volume is well worthy of its title. The theme has seldom been presented with more freshness or more force.'—*Scotsman.*

H. Morrah. THE FAITHFUL CITY. By HERBERT MORRAH, Author of 'A Serious Comedy.' *Crown 8vo.* 6s.

'Conveys a suggestion of weirdness and horror, until finally he convinces and enthrals the reader with his mysterious savages, his gigantic tower, and his uncompromising men and women. This is a haunting, mysterious book, not without an element of stupendous grandeur.'—*Athenæum.*

L. B. Walford. SUCCESSORS TO THE TITLE. By MRS. WALFORD, Author of 'Mr. Smith,' etc. *Second Edition. Crown 8vo.* 6s.

'The story is fresh and healthy from beginning to finish; and our liking for the two simple people who are the successors to the title mounts steadily, and ends almost in respect.'—*Scotsman.*

T. L. Paton. A HOME IN INVERESK. By T. L. PATON. *Crown 8vo.* 6s.

'A pleasant and well-written story.'—*Daily Chronicle.*

John Davidson. MISS ARMSTRONG'S AND OTHER CIR-CUMSTANCES. By JOHN DAVIDSON. *Crown 8vo.* 6s.

'Throughout the volume there is a strong vein of originality, and a knowledge of human nature that are worthy of the highest praise.'—*Scotsman.*

M. M. Dowie. GALLIA. By MÉNIE MURIEL DOWIE, Author of 'A Girl in the Carpathians.' *Third Edition. Crown 8vo.* 6s.

'The style is generally admirable, the dialogue not seldom brilliant, the situations surprising in their freshness and originality, while the subsidiary as well as the principal characters live and move, and the story itself is readable from title-page to colophon.'—*Saturday Review.*

J. A. Barry. IN THE GREAT DEEP: TALES OF THE SEA. By J. A. BARRY. Author of 'Steve Brown's Bunyip.' *Crown 8vo.* 6s.

'A collection of really admirable short stories of the sea, very simply told, and placed before the reader in pithy and telling English.'—*Westminster Gazette.*

J. B. Burton. IN THE DAY OF ADVERSITY. By J. BLOUN-DELLE BURTON.' *Second Edition. Crown 8vo.* 6s.

'Unusually interesting and full of highly dramatic situations.'—*Guardian.*

J. B. Burton. DENOUNCED. By J. BLOUNDELLE BURTON. *Second Edition. Crown 8vo.* 6s.

The plot is an original one, and the local colouring is laid on with a delicacy and an accuracy of detail which denote the true artist.'—*Broad Arrow.*

W. C. Scully. THE WHITE HECATOMB. By W. C. SCULLY, Author of 'Kafir Stories.' *Crown 8vo.* 6s.

'The author is so steeped in Kaffir lore and legend, and so thoroughly well acquainted with native sagas and traditional ceremonial that he is able to attract the reader by the easy familiarity with which he handles his characters.'—*South Africa.*

'It reveals a marvellously intimate understanding of the Kaffir mind, allied with literary gifts of no mean order.'—*African Critic.*

H. Johnston. DR. CONGALTON'S LEGACY. By HENRY JOHNSTON. *Crown 8vo.* 6s.

'A worthy and permanent contribution to Scottish literature.'—*Glasgow Herald.*

J. F. Brewer. THE SPECULATORS. By J. F. BREWER.
Second Edition. *Crown 8vo.* 6s.
'A pretty bit of comedy. . . . It is undeniably a clever book.'—*Academy.*
'A clever and amusing story. It makes capital out of the comic aspects of culture,
and will be read with amusement by every intellectual reader.'—*Scotsman.*
'A remarkably clever study.'—*Vanity Fair.*

Julian Corbett. A BUSINESS IN GREAT WATERS. By
JULIAN CORBETT. *Crown 8vo.* 6s.
'Mr. Corbett writes with immense spirit, and the book is a thoroughly enjoyable
one in all respects. The salt of the ocean is in it, and the right heroic ring re-
sounds through its gallant adventures.'—*Speaker.*

L. Cope Cornford. CAPTAIN JACOBUS: A ROMANCE OF
THE ROAD. By L. COPE CORNFORD. Illustrated. *Crown 8vo.* 6s.
'An exceptionally good story of adventure and character.'—*World.*

C. P. Wolley. THE QUEENSBERRY CUP. A Tale of
Adventure. By CLIVE PHILLIPS WOLLEY. *Illustrated. Crown
8vo.* 6s.
'A book which will delight boys: a book which upholds the healthy schoolboy code
of morality.'—*Scotsman.*

L. Daintrey. THE KING OF ALBERIA. A Romance of
the Balkans. By LAURA DAINTREY. *Crown 8vo.* 6s.
'Miss Daintrey seems to have an intimate acquaintance with the people and politics
of the Balkan countries in which the scene of her lively and picturesque romance
is laid.'—*Glasgow Herald.*

M. A. Owen. THE DAUGHTER OF ALOUETTE. By
MARY A. OWEN. *Crown 8vo.* 6s.
A story of life among the American Indians.
'A fascinating story.'—*Literary World.*

Mrs. Pinsent. CHILDREN OF THIS WORLD. By ELLEN
F. PINSENT, Author of 'Jenny's Case.' *Crown 8vo.* 6s.
'Mrs. Pinsent's new novel has plenty of vigour, variety, and good writing. There
are certainty of purpose, strength of touch, and clearness of vision.'—*Athenæum.*

Clark Russell. MY DANISH SWEETHEART. By W.
CLARK RUSSELL, Author of 'The Wreck of the Grosvenor,' etc.
Illustrated. Fourth Edition. Crown 8vo. 6s.

G. Manville Fenn. AN ELECTRIC SPARK. By G. MANVILLE
FENN, Author of 'The Vicar's Wife,' 'A Double Knot,' etc. *Second
Edition. Crown 8vo.* 6s.

L. S. McChesney. UNDER SHADOW OF THE MISSION.
By L. S. McCHESNEY. *Crown 8vo.* 6s.
'Those whose minds are open to the finer issues of life, who can appreciate graceful
thought and refined expression of it, from them this volume will receive a welcome
as enthusiastic as it will be based on critical knowledge.'—*Church Times.*

Ronald Ross. THE SPIRIT OF STORM. By RONALD
ROSS, Author of 'The Child of Ocean.' *Crown 8vo.* 6s.
A romance of the Sea.   'Weird, powerful, and impressive.'—*Black and White.*

R. Pryce. TIME AND THE WOMAN. By RICHARD PRYCE. *Second Edition. Crown 8vo. 6s.*

Mrs. Watson. THIS MAN'S DOMINION. By the Author of 'A High Little World.' *Second Edition. Crown 8vo. 6s.*

Marriott Watson. DIOGENES OF LONDON. By H. B. MARRIOTT WATSON. *Crown 8vo. Buckram. 6s.*

M. Gilchrist. THE STONE DRAGON. By MURRAY GIL-CHRIST. *Crown 8vo. Buckram. 6s.*

'The author's faults are atoned for by certain positive and admirable merits. The romances have not their counterpart in modern literature, and to read them is a unique experience.'—*National Observer.*

E. Dickinson. A VICAR'S WIFE. By EVELYN DICKINSON. *Crown 8vo. 6s.*

E. M. Gray. ELSA. By E. M'QUEEN GRAY. *Crown 8vo. 6s.*

THREE-AND-SIXPENNY NOVELS 3/6
Crown 8vo.

DERRICK VAUGHAN, NOVELIST. By EDNA LYALL.
MARGERY OF QUETHER. By S. BARING GOULD.
JACQUETTA. By S. BARING GOULD.
SUBJECT TO VANITY. By MARGARET BENSON.
THE SIGN OF THE SPIDER. By BERTRAM MITFORD.
THE MOVING FINGER. By MARY GAUNT.
JACO TRELOAR. By J. H. PEARCE.
THE DANCE OF THE HOURS. By 'VERA.'
A WOMAN OF FORTY. By ESMÉ STUART.
A CUMBERER OF THE GROUND. By CONSTANCE SMITH.
THE SIN OF ANGELS. By EVELYN DICKINSON.
AUT DIABOLUS AUT NIHIL. By X. L.
THE COMING OF CUCULAIN. By STANDISH O'GRADY.
THE GODS GIVE MY DONKEY WINGS. By ANGUS EVAN ABBOTT.
THE STAR GAZERS. By G. MANVILLE FENN.
THE POISON OF ASPS. By R. ORTON PROWSE.
THE QUIET MRS. FLEMING. By R. PRYCE.
DISENCHANTMENT. By F. MABEL ROBINSON.
THE SQUIRE OF WANDALES. By A. SHIELD.
A REVEREND GENTLEMAN. By J. M. COBBAN.

A DEPLORABLE AFFAIR. By W. E. NORRIS.
A CAVALIER'S LADYE. By Mrs. DICKER.
THE PRODIGALS. By Mrs. OLIPHANT.
THE SUPPLANTER. By P. NEUMANN.
A MAN WITH BLACK EYELASHES. By H. A. KENNEDY.
A HANDFUL OF EXOTICS. By S. GORDON.
AN ODD EXPERIMENT. By HANNAH LYNCH.

HALF-CROWN NOVELS
A Series of Novels by popular Authors.

2/6

1. HOVENDEN, V.C. By F. MABEL ROBINSON.
2. ELI'S CHILDREN. By G. MANVILLE FENN.
3. A DOUBLE KNOT. By G. MANVILLE FENN.
4. DISARMED. By M. BETHAM EDWARDS.
5. A MARRIAGE AT SEA. By W. CLARK RUSSELL.
6. IN TENT AND BUNGALOW. By the Author of 'Indian Idylls.'
7. MY STEWARDSHIP. By E. M'QUEEN GRAY.
8. JACK'S FATHER. By W. E. NORRIS.
9. JIM B.
10. THE PLAN OF CAMPAIGN. By F. MABEL ROBINSON.
11. MR. BUTLER'S WARD. By F. MABEL ROBINSON.
12. A LOST ILLUSION. By LESLIE KEITH.

Lynn Linton. THE TRUE HISTORY OF JOSHUA DAVIDSON, Christian and Communist. By E. LYNN LINTON. *Eleventh Edition. Post 8vo.* 1s.

Books for Boys and Girls **3/6**
A Series of Books by well-known Authors, well illustrated.

1. THE ICELANDER'S SWORD. By S. BARING GOULD.
2. TWO LITTLE CHILDREN AND CHING. By EDITH E. CUTHELL.
3. TODDLEBEN'S HERO. By M. M. BLAKE.
4. ONLY A GUARD-ROOM DOG. By EDITH E. CUTHELL.
5. THE DOCTOR OF THE JULIET. By HARRY COLLINGWOOD.
6. MASTER ROCKAFELLAR'S VOYAGE. By W. CLARK RUSSELL.
7. SYD BELTON : Or, The Boy who would not go to Sea. By G. MANVILLE FENN.

The Peacock Library

A Series of Books for Girls by well-known Authors, handsomely bound in blue and silver, and well illustrated. 3/6

1. A PINCH OF EXPERIENCE. By L. B. WALFORD.
2. THE RED GRANGE. By Mrs. MOLESWORTH.
3. THE SECRET OF MADAME DE MONLUC. By the Author of ' Mdle Mori.'
4. DUMPS. By Mrs. PARR, Author of 'Adam and Eve.'
5. OUT OF THE FASHION. By L. T. MEADE.
6. A GIRL OF THE PEOPLE. By L. T. MEADE.
7. HEPSY GIPSY. By L. T. MEADE. 2*s.* 6*d.*
8. THE HONOURABLE MISS. By L. T. MEADE.
9. MY LAND OF BEULAH. By Mrs. LEITH ADAMS.

University Extension Series

A series of books on historical, literary, and scientific subjects, suitable for extension students and home-reading circles. Each volume is complete in itself, and the subjects are treated by competent writers in a broad and philosophic spirit.

Edited by J. E. SYMES, M.A.,
Principal of University College, Nottingham.

Crown 8vo. Price (with some exceptions) 2*s.* 6*d.*

The following volumes are ready :—

THE INDUSTRIAL HISTORY OF ENGLAND. By H. DE B. GIBBINS, D. Litt., M.A., late Scholar of Wadham College, Oxon., Cobden Prizeman. *Fifth Edition, Revised. With Maps and Plans.* 3*s.*
'A compact and clear story of our industrial development. A study of this concise but luminous book cannot fail to give the reader a clear insight into the principal phenomena of our industrial history. The editor and publishers are to be congratulated on this first volume of their venture, and we shall look with expectant interest for the succeeding volumes of the series.'—*University Extension Journal.*

A HISTORY OF ENGLISH POLITICAL ECONOMY. By L. L. PRICE, M.A., Fellow of Oriel College, Oxon. *Second Edition.*

PROBLEMS OF POVERTY: An Inquiry into the Industrial Conditions of the Poor. By J. A. HOBSON, M.A. *Third Edition.*

VICTORIAN POETS. By A. SHARP.

THE FRENCH REVOLUTION. By J. E. SYMES, M.A.

PSYCHOLOGY. By F. S. GRANGER, M.A.

THE EVOLUTION OF PLANT LIFE: Lower Forms. By G. MASSEE. *With Illustrations.*

AIR AND WATER. Professor V. B. LEWES, M.A. *Illustrated.*

THE CHEMISTRY OF LIFE AND HEALTH. By C. W. KIMMINS, M.A. *Illustrated.*

THE MECHANICS OF DAILY LIFE. By V. P. SELLS, M.A. *Illustrated.*

ENGLISH SOCIAL REFORMERS. H. DE B. GIBBINS, D.Litt., M.A.

ENGLISH TRADE AND FINANCE IN THE SEVENTEENTH CENTURY. By W. A. S. HEWINS, B.A.

THE CHEMISTRY OF FIRE. The Elementary Principles of Chemistry. By M. M. PATTISON MUIR, M.A. *Illustrated.*

A TEXT-BOOK OF AGRICULTURAL BOTANY. By M. C. POTTER, M.A., F.L.S. *Illustrated. 3s. 6d.*

THE VAULT OF HEAVEN. A Popular Introduction to Astronomy. By R. A. GREGORY. *With numerous Illustrations.*

METEOROLOGY. The Elements of Weather and Climate. By H. N. DICKSON, F.R.S.E., F.R. Met. Soc. *Illustrated.*

A MANUAL OF ELECTRICAL SCIENCE. By GEORGE J. BURCH, M.A. *With numerous Illustrations. 3s.*

THE EARTH. An Introduction to Physiography. By EVAN SMALL, M.A. *Illustrated.*

INSECT LIFE. By F. W. THEOBALD, M.A. *Illustrated.*

ENGLISH POETRY FROM BLAKE TO BROWNING. By W. M. DIXON, M.A.

ENGLISH LOCAL GOVERNMENT. By E. JENKS, M.A., Professor of Law at University College, Liverpool.

THE GREEK VIEW OF LIFE. By G. L. DICKINSON, Fellow of King's College, Cambridge. *Second Edition.*

Social Questions of To-day

Edited by H. DE B. GIBBINS, D.Litt., M.A.
Crown 8vo. 2s. 6d.

2/6

A series of volumes upon those topics of social, economic, and industrial interest that are at the present moment foremost in the public mind. Each volume of the series is written by an author who is an acknowledged authority upon the subject with which he deals.

The following Volumes of the Series are ready :—

TRADE UNIONISM—NEW AND OLD. By G. HOWELL, Author of 'The Conflicts of Capital and Labour.' *Second Edition.*

THE CO-OPERATIVE MOVEMENT TO-DAY. By G. J. HOLYOAKE, Author of 'The History of Co-Operation.' *Second Edition.*

MUTUAL THRIFT. By Rev. J. FROME WILKINSON, M.A., Author of 'The Friendly Society Movement.'

PROBLEMS OF POVERTY : An Inquiry into the Industrial Conditions of the Poor. By J. A. HOBSON, M.A. *Third Edition.*

THE COMMERCE OF NATIONS. By C. F. BASTAPLE, M.A., Professor of Economics at Trinity College, Dublin.

THE ALIEN INVASION. By W. H. WILKINS, B.A., Secretary to the Society for Preventing the Immigration of Destitute Aliens.

THE RURAL EXODUS. By P. ANDERSON GRAHAM.

LAND NATIONALIZATION. By HAROLD COX, B.A.

A SHORTER WORKING DAY. By H. DE B. GIBBINS, D.Litt., M.A., and R. A. HADFIELD, of the Hecla Works, Sheffield.

BACK TO THE LAND: An Inquiry into the Cure for Rural Depopulation. By H. E. MOORE.

TRUSTS, POOLS AND CORNERS: As affecting Commerce and Industry. By J. STEPHEN JEANS, M.R.I., F.S.S.

THE FACTORY SYSTEM. By R. COOKE TAYLOR.

THE STATE AND ITS CHILDREN. By GERTRUDE TUCKWELL.

WOMEN'S WORK. By LADY DILKE, Miss BULLEY, and Miss WHITLEY.

MUNICIPALITIES AT WORK. The Municipal Policy of Six Great Towns, and its Influence on their Social Welfare. By FREDERICK DOLMAN.

SOCIALISM AND MODERN THOUGHT. By M. KAUFMANN.

THE HOUSING OF THE WORKING CLASSES. By R. F. BOWMAKER.

MODERN CIVILIZATION IN SOME OF ITS ECONOMIC ASPECTS. By W. CUNNINGHAM, D.D., Fellow of Trinity College, Cambridge.

THE PROBLEM OF THE UNEMPLOYED. By J. A. HOBSON, B.A., Author of ' The Problems of Poverty.'

LIFE IN WEST LONDON. By ARTHUR SHERWELL, M.A. *Second Edition.*

Classical Translations

Edited by H. F. FOX, M.A., Fellow and Tutor of Brasenose College, Oxford.

Messrs. Methuen are issuing a New Series of Translations from the Greek and Latin Classics. They have enlisted the services of some of the best Oxford and Cambridge Scholars, and it is their intention that the Series shall be distinguished by literary excellence as well as by scholarly accuracy.

ÆSCHYLUS—Agamemnon, Chöephoroe, Eumenides. Translated by LEWIS CAMPBELL, LL.D., late Professor of Greek at St. Andrews, 5s.

CICERO—De Oratore I. Translated by E. N. P. MOOR, M.A. 3s. 6d.

CICERO — Select Orations (Pro Milone, Pro Murena, Philippic II., In Catilinam). Translated by H. E. D. BLAKISTON, M.A., Fellow and Tutor of Trinity College, Oxford. 5s.

CICERO—De Natura Deorum. Translated by F. BROOKS, M.A., late Scholar of Balliol College, Oxford. 3*s*. 6*d*.

LUCIAN—Six Dialogues (Nigrinus, Icaro-Menippus, The Cock, The Ship, The Parasite, The Lover of Falsehood). Translated by S. T. IRWIN, M.A., Assistant Master at Clifton ; late Scholar of Exeter College, Oxford. 3*s*. 6*d*.

SOPHOCLES—Electra and Ajax. Translated by E. D. A. MORSHEAD, M.A., Assistant Master at Winchester. 2*s*. 6d.

TACITUS—Agricola and Germania. Translated by R. B. TOWNSHEND, late Scholar of Trinity College, Cambridge. 2*s*. 6*d*.

- Educational Books

CLASSICAL

PLAUTI BACCHIDES. Edited with Introduction, Commentary, and Critical Notes by J. M'COSH, M.A. *Fcap.* 4*to.* 12*s*. 6*d*.
'The notes are copious, and contain a great deal of information that is good and useful.'—*Classical Review.*

TACITI AGRICOLI. With Introduction, Notes, Map, etc. By R. F. DAVIS, M.A., Assistant Master at Weymouth College. *Crown 8vo.* 2*s*.

TACITI GERMANIA. By the same Editor. *Crown 8vo.* 2*s*.

HERODOTUS: EASY SELECTIONS. With Vocabulary. By A. C. LIDDELL, M.A., Assistant Master at Nottingham High School. *Fcap.* 8*vo.* 1*s*. 6*d*.

SELECTIONS FROM THE ODYSSEY. By E. D. STONE, M.A., late Assistant Master at Eton. *Fcap.* 8*vo.* 1*s*. 6*d*.

PLAUTUS : THE CAPTIVI. Adapted for Lower Forms by J. H. FRESSE, M.A., late Fellow of St. John's, Cambridge. 1*s*. 6*d*.

DEMOSTHENES AGAINST CONON AND CALLICLES. Edited with Notes and Vocabulary, by F. DARWIN SWIFT, M.A., formerly Scholar of Queen's College, Oxford; Assistant Master at Denstone College. *Fcap.* 8*vo.* 2*s*.

GERMAN

A COMPANION GERMAN GRAMMAR. By H. DE B. GIBBINS, D.Litt., M.A., Assistant Master at Nottingham High School. *Crown 8vo.* 1*s*. 6*d*.

GERMAN PASSAGES FOR UNSEEN TRANSLATION. By E. M'QUEEN GRAY. *Crown 8vo.* 2*s*. 6*d*.

SCIENCE

THE WORLD OF SCIENCE. Including Chemistry, Heat, Light, Sound, Magnetism, Electricity, Botany, Zoology, Physiology, Astronomy, and Geology. By R. ELLIOTT STEEL, M.A., F.C.S. 147 Illustrations. *Second Edition.* *Crown 8vo.* 2*s*. 6*d*.
' If Mr. Steel is to be placed second to any for this quality of lucidity, it is only to Huxley himself; and to be named in the same breath with this master of the craft of teaching is to be accredited with the clearness of style and simplicity of arrangement that belong to thorough mastery of a subject.'—*Parents' Review.*

ELEMENTARY LIGHT. By R. E. STEEL. With numerous Illustrations. *Crown 8vo.* 4*s*. 6*d*.

ENGLISH

ENGLISH RECORDS. A Companion to the History of England. By H. E. MALDEN, M.A. *Crown 8vo. 3s. 6d.*
A book which aims at concentrating information upon dates, genealogy, officials, constitutional documents, etc., which is usually found scattered in different volumes.

THE ENGLISH CITIZEN: HIS RIGHTS AND DUTIES. By H. E. MALDEN, M.A. *1s. 6d.*
'The book goes over the same ground as is traversed in the school books on this subject written to satisfy the requirements of the Education Code. It would serve admirably the purposes of a text-book, as it is well based in historical facts, and keeps quite clear of party matters.'—*Scotsman.*

METHUEN'S COMMERCIAL SERIES

Edited by H. DE B. GIBBINS, D. Litt., M.A.

BRITISH COMMERCE AND COLONIES FROM ELIZABETH TO VICTORIA. By H. DE B. GIBBINS, D. Litt., M.A., Author of 'The Industrial History of England,' etc., etc., *2s.*

COMMERCIAL EXAMINATION PAPERS. By H. DE B. GIBBINS, D. Litt., M.A., *1s. 6d.*

THE ECONOMICS OF COMMERCE. By H. DE B. GIBBINS, D. Litt., M.A. *1s. 6d.*

A MANUAL OF FRENCH COMMERCIAL CORRESPONDENCE. By S. E. BALLY, Modern Language Master at the Manchester Grammar School. *2s.*

GERMAN COMMERCIAL CORRESPONDENCE. By S. E. BALLY, Assistant Master at the Manchester Grammar School. *Crown 8vo. 2s. 6d.*

A FRENCH COMMERCIAL READER. By S. E. BALLY. *2s.*

COMMERCIAL GEOGRAPHY, with special reference to Trade Routes, New Markets, and Manufacturing Districts. By L. W. LYDE, M.A., of the Academy, Glasgow. *2s.*

A PRIMER OF BUSINESS. By S. JACKSON, M.A. *1s. 6d.*

COMMERCIAL ARITHMETIC. By F. G. TAYLOR, M.A. *1s. 6d.*

PRÉCIS WRITING AND OFFICE CORRESPONDENCE. By E. E. WHITFIELD, M.A.

WORKS BY A. M. M. STEDMAN, M.A.

INITIA LATINA: Easy Lessons on Elementary Accidence. *Second Edition. Fcap. 8vo. 1s.*

FIRST LATIN LESSONS. *Fourth Edition. Crown 8vo. 2s.*

FIRST LATIN READER. With Notes adapted to the Shorter Latin Primer and Vocabulary. *Third Edition. 18mo. 1s. 6d.*

EASY SELECTIONS FROM CAESAR. Part I. The Helvetian War. *18mo. 1s.*

EASY SELECTIONS FROM LIVY. Part I. The Kings of Rome. *18mo. 1s. 6d.*

EASY LATIN PASSAGES FOR UNSEEN TRANSLATION. *Fifth Edition. Fcap. 8vo. 1s. 6d.*

EXEMPLA LATINA. First Lessons in Latin Accidence. With Vocabulary. *Crown 8vo. 1s.*

EASY LATIN EXERCISES ON THE SYNTAX OF THE SHORTER AND REVISED LATIN PRIMER. With Vocabulary. *Sixth Edition. Crown 8vo. 2s. 6d.* Issued with the consent of Dr. Kennedy.

THE LATIN COMPOUND SENTENCE: Rules and Exercises. *Crown 8vo. 1s. 6d.* With Vocabulary. *2s.*

NOTANDA QUAEDAM: Miscellaneous Latin Exercises on Common Rules and Idioms. *Third Edition. Fcap. 8vo, 1s. 6d.* With Vocabulary. *2s.*

LATIN VOCABULARIES FOR REPETITION: Arranged according to Subjects. *Sixth Edition. Fcap. 8vo. 1s. 6d.*

A VOCABULARY OF LATIN IDIOMS AND PHRASES. *18mo. 1s.*

STEPS TO GREEK. *18mo. 1s.*

EASY GREEK PASSAGES FOR UNSEEN TRANSLATION. *Second Edition. Fcap. 8vo. 1s. 6d.*

GREEK VOCABULARIES FOR REPETITION. Arranged according to Subjects. *Second Edition. Fcap. 8vo. 1s. 6d.*

GREEK TESTAMENT SELECTIONS. For the use of Schools. *Third Edition.* With Introduction, Notes, and Vocabulary. *Fcap. 8vo. 2s. 6d.*

STEPS TO FRENCH. *Second Edition. 18mo. 8d.*

FIRST FRENCH LESSONS. *Second Edition. Crown 8vo. 1s.*

EASY FRENCH PASSAGES FOR UNSEEN TRANSLATION. *Second Edition. Fcap. 8vo. 1s. 6d.*

EASY FRENCH EXERCISES ON ELEMENTARY SYNTAX. With Vocabulary. *Crown 8vo. 2s. 6d.*

FRENCH VOCABULARIES FOR REPETITION: Arranged according to Subjects. *Fifth Edition. Fcap. 8vo. 1s.*

SCHOOL EXAMINATION SERIES

EDITED BY A. M. M. STEDMAN, M.A. *Crown 8vo. 2s. 6d.*

FRENCH EXAMINATION PAPERS IN MISCELLANEOUS GRAMMAR AND IDIOMS. By A. M. M. STEDMAN, M.A. *Ninth Edition.* A KEY, issued to Tutors and Private Students only, to be had on application to the Publishers. *Fourth Edition. Crown 8vo. 6s. net.*

LATIN EXAMINATION PAPERS IN MISCELLANEOUS GRAMMAR AND IDIOMS. By A. M. M. STEDMAN, M.A. *Seventh Edition.* KEY issued as above. *6s. net.*

GREEK EXAMINATION PAPERS IN MISCELLANEOUS GRAMMAR AND IDIOMS. By A. M. M. STEDMAN, M.A. *Fifth Edition.* KEY issued as above. *6s. net.*

GERMAN EXAMINATION PAPERS IN MISCELLANEOUS GRAMMAR AND IDIOMS. By R. J. MORICH, Manchester. *Fifth Edition.* KEY issued as above. *6s. net.*

HISTORY AND GEOGRAPHY EXAMINATION PAPERS. By C. H. SPENCE, M.A., Clifton College.

SCIENCE EXAMINATION PAPERS. By R. E. STEEL, M.A., F.C.S., Chief Natural Science Master, Bradford Grammar School. *In two vols.* Part I. Chemistry; Part II. Physics.

GENERAL KNOWLEDGE EXAMINATION PAPERS. By A. M. M. STEDMAN, M.A. *Third Edition.* KEY issued as above. *7s. net.*

Printed by T. and A. CONSTABLE, Printers to Her Majesty at the Edinburgh University Press